A
COURT
SO
DARK

T0363772

Ingrid Seymour is a *USA Today* bestselling author of over fifty novels. She writes new adult fiction in a variety of genres, including fantasy romance, urban fantasy, paranormal romance, sci-fi, and high fantasy – all with badass heroines and irresistible heroes. She used to work as a software engineer at a Fortune 500 company, but now writes full-time and loves every minute of it. She lives in Birmingham, Alabama with her husband, two kids, and a cat named Ossie.

Instagram: **@ingrid_seymour**
X: **@Ingrid_Seymour**
TikTok: **@ ingridseymour**
Facebook: **/IngridSeymourAuthor**

BY INGRID SEYMOUR

A
COURT
SO
DARK

III

INGRID SEYMOUR

HEADLINE
ETERNAL

Copyright © 2023 Ingrid Seymour

The right of Ingrid Seymour to be identified as the Author of
the Work has been asserted by her in accordance with the
Copyright, Designs and Patents Act 1988.

First published in 2023 by PenDreams

First published in Great Britain in this paperback edition in 2024
by HEADLINE ETERNAL
An imprint of HEADLINE PUBLISHING GROUP

2

Apart from any use permitted under UK copyright law, this publication may
only be reproduced, stored, or transmitted, in any form, or by any means,
with prior permission in writing of the publishers or, in the case of
reprographic production, in accordance with the terms of licences
issued by the Copyright Licensing Agency.

All characters in this publication are fictitious
and any resemblance to real persons, living or dead,
is purely coincidental.

Cataloguing in Publication Data is available from the British Library

ISBN 978 1 0354 1703 2

Typeset in 12/15pt EB Garamond by Jouve (UK), Milton Keynes

Printed and bound in Great Britain by Clays Ltd, Elcograf S.p.A.

Headline's policy is to use papers that are natural, renewable and recyclable
products and made from wood grown in well-managed forests and other
controlled sources. The logging and manufacturing processes are expected
to conform to the environmental regulations of the country of origin.

HEADLINE PUBLISHING GROUP
An Hachette UK Company
Carmelite House
50 Victoria Embankment
London EC4Y 0DZ

www.headlineeternal.com
www.headline.co.uk
www.hachette.co.uk

May your demons learn to live in harmony.

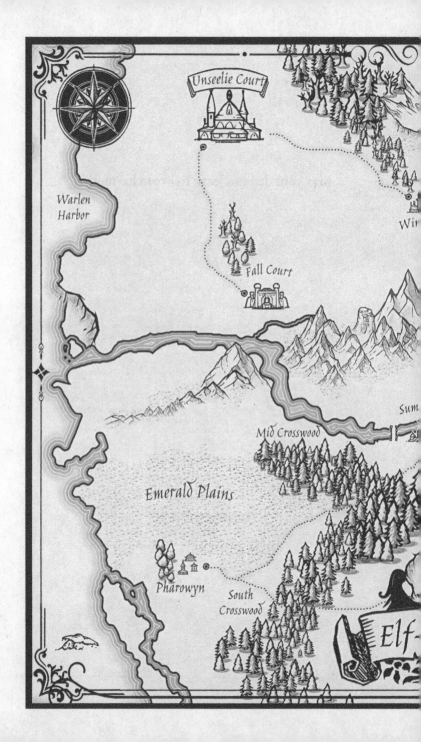

CHAPTER 1
WÖLFE

The beast tried to claw its way out of me as I squeezed the weak male's neck, but it wouldn't do to terrify my prey out of his wits. Not just yet.

"Where is he?" I demanded, my patience teetering at the sword's edge of a precipice.

A hand fell on my shoulder. "Wölfe. Please."

My head jerked back. I growled, teeth bared. "Unwise to touch me, Summer Prince."

Jeondar pulled his hand back, curling his fingers into a fist, probably worried I might bite them off. Not so unwise, after all.

I returned my attention to the coiffed male, whom I held against the wall. This was his villa. My Seelie spies had marked him as one of Cardian's allies, someone who could potentially be harboring my weasel brother.

As I squeezed his neck a little harder, Kryn came barreling through the door, followed by Silver.

"Cardian isn't here," my half-brother said. "We searched everywhere."

I narrowed my eyes at my quarry, my claws unsheathing. He whimpered as they pierced his pasty skin. A cloying sweet smell clung to him, some sort of flowery perfume. His hair was a mass of well-arranged curls on top of his head. They glittered with enough pixie dust to make a full-grown horse soar from the ground. Sweat slid down his forehead, and his tongue kept darting out like a snake's.

My fingers squeezed harder still. "I will ask one last time or I'll kill you. Where is Cardian?"

"I don't know, my king." His voice trembled.

I applied more pressure to my thumb. My claw dug in and warm blood flowed to stain his pristine white collar. I stared in fascination as it blossomed, spreading through the threads like fire through a cotton field.

"Please, my k-king," the male managed just barely. "All I know is that . . . he acquired a transfer token, stole it from your father."

For a second, I didn't move, my urge to kill him dampened by the news, then my fury redoubled and I leaned more heavily into him, the tendons around his throat feeling like flimsy twigs that I yearned to break. He made a croaking sound.

"He's told you what he knows, Wölfe." Jeondar stepped into my field of vision. "Let him go. He's not worth it."

My eyes flicked toward the Summer Prince, and for a moment, I considered his words, Kalyll trying to push his own morality on me. But the moment of insanity passed, and with a little more pressure—an effortless thing, really—I snapped the traitor's neck.

The *crack* of bones was loud in the quiet room. It reverberated like the crashing of a tree,

I let him go. He dropped to the floor in a heap of uselessness. I leaned forward, pulled an embroidered handkerchief from his breast pocket, and used it to wipe his blood from my hand. Working on one finger at a time, I turned and faced the others.

Jeondar, Kryn, and Silver's expressions were identical: wide eyes, lips pressed into tight lines, brows furrowed. They didn't approve. What a surprise.

I huffed and walked out of the room, a garish parlor with fuchsia curtains and cream cushions. My steps pounded against the veined marble floors as I made my way down a long hall. The others followed at a distance.

Two servants stood at the main door. Earlier, they had let me pass as soon as they recognized me and sensed my fury. Smart. I would've torn out their throats had they gotten in the way.

Cylea and Arabis waited outside in the courtyard under the star-covered black sky. They stayed to keep watch in case any rats scurried out of the large villa as we searched it.

"No luck, huh?" Cylea handed me Stormheart's reins, who was drinking water from a gurgling fountain.

I grunted in response.

Silver and Kryn prepared to mount, but a glare from Jeondar stopped them.

"No one's going to say anything about what just happened?" he demanded.

I looked at him over my shoulder. "You always say enough for everyone."

He met my glower, unflinching.

"What . . . happened?" Arabis asked.

Jeondar jerked a hand, pointing at the ornate house behind us. "He killed him. That's what happened."

"By Erilena." Arabis covered her mouth.

I huffed. "What would you have me do? Cuddle the traitor?"

"The king is not supposed to go around murdering denizens. Guilty or not? There should be a trial," Jeondar droned on.

"We don't have time for that. We have to find Cardian."

"Your personal vendetta should not take precedence over more pressing matters. Mythorne prepares for war as we speak."

I let go of Stormheart's reins, took a step forward, and snatched a handful of Jeondar's jacket. "Dani lies cold on a bed while my brother runs free plotting against me, against your precious realm. He possesses valuable information that can help the enemy. So I would say my *personal vendetta* aligns itself very well with your lofty goals for Elf-hame. But if you don't agree with my methods, you're welcome to scuttle back to Imbermore."

Jeondar pushed me, trying to shake himself free of my hold. I doubled down, but Kryn wedged himself between us, while Arabis came forth and placed a hand on my arm.

"Settle down, Wölfe!" she said, her Susurro powers traveling like wind over my body.

I felt the force of her command as it burrowed itself under my skin, trying to force me into compliance.

Kalyll reared his ugly head. He pushed, trying to come to the forefront and replace me, but right now his weak tactics were not needed. Right now—

CHAPTER 2
KALYLL

I t took all of my will to prevail over the darkness boiling inside me. When I came to, my head was lowered, my teeth and my fists clenched. Inhaling a deep breath, I met my friends' bewildered expressions.

"Did that work?" Arabis asked.

I nodded.

Fire burned at the tips of Jeondar's fingers. He was looking at me with a wave of anger and wariness he'd always reserved for others, not me.

Before what happened to Daniella, I had felt in control of my shadowdrifter abilities, able to unleash them when I wanted, but without her soothing presence, and with my desperation building and building, every day that had passed without her, things had become more difficult.

Finally, my restraints had snapped and Wölfe had broken free . . . allowing him to commit murder.

Jeondar fanned his hands and the fire went out.

"I apologize for my behavior," I said even as Wölfe bristled, sending bile up my throat. He was the worst of my pride, the worst of my *everything*.

Jeondar didn't acknowledge my apology, which stoked my already-incensed anger.

"As touched as I am," Cylea intervened as if to soften the blow of Jeondar's dismissal. "I don't think this is the best place for further conversation. We should go." She got on her horse in one bound and started forward, without waiting.

But I was in no mood to go anywhere with them. I kept trying to erase the image of the male's glimmering curls as I snapped his neck.

"Arabis, can you please take Stormheart with you?" I offered her the reins.

I cared nothing for the disappointment that registered in her expression as she pulled my steed away.

"How long will this go on, brother?" Kryn asked.

"You dare ask me this?" My eyes cut in Arabis's direction. He had been pining over her for ninety years. If he thought my yearning for Daniella was ridiculous, what did he call his own dogged persistence?

"Dani is—" he started, but I glared, and he held back what he'd been about to say. That she was as good as dead? That it wasn't acceptable to pine over a frozen body? A near statue?

I refused to accept what everyone thought.

"She's my mate," I spat, "but of course, you have no concept of that."

I turned my back on him and walked out of the courtyard and down the street. Stuffing my hand in my trousers' pocket, I fingered the transfer token. We were fifty miles from the Vine Tower, nearing the west boundary of Elyndell, but the distance was no matter. I had returned to see her every day since we left a week ago. Today would not be the exception.

Holding the token tightly in my hand, I let it take me to Daniella's realm. Once there, I lingered only long enough to allow the veil magic to gather and carry me straight into her chamber. Strange the way of veil magic. I could only travel quickly within my own realm if I transferred to the human realm first.

Warm light trembled within the sconces on the wall. Her narrow bed sat by the open window, well within the reach of a beam of moonlight that skidded over her frozen skin, making it glitter. I walked closer, my steps barely audible, and stopped by her side.

Her beautiful face was peaceful at rest. There was no sign of the pain she must have experienced when Varamede's attack overpowered her. In her presence, quiet as it was, the anger that roiled in my chest morphed into a sorrow deeper than any ocean.

"Can you hear me, melynthi?" I asked as I did every night and despite never receiving an answer, I didn't stop expecting it. "I feel lost without you. The rage consumes me. The others fear me . . . hate me. At least some of the time, I am sure. I need you."

I leaned forward and pressed a kiss to her cold lips. The grief that the Envoy had promised punched right through me.

My gaze got locked on something inconsequential and slowly, as I came to, I realized it was a dry petal on the floor. I glanced toward the pedestals, and for the first time, noticed the curving stems and wilted flowers. Roses. They were different from the ones I'd seen last night. Red as opposed to white. They reminded me of that day in Imbermore's gardens. I'd given Daniella a red rose that day, maybe to assuage my guilt as I tried to explain my shadowdrifter heritage without causing panic.

Reminded of something, I walked to the library, found what I was looking for inside a desk drawer, and went back.

"This one won't wither," I said as I pinned a silver brooch to her tunic.

It was the artful representation of a rose, the petals perfect and polished, the leaves carved in careful detail. The brooch had belonged to my grandmother. Roses were her favorite flowers.

"Find your way to me, melynthi." I pressed a kiss to her forehead.

The flutter of wings behind me forced me to take a step back. Larina hovered by the door, hands joined in front of her as she waited, head bowed slightly.

"I'm here to change the flowers, my king," the pixie said.

"Please, don't let me stop you," I said, finding it unacceptable that Daniella should suffer any dead blooms.

I sat on one of the armchairs by the fireplace, while Larina flew about using her magic to dismiss the dead arrangements and replace them with new ones.

"What news, Larina?"

"Two healers came this morning. They tried their best, but . . ."

She didn't need to elaborate. Many had tried to bring her back, but everyone had failed.

"I'll continue to search," she added, attempting to appear hopeful.

"What other news?" I asked, more out of obligation than any real desire to know what went on in my court.

"Your mother continues to take care of your affairs, my king," Larina said. "Today she summoned me and asked me to tell you that . . ." She stopped, seemingly unable to continue, her cheeks turning violet with embarrassment.

"You can tell me whatever it is she said."

She inclined her head. "She wishes for you to return immediately. She says you are needed here, and that . . . your blind pursuit of your brother and vengeance are misguided. That it is not the . . . worthless human who matters, but your throne and the peace of your realm."

I could feel my anger building and with it, Wölfe trying to take over once more. I stood, cracked my neck, and inhaled deeply, willing the tightly packed emotions that concentrated in my chest to spread, to diffuse. The burning under my breastbone dissipated somewhat. The anger was still there, but when it wasn't the main focus, I could keep my irrational side at bay and be a true blend of darkness and light.

Not fully Kalyll. Not fully Wölfe. But something in between.

"I'm sorry to subject you to my mother's . . . acrimony," I told the pixie. "I know she is difficult. I wish I could let you go back to Imbermore so you could be closer to your family, but I don't trust anyone else to . . ." I glanced toward Daniella, "take care of her."

"I remain here gladly. I want to be by her side. Forgive me for saying this, but Dani is my friend."

"Forgive you? I can only be grateful to you, and I hope that you also consider me your friend one day."

"Your Majesty!" she exclaimed as if I'd said something ridiculous.

I took several steps forward and approached my mate. I raised my fingers to her cold hand and stared into that beautiful face. "I have learned much from her. When she wakes up, I will marry her. She will be my queen, and together, we will change things."

Starting with the statute that said a Seelie monarch was not allowed to wed someone who wasn't of pure Fae blood. Such nonsense.

Reluctantly, I pulled away from Daniella. "I must go now. The Sub Rosa awaits. I leave her in your hands."

"Go with ease, my king. I will take good care of her."

I retrieved the transfer token and willed it to take me to the spot where I'd agreed to meet my friends.

"You're back!" Arabis shot to her feet as I materialized, a dagger in her hand with a skewered piece of roasted meat at its tip.

I found them sitting by the light of a campfire, enjoying a fresh kill, from the smell of it. Cylea had been at work with her bow and arrows, no doubt. She could always find something to satisfy our appetite.

"I thought you'd be gone much longer," she added, sitting back down.

In previous visits, I had stayed with Daniella for hours, unable to leave her side, but right now, I needed to talk to them, to find out what they thought of the bit of news we had acquired.

I found an empty rock next to Kryn and sat down. Silver offered me a plate with pieces of meat on it. I waved it away.

He shrugged. "More for me."

"We've been wasting our time searching for Cardian," I

said without a preamble. "He has a transfer token." I smack a fist into my hand. "I should've guessed."

Transfer tokens were not common. They weren't necessarily rare, but due to their high price, they were given sparingly. As a Seelie Prince, my brother would've naturally been allowed one. However, Father had denied him the privilege right after his first visit to the human realm, where he made a fool of himself, causing an embarrassing incident in a nightclub and landing himself in jail. Still, it had been stupid of me to assume he would be traveling by regular means.

"He could be anywhere now," I added, fighting my rising anger once more. I cracked my fingers as a way to focus my attention on something else.

"Do you think he escaped to the human realm?" Cylea asked.

I shook my head. "I seriously doubt it."

Cylea worked on tightening her bow. "You don't think he went to Mythorne, do you?"

"A Seelie Prince in the Unseelie Court?" Kryn said. "I don't think that would be very smart."

Arabis nodded. "I agree. Besides, Cardian is paranoid, not to mention a coward. He may have an alliance with Mythorne, but I doubt he trusts him."

Cylea nodded. "True."

They all looked at me. "I'm not sure. He's been known to do *very* stupid things. Honestly, I have no idea where he could've gone."

Since we left Elyndell proper a week ago, we'd been following a path that led to some of Cardian's closest allies—a list given to us by Naesala Roka. We had paid a visit to five lords to whom my brother had pledged prominent positions in court. Clearly, we'd been following a cold trail from the beginning.

Cylea plucked her bow string. It twanged satisfactorily. "You don't think Naesala sent us on a purposeless chase?"

She often asked questions that others might consider dense or unnecessary, but she got us talking, reflecting on every possible angle, no matter how unlikely.

"I don't think so," I said.

The others shook their heads.

"She now has a direct and important link to the Seelie King," Kryn said. "It wouldn't serve her purposes as a human spy to upset the Seelie Court."

"True," Cylea agreed.

"We have to assume Cardian had a contingency plan," Arabis put in. "He probably procured some sort of hideout in case things didn't go the way he planned."

"Yes." I rubbed my chin. "Wherever he is, though, he would maintain communication with Mythorne. Now more than ever."

The fire crackled while we sat in silence, pondering the possibilities.

"There's something to be said about trusting no one," Kryn observed.

Indeed, it seemed the only person my brother had fully trusted was Varamede. The bastard with a death sentence hanging over his head, even if he didn't know it. It was his magic that had harmed Daniella, and he would pay dearly for it.

I cracked my knuckles in frustration. So many healers, and all of them useless. Only one thing kept me from losing hope entirely: the Envoy's words. She had said Daniella would be my queen.

I stood abruptly. "We go back then. Finalize the preparations for war. My generals are restless." I couldn't expect them to make every decision while I was out here, entangled in a hopeless pursuit.

But I wasn't giving up. Sooner or later, I would have my revenge. Neither Cardian nor Varamede would get away with what they had done.

"Who comes with me?" I asked as I pulled out my transfer token.

I could take only one other person with me, and then they could come back and get the rest, one at a time. It was a limitation of tokens, one of the reasons we had ridden our horses out here. The other had been the hope of encountering Cardian on the road as he made his escape.

Cylea stood and dusted her bottom. "I'll do it. I'm dying for a hot bath."

"No." Silver shook his head. "She won't come back for us. She should go last."

"Of course I'll come back for you." She thought for a moment. "One of you at least, then that person can come back for the rest."

"That means the last person has to come back for the horses," Silver pointed out.

"If you don't make up your minds quickly," I said, "I will take Stormheart and leave your sorry asses here. The long ride might do you good." I gave Cylea a sidelong glance.

"Fine, I'll go second." Cylea sat back down and elbowed Arabis. "You go first."

Jeondar shook his head and rolled his eyes. "I vote for Cylea to go last."

"Hey!" she protested.

Annoyed by their bickering, I stepped up to Kryn—the only one who hadn't said a word—placed a hand on his shoulder, and willed us into the human realm.

"Wuh, hold on." Kryn took my arm and steadied himself. "It's been a while since I've done that, and I still don't like it." He looked ready to vomit.

We stood in the middle of a solitary forest. It was a place near the city of St. Louis. I had been transferring here for no other reason than it was close to Daniella's home. Dry leaves crunched under my feet.

Kryn took a deep breath and looked around. "What if Cardian is hiding here?"

"It's possible, I suppose. Though, something tells me he is not. He hates to lose, always has. He had time to believe himself king. That loss surely left a bitter taste in his mouth. Soon, he will make a move and reveal his whereabouts."

"Let's hope so." Kryn tightened his grip around my arm and nodded to let me know he was ready for another transfer.

In an instant, we appeared in Daniella's chamber. We hadn't been there but a second when Larina zoomed over and hovered directly in front of my face.

Adrenaline flooded me, sending my heart pounding and sharpening my senses.

Something was wrong, terribly wrong.

Kryn took out his sword. He stepped forward, eyes searching for danger, but everything was as I'd left it.

My first concern was for Daniella, but she lay in the same spot, as still as always.

"What is the matter, Larina?" I asked, realizing that my claws had unsheathed of their own accord.

The anger and darkness that fueled Wölfe also pushed to the surface, but I held on tightly to the reins and kept him under control. He had become a part of me, so entangled with my sense of self that it was impossible to tell where I ended and he began. Still, there was a sliver of shadowdrifter power that remained solely under my care. A good thing lest I grow used to murdering everyone who made me mad.

"Your Majesty," she inclined her head, her features twisted. Whatever piece of news she carried, she didn't want to deliver it.

"Out with it," I barked impatiently, hating the way I made her flinch.

"It's your mother. She . . . she is dead."

"What?" I demanded, unable to believe my own ears.

Larina's eyes wavered. Kryn absentmindedly sheathed his weapon.

"I am so sorry, Your Majesty." The pixie blinked rapidly, fighting to prevent the tears that pooled in her eyes from falling.

A terrible numbness spread over me. My mother, dead? The idea seemed as ludicrous as Father's death seemed every time I thought about it.

"What happened?" I asked, doing my best to ignore the thrashing emotions inside my chest.

"She was found dead in her workroom. She . . . she was murdered."

"Who?" I asked, but even as the question left my lips, I knew the answer.

"I . . . I don't know," Larina said. "I just found out."

Kryn and I exchanged a knowing glance.

"When did this happen?" I asked.

Larina wrung her hands. "Her . . . body was only just discovered."

My eyes cut to Daniella, then to my brother. "Kryn, stay here. Larina, find my uncle. Tell him I want his best guards to come here and protect Daniella."

She zipped out of the room.

I turned to Kryn again. "When the guards get here, come find me."

CHAPTER 3
DANIELLA

*D*arkness *smells sweet.*

That was my first thought, and my only thought, for a long time. It was maddening to perceive only that sickly smell. There was nothing else. No sights. No sounds. No brushing caress against my skin.

Only a flat, indistinguishable sweetness.

I didn't know how long I was submerged in that cloying nightmare, but at some point, the sweetness seemed to take shape and acquire a name.

Flowers.

That was what I was smelling: flowers. Soon, even that knowledge grew more specific, and I could tell the flowers were roses.

Another realization hit me. I wanted that scent. In fact, my entire being was reaching for it. At first, the scent lingered, then gradually grew weaker, until only an undertone of decay remained. When that happened, I grew restless, what little awareness I possessed reaching outward, wanting more.

But always, the sweetness returned, and I was grateful for it. I begged it to stay with me, but it never did. It always seemed to die, just to return again. Then its visits became shorter and shorter. The sweetness turning to rot far too quickly.

Hours or days passed, but eventually, the sweetness acquired a taste. It was slightly bitter in its aftermath, the way I imagined eating a handful of petals would feel. Yet, I welcomed this new sensation—one I'd nearly forgotten.

Sometime later, there were also sounds. They were distant and unintelligible, but I derived comfort from them. One in particular, I craved. It came and stayed with me for only a moment, then it was gone, and I felt its loss acutely.

Once more, sweetness renewed the scent of rot.

Fresh flowers!

I reached for them eagerly and realized that I didn't only want them. I needed them. I was drawing from them, taking what little life they had to build my strength, to heal the damage that had nearly obliterated every single cell in my body.

This was it. This was the last batch I needed to awaken. Once I was done drawing its energy, there would be enough of my own life force to let my magic work, to heal myself.

I eagerly drew and drew and drew, like sucking on a straw without taking a breath. I took everything the flowers had to give in an instant, then my healing skills kicked in and swept over my body.

"Kryn, stay here," someone said. "Larina, find my uncle. Tell him I want his best guards to come here and protect Daniella. When the guards get here, come find me."

Kalyll! Kalyll was here.

I struggled to speak, but not a word came out. I willed my

healing skills to hurry up, to push away the cold. My entire body tingled as it attempted to warm itself up.

A moment later, I came to, gasping and shivering. I wrapped my arms around my torso, trembling, nothing but a grunt escaping my lips.

"Dani!"

I blinked, and a mane of red hair took shape. "K-Kryn," I managed in a hoarse voice.

His emerald gaze snapped to one side. It looked as if he were going to call someone, but he stopped himself and returned his attention to me.

"You . . . are you all right?" he asked.

I frowned, my mind so addled that I couldn't begin to shape an answer. I grabbed Kryn's hand and tried to sit up with his help, but I collapsed back down, exhausted, my healing abilities already drained. Before I knew what I was doing, I got hold of Kryn's life force.

His eyes shot wide open as I drew from him. His energy felt like a ray of sunshine after an endless night, but I bit on my lower lip and managed to clamp down the desperate hunger for self-preservation.

I let him go, a sob escaping me.

"No, no, it's all right," Kryn said and seized my hand. "Take what you need."

I shook my head weakly.

"C'mon, Dani. We need you. Kalyll needs you." He squeezed my fingers, urging me to draw more energy from him.

"S-sometimes I can't s-stop," I said, a shiver raking its nails down my spine.

"You'll stop. I know you will."

Kalyll needs you, Kryn had said.

I needed him too. I needed his arms around me to warm me and get rid of this unbearable cold.

Without further protest, I found the spark of Kryn's life, something like a glow in the middle of his chest, and drew from it. Strength filled me. My eyes rolled into the back of my head, and I sighed as a measure of blessed warmth suffused my limbs, driving life into the tips of my frigid fingers and toes. When I opened my eyes again, Kryn was pale, his teeth bared as he did his best not to collapse in a heap.

I let go of him, even though I needed so much more. He inhaled sharply and took a step back, pressing a hand to his chest. He swayed on his feet, and I thought he would pass out, but after several deep breaths, he straightened and gave me one of his patent mean looks.

"Don't ever let me be nice to you again," he grumbled.

I was still cold, but it was bearable.

I sat up with some difficulty. There was a blanket over my legs. I fumbled with it, my hands clumsy as I picked it up and wrapped it around me, welcoming its warmth. Two pedestals with large arrangements of dead flowers sat on either side of my bed. I blinked at the dead petals on the floor.

"This is . . . incredible." Kryn looked me up and down, his eyes round.

I glanced around the room as memories slowly trickled back into my mind. The first one threatened to overwhelm my senses. It was a sharp blast of light followed by unbearable pain. I shook my head, squeezing my eyes shut. When I opened them again, I searched Kryn's green gaze.

"Kalyll . . . he's all right?" I asked.

He huffed. "You could say that."

"Varamede didn't hurt him?"

"Oh, you're talking about that. No, Varamede didn't hurt him. You were really stupid, and he hurt *you* instead."

I wanted to argue, but I *had* been stupid, or so my returning memories suggested. I'd thought Varamede's lightning attack would strike Kalyll, and I'd intervened even as he turned to shadow to avoid the strike.

Dropping the blanket, I splayed my hands in front of me and stared at them. "All that light," I said. "It came out of me."

"It sure did."

"I'd never . . ." I trailed off.

"We've speculated a lot about it. Kalyll thinks it has something to do with the bit of shadowdrifter energy that tangled itself with you that day in Mount Ruin."

I pressed a hand to my forehead and rubbed it from side to side. I barely managed to keep myself together as all the memories came at once, the realization of what I'd become hitting me like another bolt of lightning.

The energy I'd used to fight Varamede had come from the life of that poor guard I'd killed. I had taken it from him. I had kept his life force trapped inside me, unaware of it. Then I'd used it to attack with the full intention of killing once more.

Many times I'd wondered what I would be capable of for a loved one, and now I knew. I hadn't even stopped to consider my options. But even if I had, I knew my actions would have been the same.

More than once, I had tried to shame Wölfe for his selfish behavior, for always putting his happiness first. But now I knew, I would always do the same. I would defend Kalyll, my need to be with him, to love him and cherish him for as long as I could, over anything else.

"He's right," I said. "His shadowdrifter energy changed something in me."

"He explained. You can still heal and give life, but you can also take it away." As he frowned, he examined his hand, the one I had drawn energy from.

"I'm not useless in a fight anymore." I gave him a sidelong glance.

He smirked.

"Where is Kalyll now?" I asked.

Kryn winced at the question. "A lot has happened."

"How long was I out?"

"A week."

A week. It both seemed like a long time and a short time. I had been lost in an endless limbo, and it had seemed like an eternity while I tried to claw my way out from the brink of death. Seven days was nothing in comparison.

"I should have died," I said.

Kryn didn't argue with that. He simply nodded. "Silver . . . he froze you. No one could heal you. How did you . . .?"

I nodded toward the flowers. "I drew their energy. It was so hard at first. It took a long time, but as I got stronger, I was able to do it faster and faster."

"That's why Larina had to keep replacing them."

I turned my head and realized they'd moved the bed in front of the window, which was open, a tranquil moonlit night stretching far into the distance above Elyndell.

My feet dangled over the side of the bed. Kryn offered me

his hand. I took it and slid down to the floor. He steadied me, although he didn't look much better than I felt. I'd taken a lot from him—enough to make him look as if he'd just gotten over a bad flu.

"Seven days, then," I said. "What did I miss?"

Kryn winced again.

"That bad?"

"He was here just now. We've been looking for Cardian and Varamede, but no luck there, so we came back, and another blow was waiting for him."

"What do you mean?" I pressed a hand to my chest, bracing myself for it. Kalyll had been through so much already. What else could . . .?

I froze, looking over Kryn's shoulder as a warning rose in my chest. His hand immediately went to the sword at his side, and he started to turn.

"No!" I cried out as Cardian, who had appeared behind Kryn, raised a dagger and plunged it into the side of Kryn's neck.

A horrible gurgling sound escaped Kryn. Despite the terrible wound, he grabbed Cardian's wrist and whirled on him, blood streaming down his neck, staining his jacket. He drove Cardian back, using his weight, and slammed him against the wall.

Cardian pulled the dagger out, a weapon that looked more like an icepick than anything else. Now, the blood spurted from the wound in a jet. Panicked, Kryn smacked a hand to his neck to contain the flood. He stumbled backward, eyes full of dread.

"Run, Dani!" he ordered me.

When I just stood there and watched him topple to the floor, it was the pleading look in his eyes that made me hesitate. I wanted to run to him. I could heal him, give him back the life force he'd lent me. But he wanted me out of here. His eyes told me that my safety mattered more to him than anything else.

Except, I couldn't leave him on the floor, bleeding to death. I took a step toward him. I had to . . .

Cardian stepped in front of me, dagger raised.

"Run!" Kryn said again.

I shook my head.

Cardian took another step, a gleeful smile stretching his thin lips. "You're coming with me, Sleeping Beauty."

No. I couldn't let Cardian take me. For all I knew, I would end up a prisoner of the Unseelie King. They were working together. I took several shaky steps back, my eyes locked on Cardian's blood-stained dagger. Behind him, Kryn kept bleeding, and still, his only concern was for me.

"Run!" Kryn's voice again, this time accompanied by a gurgle.

I obeyed. As fast as my weak legs allowed, I ran on bare feet. I heard Cardian behind me, his boots tapping with purpose. My knees wobbled. My head swam. I was too weak to escape.

I made it to the door and staggered into the hall.

Cardian laughed. "You're not going anywhere."

Holding on to the wall, I managed to go down the first flight of the tower's winding steps. At the landing, there was a fork. The one to the left led to a door that spilled into a garden, while the one to the right led deeper into the palace.

That was the way I should have followed, but I kept leaning on the wall and veered left, too weak to move away from its support.

Suddenly, I heard voices and rushed steps coming from the right. Help was on its way. I stopped and glanced over my shoulder, my vision going dark around the edges.

Cardian was a few steps up, dagger still in hand. He was frozen with indecision, his head cocked toward the approaching sounds. He glanced in my direction and met my eyes for just an instant before he tightened his hand around something and disappeared, leaving nothing behind but air.

The darkness encroaching on my vision rapidly shrank. I stood there for a few seconds, my body swinging precariously. Through my blurring vision, I saw several shapes run past, bounding up the steps, dashing through the exact space where Cardian had been standing just a moment ago.

They'll help Kryn, I thought. *He'll be all right.*

But the sounds of a struggle ensued. Why? Had Cardian gone back to the room?

Weakly, I reached out a hand and murmured. "Kryn."

Then I toppled backward and rolled down the stone staircase, unconsciousness sinking its claws into me, even as the pain of the fall jarred my bones.

CHAPTER 4
KALYLL

"Kryn, stay here. Larina, find my uncle. Tell him I want his best guards to come here and protect Daniella," I told them.

Kryn gave one solemn nod, and I knew he understood watching Daniella was the most important thing I could ask of him.

"When the guards get here, come find me," I urged as I hurried out of the chamber and rushed down the winding steps of the tower. As soon as I abandoned the area, there were signs of disarray. Servants and guards hurried down the long corridors, looking panicked.

"Does anyone know where to find the king?" I heard someone shout down the hall. "He needs to know what happened."

I clenched my fist as I marched past a couple of startled page boys. I hadn't been here to guard my home, and now my mother was dead.

As soon as I passed them, one of the page boys ran in the opposite direction.

"The king is here. The king is here," he went calling.

The doors to my mother's workroom were thrown open.

Several males stood guard, their expressions grim. When they noticed me, they bowed deeply, and I sensed a combination of sorrow and guilt. The queen mother was dead, so I understood the sorrow. But the guilt . . . I was sure it was misplaced.

I was the only one to blame for this. I should've been here to protect her.

My steps echoed in the large space. More guards stood inside, facing the door I'd just walked through. Their backs were turned to the chaos.

This workroom had never been the tidiest of places. There were always canvases everywhere. Brushes, pallets, and half-spent tubes of paint lying around, but now . . . there was no disarray, only destruction.

Easels sat broken on the floor, their canvases trampled and torn. A tube of bright yellow paint lay busted, boot prints smearing away from it toward the center of the room, where a shape bulged under a heavy tarp, and my uncle, his wife, and two council members stood.

Everyone turned to face me as I approached.

"My King." Captain Loraerris pressed a fist to his chest. His eyes were red-rimmed, his entire demeanor crestfallen.

If I still harbored any doubts that my mother was dead, his expression erased them. That was his sister on the floor, under the tarp.

My uncle's wife was deathly pale, clinging to her husband's arm. The council members—one male and one female, who had always been close to my mother—appeared just as distraught.

Reluctantly, I lowered my eyes to the floor. There were red

splatters everywhere. I wanted to tell myself they'd been caused by paint, but I knew better. I'd seen enough violent acts to know that these patterns spelled brutality. I moved closer and lifted the piece of cloth. I was only able to handle the sight for a couple of seconds before I pulled away.

Dry blood stained her beautiful hair, which looked matted. Her face was unrecognizable, a deep cut slashing her from temple to jaw. And beyond that, her neck . . . a puncture.

"Did anyone see what happened?" I asked, forcing hoarse words past my tight throat.

"I got here too late," a small voice said behind my uncle.

Someone I hadn't noticed stood on the corner of one of the still-standing canvases. It was Shadow, my mother's closest servant, the sprite who had once been a slave to a wealthy lord for many years and whom my mother had liberated by paying a substantial sum. Strangely, instead of using her freedom to go back to her land, Shadow decided to stay beside my mother.

I turned to face her. She looked beyond sorrow. She was angry. I recognized my own fury in her expression.

"But I did see who did it," she said, without taking her eyes from my mother's motionless shape.

"Cardian," I said, without hesitation.

Her gaze cut to me. She seemed surprised, but for only an instant, then she nodded.

"How did he get in?" my uncle asked. "The guards at the door never saw him."

"He has a transfer token," I said.

Shadow startled. "That's how he got away so fast when I went after him." She clenched her small hands.

Cardian better hope I got a hold of him before the sprite did. She was vicious, a Sunnarian warrior known to have defeated more than one powerful foe, just the reason my mother had welcomed her request to remain by her side.

Though the way that Wölfe was thrashing inside me made me wonder which of the two would make Cardian wish he'd never been born.

I started pacing. If I didn't move, I would crumble like a too-old statue battered by a tempest. In the expanse of two weeks, I had lost my father, my mother, my brother, my mate.

All I had left was this useless kingdom and an all-consuming desire for revenge.

Wölfe whispered in my ear.

You chose this godsforsaken place over her. It's your fault she's frozen in time. You had to take the crown from the little prince, so you could wear it. Now, we both suffer. Now, we both mourn her. You don't deserve her—not when you don't put her first. You killed her.

No! I have not lost her. She's still here, and soon she will awaken.

And once she was back, she would soothe all this pain away with only a smile. And her mouth and smooth skin would provide refuge. Her touch would be a salve to all this loss.

How selfish are you? Can't you think of anyone else but your-self? No matter. While you cry like a weakling, I will be the one soothing her, protecting her, making sure she's safe.

I shook my head, a growl escaping me.

They all looked at me strangely. I had the urge to tamp the darkness down, but I didn't have to anymore. They all knew what I was. Mother had weaved her lies artfully, so I could remain the legitimate king, so I could spare the people of Elf-hame a gruesome war.

But that was before.

Before Cardian and Varamede brought pain upon my mate. Before *I* brought all of this on Daniella. Because Wölfe was right. *I* was responsible for her awful fate, and that meant now there would be no peace. There would only be destruction until those directly or indirectly responsible paid the price of her pain in blood.

Peace was not meant to be a burden for one person to bear. It was a shared dream, a collective purpose that everyone needed to uphold. I'd been trying to bear the Unseelie King's duty as well as my own, and in the process, I had forgiven many of his transgressions. But no more.

I had left his trespasses unanswered for far too long, and he had grown bold. He thought he could act with impunity. For the sake of sparing the many, the few—like Valeriana and her Dryad clan—had paid dearly. But now, it was time for the likes of Kellam Mythorne, Cardian, Varamede, and anyone who shared their boundless greed to pay for their crimes.

"I must talk to my generals," I said.

My uncle inclined his head. "I will make sure the arrangements are made for Eithne's sendoff."

"Thank you, uncle. Forgive me that I can't be of help at the moment, but—"

He shook his head. "No need to explain. You are needed in the war room, my king."

Uncle Vul Loraerris, forever faithful, first and always the captain of the palace guard, even when it meant taking on the painful burden of putting his sister to rest.

I placed a hand on his shoulder. "Thank you."

He opened his mouth to say something, but voices and the frantic whirring of wings stole his attention. His head snapped to one side and so did mine.

Larina hovered by the door. Her blue skin appeared nearly gray with fright, and the guards who had been outside were now standing behind her, looking unsure of whether or not to swat her down like an overgrown bug.

"There's an attack in the tower," she cried out.

A burst of dark energy shot through my body, and in the next instant, I dashed out the door, a ball of dread lodged in my throat. I was dimly aware of my uncle and the guards following my tracks, but one thought took center stage.

Not her. Not her. Not her.

My blood pumped, and my heart pounded like a giant fist as I bounded up the stairs faster than I'd ever run in my entire life. When I reached the landing and was able to see the door to her chamber, I nearly came to a halt.

A body—a guard judging by the uniform—lay on the floor in a puddle of blood.

Horror gripped me. If I stayed out here, I could pretend Daniella was all right, that no harm had come to her. But the hope that I wasn't too late spurred me on, and I dashed past the door, my boot splashing the male's blood without care.

The sight that welcomed me next arrested me in place. It took all my strength not to fall to my knees and bellow at the sky.

Two more guards lay on the floor, punctures in their necks.

And Daniella . . . she was gone.

Her bed was empty—the pedestals with their wilted flowers the only witnesses.

A moan from behind one of the armchairs snapped me from my stupor. I rushed there and found Kryn holding a hand to his neck as blood squirted through his fingers.

"Brother!"

He reached a hand toward the bed and attempted to speak, but only a gurgle came out.

"Don't speak."

He was deathly pale, even his eyes didn't look as green as normal as he blinked in a daze. I had to fight to keep my focus on him and not on the absence of my mate. Tearing a sleeve off my shirt, I removed his hand from the wound, pressed the cloth to it even as blood shot out.

"Hold this as tightly as you can," I ordered him.

He obeyed, and I willed his healing powers to work faster and save his life. I couldn't lose him too. As I sprang to my feet, eyes searching for any sign of Daniella, my uncle and his men rushed into the room, weapons at the ready. They froze as I had, though their eyes searched every corner, and under my uncle's orders, they quickly spread out to search the bathroom and the closet.

Larina flew without a care for her safety and stopped to hover right over the empty bed. "Oh, no! Where is she?"

"Tend to my brother," I ordered her as I rushed past the library doors, throwing them open and finding nothing but emptiness. "Daniella," I bellowed, my voice echoing through the three stories of useless shelves and books.

As the guards came out of the closet and bathroom, their blank expressions suggesting they found nothing, I ordered them to search the library from top to bottom. They rushed in and efficiently spread out, two staying on the first level, and the other two bounding up the stairs. They dashed between the shelves, but I suspected they would find no one there.

I started to turn away from the library when my uncle cried out a warning.

"Kalyll! Behind you!"

I had no time to react as I noticed my brother appear out of thin air. A stab of pain went through my neck. The world turned completely black. I tried to lunge for him, to wrap my hands around his neck and strangle him, but the floor seemed to shift under my feet, and I fell, tumbling into the gloom until I knew no more.

CHAPTER 5
DANIELLA

Heat seeped into me. The image of a kindling fire floated inside my head. It was comfort and warmth and arms wrapped around me. Kalyll's mouth on mine. His body on top of my own, driving me to ecstasy, my entire being smoldering from the inside out.

I sprang to a sitting position, calling his name.

A strange male sat next to me. I pushed away from him, my arms and legs feeling strong, unlike the last time I'd been awake.

He put both hands up in a pacifying gesture.

Arabis was next to me in an instant. "It's all right. No need to panic. He's a healer."

He had graying hair, which fell in strands as he inclined his head and quietly walked out of the room.

I collapsed back onto the pillow, feeling dizzy. When the spell passed, my gaze danced around. I was back in my chamber. Something pinned to my chest caught my attention. It was a silver brooch in the shape of a rose. It was beautiful and delicate.

Where had it come from?

A memory rose like a phantom from the back of my mind.

"This one won't wither. Find your way to me, melynthi." Kalyll's voice. He had given me this. I didn't know how I knew, but I did.

I sat up slowly, searching every face, aching to see him.

Cylea was there, and Larina too. They wore matching concerned expressions that gradually seemed to ease as they offered me a weak smile.

"Kryn!" I exclaimed.

No one said anything.

Tears filled my eyes.

"No, no, no." Arabis took my hand and squeezed it. "Kryn is fine. He'll be all right."

There was great relief in her voice. I still didn't know where their tumultuous relationship stood, but at least she didn't want him dead.

"And . . . Kalyll? Where is he?" I asked, a smile starting on my lips at the thought of him.

"He . . . um . . ." Arabis shook her head, unable to finish.

The smile never developed, and the tears that had gathered in my eyes spilled, streaking down my cheeks. Was he dead?

"I think he's fine," Cylea blurted out. "I mean . . . as fine as anyone who's been kidnapped by his vengeful brother can be."

"Kidnapped?"

Cylea nodded.

An odd mixture of relief and panic assaulted me. The relief dried my tears immediately, while the panic sent my heart into a frenzy and slowly started morphing into anger.

"Cardian stabbed Kryn." I placed a hand on my neck.

"We know." Arabis nodded. "He told us what happened.

Cardian wanted to take you, and when he couldn't, he went for Kalyll instead."

"He's going to . . . kill him. We have to find them."

Once more, everyone went silent.

I extricated my hand from Arabis and jumped off the bed. "We have to go now. He may not have long." I chose to believe Kalyll was still alive, but I also understood that Cardian could kill him at any moment. "Where are the others? We need everyone. Silver, Jeondar. I'll finish healing Kryn if he needs it."

Everyone stared at me blankly.

"Why are you just standing there?" I demanded.

"Well," Arabis shook her head, a maddening sadness in her eyes, "we don't know where to look. Cardian has a transfer token. We've searched everywhere already, but he has eluded us thus far."

"No," I said emphatically. "That's just . . ." I didn't know what it was, only that I couldn't accept it. "There has to be a way to track him."

Larina, who had been hovering by the foot of the bed, frowned as she noticed something and flew toward a small table partially tucked behind an armchair. Suddenly becoming flustered, she hurried back on whirring wings, waving her little arms.

"What is it, Larina?" Cylea asked.

The pixie pressed a finger to her lips, urging us to be quiet, then pointed frantically toward the table.

With a frown, Cylea walked over. Arabis and I moved closer. Cylea placed her hands behind her back and leaned forward to examine the small figurine, eyeing it with a sneer.

She glanced in my direction and pointed at it. Her expression seemed to ask *do you recognize this?*

I shook my head. I'd never seen it before.

Larina flew to Cylea's ear and leaned in to whisper something. Cylea's eyebrows went up. Larina then zipped toward the clock on the mantel and pointed at a small knob on top of it. Understanding her meaning, Cylea approached the clock and twisted the knob.

Orange tendrils of energy emanated from the device and quickly swept across the room. They scoured every corner, going in and out of the adjacent washroom and closet. One tendril came to rest at the small table. There, it gave up its search. The rest of the tendrils continued flitting around the room, but when they got to the table, they also stopped. Quickly, every bit of luminous energy had gathered there by the small crystal bird, illuminating it in sharp relief.

Cylea sighed loudly. "I don't know about you, but all this midnight excitement has made me hungry and thirsty. Larina, is there anything good in the kitchen that we can pillage."

"A thing or two," she said, catching on quickly.

"I can eat," I said.

We all filed out of the room without saying another word. Instead of going to the kitchen, Cylea led the way to her chamber where she twisted a knob in one of the fairy-light sconces, and similar tendrils of energy crisscrossed the room, checking for anything that wasn't supposed to be there. When every inch of the place had been examined, the magic returned to the sconce, a clear indication that it hadn't found anything out of place. We were free to speak again.

"That good-for-nothing left a mole to spy on us," Cylea spat. "Did we say anything he can use against us?"

"I don't think so," Arabis said after a moment's thought.

I shook my head. "I don't think so either, but let's forget about that. What matters is that we find Kalyll. We need to track him. My sister. My sister can find him. We have to go and get her. She can find anyone. Anywhere."

"We have trackers here, Dani," Cylea said. "Kalyll used several. They found no trace of Cardian."

"My sister is better."

"Wherever he is, Cardian's using powerful magic to conceal his whereabouts."

My sister had once found someone who had been kidnapped by a powerful vampire. That vampire had also used powerful magic, and Toni had still been able to find him.

"My sister can find him," I insisted.

Arabis tried to place a hand on my arm, but I stepped away. "Kalyll had already thought of that, but he didn't want to involve her. He already felt guilty for bringing you into this. He derailed your life, and he didn't want to be responsible for bringing more turmoil to your family."

I grabbed my head and backed into an armchair. I collapsed into it, the whirring of Larina's wings serving as background noise to the whirring of my own brain. It *would not* be fair to bring my sister into this. She had her own life, which she would abandon the moment I asked for her help. And if the obstructing magic Cardian was using interfered with her tracking skills, then what? She would be stuck in an impossible situation, feeling responsible for her inability to find Kalyll.

No. I couldn't do that to her. Kalyll had been right not to bring her here.

"If you would allow me . . . I can help you find the murdering prince," a new voice called from the door.

I looked up to find a sprite in the room. I had seen her before, the day I made that blood pact with Queen Eithne. She had allowed me into the queen's workroom. Her wings were iridescent, like Larina's. Her skin was gray and her eyes were narrow slits with all-black eyes. Her nose was flat, almost non-existent, and her thin-lipped mouth was filled with rows and rows of curved teeth. She was a creature of beauty and terror.

Larina turned violet and dashed behind Cylea. She hovered over her shoulder, her blue skin camouflaging perfectly with Cylea's hair. She was intimidated by the new arrival, which seemed odd since they were the same size.

Arabis examined the sprite with care, though her expression was skeptical. "Shadow, I'm not sure how you could help us find Cardian. Not even the court spies know where he is. We *questioned* all of his allies and got nothing."

The way she said *questioned* made me wonder exactly what they'd done to the people who had offered their support to the younger prince. Something told me they were now regretting their alliance.

"We minor folk have our ways," Shadow said.

She and Larina exchanged a knowing glance. Larina abandoned her hiding spot, as if she were reassessing Shadow.

Arabis still didn't look convinced, but she said, "We'll take any help we can get."

"There is one condition," Shadow said.

Cylea bristled at that, and Arabis also appeared displeased by this. For all we knew, the sprite was one of Cardian's supporters, and she would send us on a wild goose chase, straight in the opposite direction of where we needed to be. Or worse yet . . . into a trap. We couldn't have that. At Cardian's mercy, Kalyll's days were surely numbered. There was no time to waste.

"What condition?" Cylea demanded, looking ready to throttle the sprite if her stipulation turned out to be something ridiculous or outright extortion.

"I want to be the one to kill Cardian Adanorin," Shadow declared, surprising us all.

Larina nearly choked.

I stood up, anger and darkness driving me to my feet. Before I could think what I was saying, Dark Dani was in control. The image of Cardian driving that knife into Kryn's throat took center stage in my mind.

"*I* will kill that bastard," I said.

"As eager as we all are to take our revenge," Arabis said, "our king may not want his brother dead. So it isn't up to us to decide Cardian's fate."

"I could content myself with plucking his eyes out." Shadow huffed and thrust her hand forward in a stabbing motion.

Cylea shrugged. "I'm sure something can be arranged."

"No." Arabis shook her head. "Those things are not for us to decide. Our only concern should be to find the king and bring him back safely."

Shadow rolled her eyes. "Fine. I will make this request from the king when I find him." Rotating her fluttering wings slightly, she turned in midair and left the room.

"She's mad," Larina said. "I kind of suspected that already, though."

"What are you saying?" I asked. "That we can't trust her to find Kalyll?"

Larina opened her mouth to answer, but Arabis cut her off.

"Shadow was faithful to Queen Eithne for over a hundred years. We can trust her."

"Was?" I asked.

Arabis nodded sadly. "She's dead. Cardian killed her. Shadow witnessed it. She went after him, but he has that transfer token and he disappeared before she could reach him."

I didn't know what the tiny sprite could have done to stop Cardian, but at least I now understood why she wanted him dead so badly.

A lump formed in my throat as I thought of Kalyll. He had lost both his father and mother in such a short time. I hadn't particularly cared for the queen and the way she treated her son, but my heart ached for Kalyll. He had taken so many blows, and yet he'd remained strong. I had to wonder how much of it was a façade, though. Oh, God, I wanted so badly to wrap my arms around him and offer him what little comfort I could.

"How could Cardian kill his own mother?" I asked.

"Because he's a miserable bastard who cares only for power," Kryn said from the door.

Arabis's blue eyes cut in his direction. A spark of relief flashed on her face at seeing him there. He noticed and gave her a grateful nod, something like hope sparking in his features. Jeondar and Silver were with him. They walked in, looking imposing and determined.

Now that they were all here, I didn't feel so lost.

"We won't just rely on Shadow, right?" I said. "We have to go look for Kalyll."

The males frowned in unison. Arabis explained about the sprite's offer and the listening mole in my chamber.

"Her help could turn out to be invaluable," Jeondar said after considering for a few beats. "The minor folk do have their ways. They are incredibly connected." He looked over at Larina who nodded once. "Still, you're right, Dani. We need to do more."

"What do you suggest?" Cylea asked.

"We've been talking." Jeondar looked at Kryn and Silver. They nodded.

"We think Dani should see the Envoy."

42

CHAPTER 6
DANIELLA

I did not want to visit the Envoy. No way in hell. That creature was terrifying, and I was sure it was some sort of trickster demon, one that found its way into Elf-hame the same way that Caorthannach—that Mount Ruin bitch—had. No demon could be trusted, but trickster types were the worst. I knew it from my sister Lucia, who was studying at the League of Demon Hunters in New York. She had suffered at the hands of a trickster demon and nearly ended up possessed by it. She escaped that particular fate, though she'd suffered much worse at the hands of Lucifer's son himself. That was an interesting story, which I hoped would have a happy ending.

Under any other circumstances, I would've heeded Lucia's advice and stayed away from the Envoy, but what else could I do? Not to mention that I would go to the end of any realm—Elf-hame, my own, or even hell—for Kalyll.

Straightening to my full height, I talked with more conviction than I felt.

"Let's go then." I headed for the door.

"No can do." Silver waved a finger, then looked at Cylea for approval of his use of a human phrase.

Cylea nodded to indicate he'd gotten it right.

"Why not? We have no time to waste," I protested.

"You can't visit the Envoy during the day," Jeondar explained. "We have to wait until midnight."

"Are you kidding me? So what do we do now? Just sit here with our thumbs up our asses?"

Silver blinked several times. "Now, that is an interesting phrase worth remembering."

"Shut up, Silver. Don't make me regret interceding for you."

He put both hands up, rolled his eyes to the ceiling, and gave a lazy step out of the way, whistling casually. "I did save your life, you know?"

"You turned me into a popsicle is what you did."

"A what?"

"Oh, never mind." I batted a hand at him, but I definitely owed him my gratitude. "But thanks, for . . . helping me."

"Don't mention it."

"No. We won't be doing any of that," Jeondar said, wrinkling his nose as if he were actually picturing us doing exactly what the crude phrase suggested.

Seriously, did they have to take everything so literally?

"A visit to the Envoy isn't like walking into a tavern, Dani," he continued. "You need to prepare for it. We have to think carefully about what to ask."

Right. The Envoy would give us tricky answers, and if we weren't careful, we could end up wasting an entire day just to end up with vague, useless information.

I still didn't like the idea of sitting here chatting. I needed action, needed to feel like I was doing something to actively find Kalyll, but this was the best we had, so we had to nail it.

"So how does it work?" I sighed. "I assume you guys have visited that fucking demon and have some experience with it?"

"Demon?" Arabis asked.

"Yeah, that's what it is. At least that's what I think, but it doesn't matter. What exactly do we need to ask? *Where is Kalyll?*"

Kryn shook his head. "That won't work. You need to ask *yes* or *no* questions."

"Oh, yeah." Kalyll had explained how it worked.

It was so dumb. You had to ask *yes* or *no* questions, yet the creature only answered straight up when the answer was *no*. If the answer was *yes*, it would instead offer additional information that was vaguely related to the question.

Like when Kalyll asked *"will the one I love be my queen?"* and the trickster answered *"you will mourn her. Deeply."*

At the thought, my heart constricted. While I'd lain on that bed for an entire week, Kalyll had ached, the pain driving him to do who knew what. The others hadn't explained yet, but I had a feeling Wölfe had made an appearance, which surely only added to Kalyll's torment. Worse yet, as I stood here, he didn't know I had awakened, and so his torture and mourning continued.

Witchlights! We had to find him.

I put on my thinking cap. "So how many questions can I ask?"

That was something Kalyll hadn't mentioned.

"Two," all six of them replied in unison, even Larina up on the mantel.

"Two?! That's it?"

"Yes, that's all we have to work with." Jeondar shrugged.

"Okay." I thought for a moment. "Assuming that Cardian took him to the Unseelie King, we could ask *is Kalyll in Nerethien?*" That was the name of the city where the Unseelie Court was located.

Cylea nodded. "Yes, that's on the right track, but maybe we should be more specific. We could ask something like . . . *is Kalyll in Highmire?*"

"Highmire?" I echoed.

Cylea nodded, her blue hair swinging back and forth. "Mythorne's castle."

"Oh, that's right." I had forgotten its name. After thinking for a moment, I asked, "But couldn't being too specific cause problems? At least being broad would give us a general idea of where he is. He could be in Nerethien, but not specifically in the castle. I'm sure Mythorne has other places for prisoners."

Silver reclined against the wall. "For all we know he's in *your* realm, Dani. I just can't imagine Cardian having the balls to face Mythorne or place himself anywhere within his reach."

Damn! This was harder than I thought. Trying to locate one person in two vast realms with almost nothing to go on was like trying to carve Mount Ruin with a spatula.

My frustration mounted, and I had to fight the urge to pull out my hair and scream. I felt like a nuclear bomb ready to obliterate everything around me. I had to . . . do more.

"I need pen and paper," I blurted out, then marched to a nearby desk.

When I found what I needed I sat down and started jotting questions down. Anything that popped into my mind, I wrote it down—no matter how stupid.

Arabis sat across from me and also procured a piece of

paper and did the same. The others remained quiet, meandering through the library, deep in thought.

All the nervous energy poured out of me and onto the page until I could think of nothing else to write. I straightened, looked up over what I had written, and underlined the things that had merit.

It was a lot.

I slammed my hands on the desk and stood, knocking my chair over. "Why only two questions? It's not like it would kill the Envoy to be more helpful."

My question made me wonder for the first time why the Envoy was answering any questions at all. Did it gain anything? And if it did? What if we offered it more of whatever it wanted?

"What is the Envoy after, anyway?" I asked.

They all looked at me with matching frowns.

I elaborated. "I mean, what does it gain? Does it want gold? Jewels?"

"Oh, you don't know?" Arabis looked chagrined.

I waited for her explanation, but she only exchanged glances with the others.

"What is it?" I demanded.

"The Envoy shaves days from the end of your life." Silver was now reclining against a bookshelf, inspecting his fingernails. He shared this piece of information as if he were talking about the weather.

"You're kidding, right?"

"No."

"That's just . . . wrong! How many times has Kalyll been to visit the Envoy?"

"Only twice that I'm aware of," Kryn said. "But I think—"

I cut him off. "So let me get this straight . . . he's going to live fewer days than he would have otherwise?"

"That's the idea."

A lot of messed up scenarios crossed my mind. What if someone died before saying *I'm sorry* to a loved one? Before signing an important peace treaty? Before running over a serial killer with their car? Before conceiving a baby with their wife? The list was endless. One day, one hour, could make a huge difference, and the realization made me feel as if I was really going to explode.

So no gold or jewels for the fucking Envoy. Even one question seemed too much already. Two could break someone's entire purpose for living. What if the baby the wife would've conceived was someone like Marie Curie?

Witchlights! I had to stop thinking about it that way. For all I knew, it was more likely that the Envoy was shaving off crappy days from crappy old age.

"Are you all right, Dani?" Arabis asked.

I must have looked how I felt—ready to blow up and make a bloody mess—because she looked truly concerned for me. Clenching my fists, I reminded myself to be strong. I couldn't fall apart. Still, I had to ask my next question.

"Why do I have to go to the Envoy? Why not one of you?"

"Because we've all been already," Jeondar explained.

I shook my head, confused. "But Kalyll went twice."

"What I was going to say when you so rudely interrupted me," Kryn said, "is that I think Kalyll went once, and Wölfe went a second time."

My mouth opened. I wanted to argue the point, but I knew

very well that Kalyll and Wölfe were two entirely different people. Even if the night we visited the Envoy Kalyll had felt in charge, he must've found a way to let Wölfe take the wheel.

I smiled sadly. Kalyll was clever. If only he was clever enough to escape Cardian *right now*. I glanced toward the chamber door, willing it to open and let him in. I could almost picture him there, hands outstretched, a wolfish smile on his lips: *Here I am, were you unnecessarily worried?*

But he didn't appear, and my heart ached with his absence.

"So what questions did you come up with?" Arabis pointed toward my piece of paper on the table.

Cylea came behind me and righted the chair I'd knocked down.

Rubbing the back of my neck, I picked up my notes, reminding myself to be strong once more. Yes, Kalyll would do everything in his power to escape, but Cardian and Mythorne would not make it easy for him. They knew he was a shadowdrifter. They would take precautions against his power to turn into smoke and his ability to morph into a powerful beast when the sun came down. So I had to do my best to find him and set him free because it was possible we were his only hope.

Eyes roving over the list, I read the first idea I had underlined.

"I could ask if I will see him again?" Re-reading the question out loud made the idea sound stupid—not to mention that it also made my knees wobble at the possibility of the Envoy's answer being a *no*. I would not be able to survive that blow. When I wrote and underlined the question, I'd only been thinking of receiving a positive answer.

Silver shook his head. "Not a useful question. You might see him again, but that doesn't mean he'll be alive when you do."

I placed a hand on the table to steady myself.

Cylea swatted Silver's arm. "Shut up, you insensitive bastard."

I went over the rest of the list, then crumbled it in anger. None of the things I'd written were any good. All the questions were a reflection of my desire to know that Kalyll was all right, that his traitorous brother hadn't murdered him already.

"This will sound terrible," Kryn said, "but you need to get a grip, Dani. Kalyll's life depends on that visit."

"I know. I know." I beat a fist on my forehead and took several deep breaths. Looking inward, I found the place where I liked to relegate Dark Dani. I needed her cold determination, her calculated way of thinking.

Not her *determination,* she seemed to say. Our *determination. Kalyll has accepted all aspects of himself. You need to do the same if you want to see him again. Alive.* She pointed out that last bit, adding an edge of sarcasm to the word.

Dark Dani wasn't one hundred percent me, but I could be like her. I *had* been like her in the past. Gently, careful not to let her overtake me completely, I invited her in.

Immediately, I felt my pulse slow, and my mind clear. The edge of desperation was still there, but it was less sharp. Manageable.

Rolling my shoulders, I glanced around the room, meeting everyone's gazes. They all seemed calm, ready to confront any news the Envoy might deliver. For a moment, I found it surprising that Kalyll had surrounded himself with such a glacial bunch. Then I realized they were exactly what a Seelie Prince needed to help him perform his duties. Emotion couldn't rule in court, just like it couldn't rule in the emergency room or the operating table.

And that was when it hit me—Dark Dani had always been with me. She was the one who healed with steady hands when there seemed to be no hope. She was the one who issued clear commands to the staff when gauze, retractors, forceps, or scalpels were needed. And that was exactly who I needed to be right now. This was how I would be strong for Kalyll.

"Okay, this is what I'm thinking," I said, taking charge of myself and the situation. "It's best to ask questions that we think have a positive answer, right?"

"Right," Jeondar said. "That way she will provide additional information."

"It would be nice if said additional information was useful, but from what I experienced last time, I bet it won't be."

"Sometimes it is." Arabis shrugged and glanced toward Kryn, making me wonder if, during her visit to the Envoy, she'd asked something about their relationship.

From the way Kryn was frowning, it was easy to guess he was wondering the same thing. *Witchlights!* I would be glad if these two got their stories straight. It was heart-wrenching seeing them pine over each other day in and day out. I wasn't sure how the others had endured the tension for so long.

"*Is Kalyll in Elf-hame?*" I said, pushing thoughts of Arabis and Kryn aside. "What do you think of that as the first question? It's broad, but we need to discard the possibility that he's in my realm. Besides, I have a feeling he's still here, so the Envoy's answer should be *yes*. But you guys know

Cardian better than I do. Do you think he took him elsewhere?"

Arabis shook her head. "Cardian isn't familiar with your realm. When he first visited, he behaved *like a horse's ass*, as the saying goes in your realm. That was when King Beathan took away his transferring privileges. It's the reason we never suspected he had a token. He might be using it to travel faster within Elf-hame, but he has no friends on the other side of the veil. All his allies are here."

"I agree." Kryn nodded.

The others did too, making me feel better about using this as my first question.

"Okay, so I'll ask *is Kalyll in Elf-hame?* and when she says *yes*, she'll provide additional information. If it's useful, my next question can be based on whatever she says. If it's not, then my second question could be *is Kalyll in Nerethien?* Again, I have a feeling that's where Kalyll is, but maybe you all know of a more likely place where Cardian could have taken him."

"He could be right under our noses, for all we know," Cylea said. "Right here in Elyndell."

Jeondar paced, a fist rubbing his chin. "We paid a visit to Cardian's closest, most powerful allies, and after the scare Kalyll gave them, I don't think they would dare lend the coward a hand any longer."

"One of those allies literally can't," Kryn said with a chuckle.

Arabis threw a disapproving glance toward Kryn, while Silver laughed and the others just shook their heads. I frowned and suspected they were talking about something Wölfe had done. I didn't want to know, so I didn't ask.

"Elyndell would be too difficult a place to keep Kalyll hidden," Jeondar added.

"Maybe you're right." Cylea nodded. "What about Pharowyn? The little prince has a couple of allies there."

"I doubt he does anymore," Jeondar disagreed. "News travels fast. I bet they're not even in Pharowyn anymore. I bet they heard the king was on a westbound extermination path and found suitable hiding places to fare the storm."

Cylea lifted her arms to the heavens. "Then Nerethien sounds like the most likely possibility, after all."

The others thought for a moment.

Jeondar started nodding to himself. "At this point, Mythorne might be the only ally of any considerable strength left to Cardian. Maybe the only one who would dare try to contain Kalyll, especially now that his reputation as a ruthless shadowdrifter has everyone talking."

"Then it's settled," I said with more confidence than I felt. "We have our questions."

Now, all I had to do was wait until midnight without losing my mind in the meantime.

CHAPTER 7
DANIELLA

While we waited for midnight to arrive, I stayed in my chamber—we didn't want Cardian to know we'd discovered his magical mole—while the others tried to do damage control and got ready for a potential trip to Nerethien.

Jeondar, as the highest ranking of the five, met with the council members and dispatched several messages to his father at the Summer Court, as well as to the Spring, Fall, and Winter Courts. He reiterated previous messages from Kalyll, warning them about Mythorne and Cardian's intentions of taking control of the minor courts. The messages also entreated them to be ready to defend their domain from hostile forces from the Unseelie King. Among other things, Jeondar also expedited things with the council members so that Kalyll's uncle was placed in charge of any decisions while the king was absent.

In the meantime, the others gathered supplies that we might need during our search for Kalyll, including healing ingredients from a list I put together.

When I got tired of the silence, I gestured to Larina to follow me, and we went to Cylea's chamber. No one else was there.

"That's all I'm good for. Lists," I complained to Larina, while I meandered through the room and walked into the closet.

I paused to look in the mirror. The Fae features Naesala Roka had forced on me remained in place and would for who knew how long.

"For now," Larina said. "Once you become queen—"

I put a hand up to cut her off. "I don't wanna think about it. That's a whole other battle. I can't even look like myself. I have to stay like this so I don't raise eyebrows wherever I go. If we ever get through this—"

"When," Larina put in. "Let's be more optimistic."

"When," I repeated, inwardly thanking her. I *had* to stay positive or I'd go mad. "*When* we get through this, I'll still have to deal with all of that . . . the court accepting me for who I am, figuring out how to be a queen to people I don't understand, and who knows what else."

"I think you will make a splendid queen."

I smiled up at her as she hovered above my head. "Thanks for the vote of confidence. You will be there to help me, won't you?"

Larina's cheeks turned violet with embarrassment. "Of course I will," she said once she recovered.

"As my friend, as my confidant, right?"

Her cheeks grew brighter still. "It will be my honor."

"And mine, you're an amazing pixie. The best friend I could've asked for."

She fluttered to my shoulder and hugged a strand of my hair. I wanted to hug her back, but she was so tiny I was afraid to crush her or damage her fragile wings.

"Will you come with us to Nerethien?" I asked. "I know it's selfish of me to—"

"I will," she blurted out without hesitation. She let go of my hair and fluttered back up. "I want to help as much as I can."

"Thank you, Larina. I may be overstepping but . . ." I stood and straightened to my full height.

The pixie hovered right in front of my face.

"I declare you a member of the Sub Rosa," I announced.

Larina blinked, looking taken aback. "I don't know what to say."

"You don't have to say anything, and *when* Kalyll is back, I will make sure he makes this official."

Even though I didn't know where I was going, I kept getting ahead of everyone, marching down the road with firm steps.

"Dani, this way," Arabis said, pointing to the path leading to the left, which I'd just passed.

I backtracked and, undeterred, marched ahead again.

They had to keep calling me back to the correct zigzagging alley, but I couldn't help myself. There was too much restless energy in my muscles to do anything else.

I was dimly aware of the beauty that surrounded us: the starlit sky, the moss-covered paths that felt like walking on lush carpets, the swinging bridges connecting tree-like homes and illuminated by fairy lights. Not once had I been able to walk the streets of Elyndell and enjoy its beauty. It seemed I was condemned to skulking around at night like a thief.

As we got closer, I recognized the way and hurried ahead with more confidence. This time, Arabis didn't correct me when I took a sharp right and found myself in a narrow corridor. I stood in front of the thick tree trunk that acted as one of the flanking walls.

The others caught up with me. Only Larina and Jeondar had stayed behind, the former ensuring everything was ready for a swift departure, and the latter doing his best to leave a firm chain of command behind.

My stomach turned with nerves. We had agreed that Arabis would go in with me. I was terrified of entering by myself, and when she offered to accompany me, I immediately seized the opportunity. The others had only looked relieved that all they had to do was stand guard outside.

"What now?" I asked.

Arabis stopped next to me and whispered in my ear. "Say the following, *anolen lathwen.*"

I nodded, then repeated the words.

"Anolen lathwen."

The texture of the tree changed, growing transparent.

Arabis gestured encouragingly. My heart started hammering. Arming myself with all of Dark Dani's courage, I stepped into the dark circular space. The temperature seemed to drop several degrees as the Envoy's lair swallowed us. The same oil lamps as before rested inside small crevices in the walls and cast their dim, wavering light.

My hands tingled as a dark pool materialized on the floor. It shone like a puddle of oil, absorbing the light from the lamps. Circles rippled outward from the center, growing larger. The hair on my arms and neck stood on end. The ripples continued, and then the Envoy's impossibly clean head rose slowly.

The atmosphere around us changed, and it became harder to draw breath. I didn't know if the air had grown thicker or if my lungs were refusing to work properly.

When the Envoy's head finished appearing in the center of the well, I clutched Arabis's hand. For a moment I was embarrassed, until she squeezed back, needing my support as much as I needed hers.

The rest of the Envoy's body surfaced and hovered, her bony feet inches from the pool. She was spotless—same as her white gossamer dress—despite the fact that she'd just climbed out of a foul pit.

As I stared at her face wrapped in all those pieces of fabric like a mummy's, I remembered how her face changed every time she spoke, and the armor I'd donned earlier felt ready to slip off. Gritting my teeth, I held on to my courage. I was grateful to Arabis for being here with me and giving me the added strength to ask my first question.

"I would like to know if King Kalyll Adanorin is in Elfhame," I said.

My question echoed in the cavernous space.

He suffers at the hands of his enemies, the Envoy's androgynous voice answered. All-black eyes and a grotesque, rot-filled mouth flashed for an instant, then disappeared.

I tried not to think of those sharp teeth and how easily they could rip through our flesh if the demon decided to make a meal out of us, which wasn't hard to do, not when her answer both tore me apart and gave me hope.

Kalyll was alive, but he was being tortured.

I shook my head, trying to focus on my relief only. They hadn't killed him, and that was my selfish hope. I would see him again.

I inhaled, ready for the next question. "Is King Kalyll Adanorin in Nerethien?"

"No." The Envoy's mouth appeared and snapped the word through its teeth. Before it disappeared, it grinned with satisfaction.

Anger rose in me at the sight of the creature's glee.

"Where is he then?" I demanded.

"Dani, no." Arabis pulled my hand, trying to drag me toward the exit.

I freed my hand. "Where is he, you infuriating creature?"

In the blink of an eye, the Envoy swooped down from her hovering height, headed straight for me. My anger served as stupidity because as she came for me, I didn't move. I stood my ground, holding my head high, even as her teeth snapped an inch from my nose.

"Give me more," she hissed.

The scent of rot invaded my nostrils, pushing against me like a physical force. A forked tongue, three times as long as it should have been, snaked out, tasted the air, then proceeded to lick the upper lip from one corner to the other as if tasting something delicious.

And I supposed she was. It had just drained two days of my life, and she wanted more. That was why my failed question delighted her.

I opened my mouth, my head churning with insults, but also with possible questions that would guide me to Kalyll. He needed our help. He was being tortured, and I couldn't allow that to go on. I had to do everything I could to save him.

But what question was the right one? They all crowded in my throat.

"Let's go." Arabis grabbed my arm, but I shook her off, staring at that faceless creature as it bore down on me.

Now that the Envoy was close, I heard her breaths. They were shallow and rattling, sounds I'd heard more times than I cared to admit. She breathed the way the dying breathed.

"Give me more," she demanded in her eerie voice.

"Is King Kalyll Adanorin in the human realm?"

"No," she answered, then cackled with delight, throwing her head back and licking her lips again, this time loudly as if she'd eaten her favorite meal.

Shit! Why had I asked that? I already knew he was in Elf-hame.

"We need to leave." Arabis tried to pull me away, but I wouldn't have it.

What was one more day shaved off my life? Maybe if I were still contemplating a human life, but Naesala Roka was going to help me live longer. I was going to live three hundred years instead of a third of that.

"Is King Kalyll Adanorin in Elyndell?" I flung the question at the Envoy, a strange heat spreading inside my chest.

"No." Another delighted cackle issued from her nasty mouth.

Maybe I was imagining things, but it looked as if the demon had gotten bigger. I swallowed thickly, my throat burning with bile.

"Dani, this is madness." Arabis grabbed me by the elbow

and shook me. "You have to stop. This can't be good. You'll die."

No, I would not die. Once I started my training with Naesala, I would have tens of thousands of days at my disposal. A few wouldn't make a difference—not after Kalyll and I had spent several lifetimes together.

"Let me be." I shoved Arabis away.

She stumbled backward, her arms thrashing for balance.

"Is King Kalyll Adanorin in Pharowyn?" I wiped a hand across my feverish forehead. I was sweating, and the small alcove seemed to be closing in on me.

"No."

"Is King Kalyll Adanorin in Imbermore?"

"No," the Envoy answered, her voice an elated whisper that made me think of a Scroogelike person counting their coins and hoarding them close to their chest, afraid someone might steal a single one.

"Is King Kalyll Ad—"

"I'm sorry about this, Dani." Arabis stepped in front of me, pulled her fist back, and decked me harder than her petite body had the right to.

The last thing I registered was falling backward, the question dying on my lips as the back of my head hit the stone floor, and I lost consciousness.

CHAPTER 8
KALYLL

"Your Sub Rosa friends are off to visit the Envoy, likely to find out where you are," Cardian said, leaning close enough that I could have reached out and strangled him, if not for the magical barrier between us.

"How predictable?" He went on, so pleased with himself. "Of course, they're wasting their time. They'll never find you."

His small eyes shone with what he left unsaid, that I would stay here, at his mercy, for as long as he wanted me to. Though the word *mercy* didn't really factor into the equation.

I looked at my hands, at the unnatural angle at which my fingers were healing. From outside this magical bubble, he could have his sorcerer do whatever he wanted to me. And he was enjoying himself so much that I'd begun questioning every single moment, every single interaction, I'd ever shared with him.

He hated me. Truly hated me.

I had to believe there was something I'd done or not done to deserve it.

My mind riffled through countless memories of our childhood and adolescence. I searched through each one of them, trying to see if I'd been cruel, if I'd hurt him in some way, but the more I went over our past, I realized that I'd been vastly absent. My duties as future king had kept me away.

While he played, I sat with tutors most hours of the day. I barely had time for anything other than studying and attending council meetings, during which I was only allowed to listen and learn.

While he partied and lived the pampered life everyone thought a prince should have, I learned battle strategies, drilled in the training grounds, and soaked my bruises at night, all so I could do it over again the next day.

So no, I hadn't had time for my brother—my *half*-brother, I reminded myself. Had he wished I had? He never gave me any indication that he wanted me near him. On the contrary, he often complained that my presence felt stifling, that I *killed the fun*. If I was honest, there was no love lost between us.

From the start, he saw me as a suffocating authoritative figure, and I always saw him as a brat.

Would it have been different if we'd shared a father? If the blood bond had been stronger between us, if our connection hadn't been diluted?

It was impossible to answer that question. We couldn't change what it was. There was no point in wondering about it. Whatever had caused his hatred, it had brought us here.

A point of no return.

Weak. You're so weak, Wölfe whispered in my mind. *None of that matters. He signed his death sentence the moment he hurt Dani.*

An involuntary growl escaped me.

"The decorous prince is nothing but a beast and always has

been." Cardian laughed, delighted by the irony. "Growl all you want, Kalyll. Shift into that hideous monster and claw away at your prison like you did last night—I must admit, it was quite entertaining to watch—but it won't serve you. Best to save your energy because you're not going anywhere." He batted a hand in the air. "But what am I saying? Keep on with your ridiculous behavior. You are quickly becoming my favorite sport. If you suffered with resignation, it wouldn't be half as amusing."

The energy field that surrounded me crackled as, from the shadows that lurked behind Cardian, that hooded figure reappeared. Woven with threads of silver and gold, the cloak and hood shimmered as though imbued with enchantments. Its length was long and flowing, and its hues seemed to shift with the light. This was the powerful sorcerer my brother had tasked with torturing me. I speculated he was a male. He was taller than Cardian, thicker too, a male's build for sure.

He was responsible for the force shield that kept me and the beast contained. Yesterday, I had waited for nightfall, hoping the beast would be able to rip through the shield. I'd clawed at the barrier, rammed my shoulders against it, exhausted myself trying, but it had been useless. I ended up battered, my clothes in tatters, and my fury quickly morphing into frustration and hopelessness.

The sorcerer appeared faceless, only a black hole edged by the cowl of his cloak. His hands—also those of a male—were interlaced in front of him. An unnecessary amount of fabric draped around his arms, the end of the sleeves hanging around his wrists.

Gently, each movement practiced and graceful, he waved a

hand in the air, and my ripped jacket, shirt, and boots which were discarded at my feet disappeared. I had been using the tatters as a pillow when I tried to sleep. It had been little comfort, but they wouldn't even allow me that much.

"Lucky thing you kept your pants," Cardian said, his mouth twisted in disgust, as if he were trying not to imagine me totally naked. "Still, you're about to wish you had kept on more than that."

There was a spark in his eyes that caused an involuntary shudder to go through me. He watched me closely, likely searching for a reaction, but I kept it hidden, revealing nothing and resisting the urge to tighten my broken fingers into fists that ached to pummel him.

Cardian nodded to the sorcerer, smiling.

The hooded figure moved his hands in an arc as if to encompass the sphere that held me. My entire body tensed as I braced myself for the pain of more broken bones, but nothing happened. Not at first.

Then a shiver ran down my spine, and I noticed a marked change in temperature. Soon, the air inside my prison turned frigid. My skin tightened around my bones, every hair standing on end.

"You've always enjoyed a nice fire, haven't you? Lit year-round in your chamber. Why is that exactly? Is it its warmth you crave? Or is it its cozy comfort and glow?"

On the few occasions when he had visited me in my quarters, he had complained about it being too hot and stuffy. I had never liked the cold. I was surprised he remembered such a small detail.

My teeth began to chatter. I tightened my jaw and fought

not to rub my arms or hug my torso to preserve the quickly fading warmth of my body.

Cardian took a step closer and watched me from head to toe. "Oh, your skin is starting to match your hair." He glanced over his shoulder and said to the sorcerer, "Make sure it doesn't kill him. Just barely."

The male gave a single nod.

"I would love to stay and watch you freeze," Cardian said, returning his attention to me. "But I have pressing matters to attend to. Elyndell has been left leaderless. We can't allow that. Not to mention there are a few pests that need my attention."

I rushed to the barrier and pounded my fist on it. Its surface crackled, distorting the space beyond, making Cardian and the sorcerer appear blurry.

"If you hurt any of my friends, I will kill you," I shouted, my throat raw with the force of my voice.

Cardian only shook his head and smiled sadly as if to highlight the improbability of that pathetic threat ever coming to fruition.

"I'm sure you understand why I can't allow them to . . . carry on. I can promise you that they'll go swiftly. All except for one. I'm curious about your Jovinian girl. What's so special about her? I'm really intrigued."

I growled through my clenched teeth. "I will rip you to pieces."

"My, my. She must be something. She did jump to save you when Varamede attacked. That kind of loyalty from a subject is admirable. What did you offer her? A prominent position in court? Gold? Or was it *love*?" He said the word with mockery, as if love were a tall tale, a mythical creature that didn't exist.

But of course, he would think that. He thought loyalty could be bought. He didn't understand that to receive something you had to give it first. I would give my life for every single member of the Sub Rosa. If they did the same for me, I could only count myself lucky.

And if he didn't understand loyalty, how could he ever understand love?

I pity you, I wanted to say to him, but I kept my mouth shut. It was infinitely better if he thought my relationship with Daniella was a transaction.

"She's at least as powerful as Varamede," Cardian went on, "and that is saying something. She's new to your group, so I'm sure it won't be too hard to sway her loyalties. Not with the right offer." He paused and made a show of pondering something. At last, he asked, "Are there any other services she might provide besides hurling herself in front of an oncoming attack? You know, is she . . . a good fuck?"

"Bastard," I spat, tamping down the bulk of my anger, though not without effort. I wanted to hurl insults and curses. I wanted to strangle him with my bare hands for even daring to think of touching her. But I contained my trembling ire, disguising it with a shiver that he would attribute to the cold.

"*Tsk, tsk,* you're the only bastard here. Literally." He smirked, then whirled on his heel and left me with the sorcerer.

I took a step back. My arms moved up of their own accord as a violent shiver ripped through me. Breathing hurt my nostrils, my throat, my chest. The air was frigid.

Turning my back on the sorcerer, I lowered myself and huddled in a tight ball. I trembled violently, my body's movements completely outside of my control.

I wished for the tattered coat, then imagined a warm fire and Daniella sitting by my side. Soon, I went numb all over. I couldn't feel my hands. I stared at them for a long moment. Absently, I grabbed one of my broken fingers and set it straight. There was a crack, but I felt no pain. In fact, I felt nothing at all.

Almost amused, I straightened the others. I couldn't bend them or feel them, but at least they looked right.

My eyelids closed and froze shut.

CHAPTER 9
DANIELLA

"Ow." I wiggled my jaw from side to side and massaged it. Placing my fingers on each side of my face, I slowly allowed healing magic to seep in and take away the dull ache.

"I'm sorry I had to do that," Arabis said, "but you lost it."

"Did you have to sock me? You could have *Susurro'd* me instead."

"I don't do that to my friends."

"You do it to Kalyll all the time when he loses it."

"He asked me to. I'm sorry."

"You don't have to apologize." I sighed as the pain dissolved. "I deserved it."

More than ever, I was sure that the Envoy was a trickster demon. True, I had been desperate to learn where Cardian was keeping Kalyll, but there had been more to it, some sort of compulsion caused by the creature, something I had been unable to control.

While I was unconscious, Arabis and the others brought me back to Cylea's room in the Vine Tower, and so we were back right where we'd started, with no idea of where to begin our search.

"What are our options now?" I slumped on an armchair by the fireplace and looked to the others for answers.

Larina was sitting at the edge of a table. Cylea lounged on the bed, her posture unconcerned, although her pinched face revealed the opposite. Jeondar, Kryn, and Silver stood close to the open window, while Arabis paced by the door.

"I still can't get over the Envoy's trickery," Silver said, running a hand through his platinum-colored hair. Moonlight came down in shafts through the window, making the short strands shine. "They always warn you about going over two questions, but they could have been more specific about what would happen if you did."

"No kidding," Cylea rolled onto her stomach, kicking her feet up. "Maybe no one ever got out of there alive to share the details."

"Very likely," Jeondar put in.

"How do we find him now?" I insisted.

I didn't care about the Envoy anymore. That avenue was shot. If I lost more than two days of a very long life, I didn't care anymore. I only wanted to figure out where to find Kalyll.

"Word is being spread out across the kingdom," Jeondar said. "Everyone—soldiers, dignitaries, guards, spies—they all have instructions to keep an eye out. Sooner or later, we'll hear something." I knew he was trying, but there was no confidence in his voice. He didn't believe what he was saying.

"Sooner or later isn't good enough," I said. "What about Shadow? Has anyone talked to her? Was she able to find out anything?"

"I wouldn't put your hopes on a *sprite*," Kryn said.

The way he said *sprite* sounded dismissive as if nothing could ever be expected from someone so tiny and inconsequential in his view. On the table, Larina shifted uncomfortably from side to side.

"Don't be an ass, Kryn," I snapped.

"I'm not being an ass. I'm just . . ." At a sidelong look from Arabis, he seemed to shift gears. "I . . . I'm just trying to say that we should think of something *we* can do other than waiting."

I knew that wasn't what he'd been about to say, but I couldn't disagree with him and had to give him credit for amending his attitude. It was more than he would've done when I first met him.

Halfway to opening my mouth to say something, a tiny knock came at the door. Arabis opened it, and as if I'd conjured the sprite with my words and thoughts, Shadow flew in on translucent wings, a determined expression on her fierce face.

Cylea jumped off the bed, reclined on one of the posts, and crossed her arms. "We were just talking about you. Any news?"

Shadow inclined her head in the affirmative.

I jumped to my feet, too. "What have you learned?"

The sprite looked down at me from where she hovered a couple of feet above my head. Due to her all-black eyes, it was impossible to judge what she was thinking. How much did she know about me? Had Queen Eithne told her who I really was?

"I know where King Kalyll is," she said, turning her full attention to Jeondar, the highest ranking of all of us.

"Where?" the Summer Prince demanded.

"He is in Nerethien."

Jeondar narrowed his eyes.

I shook my head. "No, he's not there."

Shadow turned her face in my direction, her movements slow and calculated. A shiver went across my back, and a slash of fear stabbed my gut. It was ridiculous. How could I feel afraid of someone so tiny? And yet, I did. Some instinct told me this was the kind of person with whom you needed to tread carefully.

"My source is trustworthy. King Kalyll is in Nerethien," she reiterated.

"I don't know who provided your information," Kryn stepped forward and placed his closed fists on his hips, "but ours comes from the Envoy."

Shadow scoffed. "That trickster? Then I know for a fact you are mistaken."

"I'm sorry, Shadow," Arabis said, "but we have all visited the Envoy and received accurate information, including the king."

"That may be so, but you cannot deny that she isn't necessarily forthcoming. The king is being held in Highmire at this very moment. We shouldn't waste time. We should make plans to go immediately."

"We, huh?" Kryn said. "And how do we know we can trust you?"

"I was loyal to Queen Eithne for a long time. How can you doubt me?" Shadow sounded injured at the suggestion that she was being anything but honest and loyal to the crown.

"Queen Eithne wasn't exactly a bastion of virtue," Kryn said.

One moment Shadow was hovering in midair and the next she was rocketing toward Kryn's face, a sharp spear appearing in her hands, which she aimed directly at one of his eyeballs.

A collective gasp swept through the chamber. Arabis opened her mouth surely to issue a Susurro command, but Shadow was too fast, even faster than Kryn, who had started drawing a dagger from his belt at the same time as he tried to duck.

To everyone's surprise, it was only Larina who was able to match Shadow's speed, and it was her magic that made the sprite's spear vanish and saved Kryn from ending up looking like a pirate for the rest of his life.

Somehow, Shadow put the brakes on her plummeting advance and stopped mere inches from smashing into Kryn's nose. She stared at her empty hands for an instant, then flashed in Larina's direction barely avoiding a slash of Kryn's dagger, who seemed ready to murder her for daring to attack him.

"How dare you, pixie?" Shadow demanded, flying toward Larina. "Give it back."

It might not have been the best idea, but I took a step sideways and blocked Shadow's path. I braced for a collision, but her control was amazing. She stopped on a dime, or more likely an atom. Veering left, she tried to bypass me. I lifted my hands and waved them around. She pivoted from side to side, trying to get to the pixie, but there was no way I would let her hurt my friend.

"Stop, Shadow," I commanded in an authoritative tone that surprised me.

The sprite literally froze in midair as if by some sort of

magical spell. I blinked up at her, wondering if Larina had done that, but then I noticed Shadow's stern expression.

"Thank you," I said.

Shadow frowned at my words of gratitude.

What now? What would a queen do? Okay, Kryn had insulted her, so diplomacy was needed.

"Um . . . Kryn didn't mean to doubt you, Shadow," I said.

"The hell I didn't," he growled, dagger still in hand.

I shot a loaded glance in his direction.

He seemed ready to argue but must've thought better of it because he pressed his lips into a tight line and batted a hand as if to dismiss the entire situation.

"He needs to apologize," Shadow said.

"We all apologize." I inclined my head.

I knew Kryn well enough to realize he wasn't going to apologize, so I took it upon myself to make things right.

"Shadow is trying to help," I said, addressing everyone. "We need to be grateful and respectful of that fact."

Jeondar's amber eyes scrutinized me with interest. A slight smile stretched his lips as if he approved of what I was doing. I felt glad for his support because I was nobody in Elyndell, and I was overstepping.

Still, it wasn't for Shadow to decide what we needed to do next, and it wasn't unreasonable for Kryn to want to keep things within the Sub Rosa.

"We appreciate the information you have delivered to us," I said. "Now, we need to discuss what to do next based on what we know. Would you mind giving us some time?" I glanced toward the door, donning a gentle smile.

Shadow appeared conflicted. She knew I had no authority

here, but she didn't have any either. Who was she without Queen Eithne? Where did that leave her in the palace's hierarchy? Given how things were with the minor folk, I wouldn't be surprised if she'd fallen to the very bottom of the ladder.

She didn't appear happy. Nevertheless, she bowed her head and flew toward the door, though not without shooting Kryn a death glare.

Arabis closed the door once the sprite had left.

Larina shivered, her translucent wings making a whirring sound as she did so. "I'd heard Sunnarian were intense, but that was terrifying."

"It really was," I agreed. "I don't understand how someone so small can produce such an impact."

"Sunnarian armies are legendary," Arabis said.

Larina shivered again. "I never want to face an army of Shadows."

"I had it under control," Kryn said.

Arabis sputtered. "Really?"

Silver slapped a hand on Kryn's shoulder. "There's no shame in it, my friend. What is shameful is that you haven't thanked Larina for saving your pretty eyeball."

Cylea laughed, her blue hair swinging as she shook her head from side to side. She sobered quickly and addressed Larina.

"I thank you on behalf of all of us. Kryn is an insufferable babe when he gets hurt."

Kryn turned red and seemed ready to go to battle with the others, but as much as I enjoyed and needed the lighthearted mood, we didn't have time for it.

Ignoring the banter, I turned to Larina. "What do you

think of what Shadow said? Can we trust the information she provided?"

Larina appeared taken aback at being singled out. "Um."

She wrung her dress, a blue affair that matched her skin to perfection, and puffed out around her hips. It looked like a tutu, and if she exchanged her tall boots for a pair of ballerina slippers, I could have easily imagined her twirling around like one of those little dolls in a music box.

"I think . . . I think . . ." The pixie seemed afraid to speak, but then she took a deep breath, straightened her spine, and said, "I would trust her information."

Confused, I turned to the others. "Are you sure the Envoy is never wrong?"

They all nodded.

"Maybe . . ." Larina started and only continued when I faced her again. "Maybe, King Kalyll was not in Nerethien at the exact moment you asked the question."

"Maybe."

"If Prince Cardian is using a transfer token, they could come and go within seconds," she countered.

"True," Jeondar said, "but I can't imagine Cardian easily moving Kalyll from one place to another. Unless . . ."

"Unless what?" I asked.

"Unless Kalyll is unconscious."

Everyone grew quiet, considering this.

Shame came over me as I said, "*We* have kept him unconscious to subdue him."

Kryn rubbed the back of his head, looking chagrined. Cylea shifted from foot to foot, and I felt bile rise up my windpipe.

"Kalyll submitted himself willingly and allowed us to do that," Arabis said. "If Cardian is drugging him against his will, there is no comparison. So let's stop feeling bad about that."

Kryn huffed. "I highly doubt that's what's going on. That coward wouldn't miss the opportunity to torture Kalyll."

"Agree," Cylea said. "Cardian is cruel. Once, I watched him beat a horse because he lost a stupid race against his friends. It didn't matter that he's a lousy rider. He took it out on the poor animal, and I'm certain he felt no guilt afterward."

"He's a psychopath," I said, my insides trembling.

"Psychopath?" Larina echoed, eyebrows drawn together.

"In Dani's realm," Cylea said, "they have a name for everything. In their dictionaries, when you look for the word psychopath, you find Cardian's portrait."

"Oh." The pixie's mouth formed an "O" as she considered this. She seemed unsure of whether or not this was true, so I had to set the record straight.

"Cylea is joking, Larina."

I fought against the image of the poor horse, which Cylea had painted in my mind and my imagination had embellished. I didn't want to think about Kalyll in the hands of a psychopath.

"Let's focus on the matter at hand." I cleared my throat. "So, we think it's possible that when I asked the Envoy if Kalyll was in Nerethien that he was *momentarily* elsewhere."

Cylea twirled a strand of her long hair, appearing deep in thought. "What if he knew we were going to see the Envoy?"

"We didn't tell anyone," I said. "We didn't speak of it in my chamber either."

Kryn's green eyes wandered to Larina.

"Don't you dare, Kryn." I pointed a finger straight at his nose.

"I'm sorry, Dani, but she's the latest addition to the group. We barely know her, and it wouldn't be the first time she'd betrayed you. She did put that necklace in your bag in Imbermore."

I turned to Larina. "Don't let him bother you. Most of the time, he's a jerk. He has his moments, but this is clearly not one of them."

Kryn huffed. "I'm just trying to make sense."

"Hundreds of people live in this palace," I snapped. "For all we know, Cardian still has spies here. Maybe someone followed us out of the palace. That's not so hard to fathom."

Jeondar nodded pensively. "It seems our plans to go to Highmire stand. We can sleep for a few hours, then go at dawn. We can leave from here, and maybe we can come up with a way to throw Cardian off our scent by using that crystal bird to our advantage."

"We should leave now," I said.

"Dani, you need rest," Arabis said, placing the barest of emphasis on the word *you*.

I was the human who was slowing them down. With their Fae stamina, they could probably go for days without sleep and rest, but not me. The worst part . . . I *was* tired. To the bones. It had been a long day of stress and many waking hours. Still . . .

"We can at least go to Nerethien now, can't we? We could

rest there." Something told me that if I was closer to Kalyll, my heart would be at ease because I would be able to feel him.

They all exchanged glances, considering.

"Everything is ready, correct?" Jeondar said. "I've done all I can on my side to set order among the council members and generals, in case there is an attack from the Unseelie Court."

"I'm packed and ready to go," Cylea said. "I couldn't decide if I would need a gown, though. What do you think?"

Arabis shook her head and rolled her eyes. "I'm ready too."

I looked expectantly from Kryn to Silver. The former simply nodded, while Silver punched a fist into his open palm.

"I'm ready to get out of here," he said. "Ever since I spent time in its dungeons, I don't care for the Vine Tower all that much."

"As if Highmire's dungeons will be any better," Cylea put in. "So we agree then? We leave tonight?"

Everyone nodded.

Cylea pulled something from her tunic's pocket. "Good thing Kalyll left this with us."

She held a transfer token, a wooden coin with the carving of a snake in the middle. It was the same one Kalyll had let me use when he sent me back home after Mount Ruin. The same one Wölfe had used to get me right back.

My spirits lifted slightly. In a few moments, we would be closer to Kalyll, well on our way to rescuing him.

"I'll go get my things," I said.

Jeondar stopped. "While you're in your chamber, mention casually that we're going to Imbermore. Hopefully, that will keep Cardian looking in the wrong direction."

I nodded and while Larina and I retrieved my backpack, we did as Jeondar instructed. For ten minutes we stood gathered in a circle. My bag's strap rested across my shoulder and its weight on my hip. We only had a few necessities. Jeondar had said that if we needed anything else, we would purchase it.

"Who'll go with me first?" Cylea asked.

Arabis put a hand up. "I think I will be the least conspicuous, so I should be the one to procure our lodging."

"Let's go then." Cylea took Arabis's hand, and in the next instant, they dissolved into thin air.

They all looked at me.

"What is it?" Jeondar asked.

"I forgot something. I'll be right back." I ran out of the room, headed for my chamber. When I had changed, the brooch that Kalyll gave me stayed on the dress. I had to get it back.

"Hey, wait," Jeondar called.

Wings whirred behind me as I ran down the hall, headed back to Kalyll's tower.

"Wait, Dani," Larina called behind me. "I can get it for you. It will only take me a second or two."

I stopped and glanced back. "Okay."

Using her magic she flew past me at a prodigious speed. I smiled as glittering dust rained down on me, giving me a tingling sensation.

Marching steps sounded from the hall to my left. I turned to find a host of guards crowding the tight space. They were led by Cardian.

CHAPTER 10
KALYLL

Something woke me. The numbness turned to pain. As I opened my eyes, the first thing I noticed was the bitter cold that still clung to me. I was still trapped in the force field, which pulsed with a soft blue light. I shivered uncontrollably, trying to make sense of what had happened.

Slowly, the memories of the sorcerer's spell came flooding back to me. His spell had lowered the temperature so drastically that I had fallen unconscious within minutes. How long had I been out? I wasn't sure.

As I tried to sit up, I realized how weak and stiff my limbs felt. My fingers and toes were numb, and my face and ears burned with a painful sensation. I took a deep breath, trying to push away the fog that still lingered in my mind.

A movement caught my eye. Someone came into the room, steps light and measured.

"So you are Kalyll Adanorin?" a serene voice asked. "The great Dragon Soul."

I struggled to focus. At first, the shape was blurry, then it sharpened into a tall, thin male with a bony face and hook nose. I had never met him, but I immediately knew this was Kellam Mythorne, the Unseelie King.

"You're not much to look at." He paced in front of the sphere, looking me up and down. "Though you're not as insignificant as your brother. He's not *legendary* like you, after all."

I forced myself to stand up, even though every muscle in my body protested, and the cold bit at my skin. I watched him, wondering why he'd come. To taunt me? He would not succeed in that.

"Let me out of here," I said, my voice a raw rasp.

"And then what? You will fight me? Perhaps another day. You're not in any shape to do much at all. And after Runik has another go at you, even less."

Runik? That was the sorcerer's name?

Runik Begallard was a name almost everyone in the realm knew. He had served Queen Rothala, Mythorne's mother. He was the one who, during The Slaughter at Stone Peak, summoned a massive storm that raged across the battlefield, raining down lightning and hailstones upon the Seelie army. The storm was so fierce and destructive that it nearly turned the tide of the battle in their favor. He was a legend all by himself.

"I was only mildly curious to see you. You killed my son, after all," Mythorne said, "but I find that I've already lost interest. So . . . I leave you with Runik."

Mythorne left, the sorcerer took his place, and I braced myself for more pain.

CHAPTER 11
DANIELLA

"Just who I was looking for," Cardian said, wearing a thin smile.

How was he here? And with so many guards? My stomach tumbled, and I felt sick.

I took several steps back and tried to run the way I'd come, but Cardian flicked a hand at one of the guards, and he jumped to block my path.

I flexed my fingertips. Cardian was about six feet away from me. That wasn't much—not when death dwelled in my hands. I lunged in his direction. Cardian's eyes grew wide with panic, but the guard was faster than me. He wrapped an arm around my waist and held me back, while I kicked and wriggled, trying to get free.

"I'm going to kill you," I cried out.

The commotion was enough to draw the remaining Sub Rosa out of Cylea's chamber. Kryn and Silver came running down the corridor, their swords raised, battle cries issuing from their throats.

"Kill them," Cardian ordered his guards, then pointed at the one holding me. "You, let's go. You, too." He pointed at a second guard.

They marched in the opposite direction to my friends.

"Stop!" Kryn shouted as the sound of steel against steel filled the air.

"Kryn! Silver!" I kept fighting, kicking and jabbing my elbows backward, doing my best to hit the guard. But he was tall and strong, and my efforts were in vain. "Let me go, you bastard." I tried clamping my hands around his forearms, but he was wearing leather gauntlets, and I couldn't make contact with his skin.

If only I'd had some of the light magic I'd used against Varamede, I would've blasted Cardian to the confines of hell. But I needed to kill someone in order to harness that kind of power.

As we turned the corner, I caught a glimpse of Larina. She was coming around the bend in a hurry. I shook my head, warning her to stay away. Cardian marched in front of me—not in the least worried about the scuffle taking place behind him.

Down the hall, we ran into a second group of guards.

"Go help the others," he ordered.

They ran past us, drawing their weapons. There were at least ten of them. The Sub Rosa would be utterly outnumbered.

"Let. Me. Go." I pounded on the guard's arm.

"Quit it, you whore." He shook me violently.

My brain rattled. I blinked, trying to clear my vision. Out of the corner of my eye, I noticed something, then felt a slight touch on my shoulder. I glanced over and found Larina scampering along my collarbone, and sliding into the breast pocket of my tunic, unnoticed by anyone but me.

As she fell inside, she wiggled. A fresh rush of panic hit me. Her precious wings would be crumpled. What was she doing?

I waited for something to happen. Maybe she could help me get free with her magic. But a few beats later—the guard carrying me down a set of steps and jarring my teeth—I realized I didn't really know the extent of Larina's magic. I'd seen her appear and disappear things like food and Shadow's spear, use her pixie dust to fluff my hair and speed up her pace, but maybe she couldn't do much more, especially not against someone so big.

Part of me was glad for her company. Wherever Cardian was taking me, I wouldn't be alone, but I was also afraid for her. She could get badly hurt, crushed. I shook my head. No, nothing bad would happen to her. I would make sure of that.

After traversing several long corridors, we entered a waiting room outfitted with armchairs and tea tables. A large painting in a style I recognized hung on the wall across the door. Cardian came to a stop in front of it and regarded it, hands clasped behind his back.

The guard tossed me into a chair as if I were a misbehaving child. I rolled to one side, making sure to land on my back so as not to hurt Larina.

He took several steps toward the door, waiting for Cardian's orders.

"Don't leave, and remain vigilant."

"Afraid of me?" I asked as I stood and straightened my tunic.

"You do have powerful magic, but Cedric is a neutralizer. So don't try anything stupid."

I frowned. What was he talking about? Glancing back at the guard, I figured he must be Cedric. A neutralizer? Within this context, it wasn't hard to figure out what the brute was capable of doing. He dampened magic. So even if I had been able to touch him skin to skin, he would've been all right. Even if I had been able to grab Cardian by the neck when I lunged for him, I would've accomplished nothing. Maybe that was why Larina hadn't been able to do anything either. I could only guess.

"Where's the king?" I demanded.

Cardian turned from the painting—a scene depicting a castle built on top of fluffy white clouds. "You are looking at him."

"It can't be," I said under my breath.

Jeondar had said that he'd left everything in order with the council members and generals. How could Cardian be back?

The answer came to me in an instant . . . because he had more allies in Elyndell and inside the Vine Tower than we ever imagined.

We had underestimated the weasel. I imagined I could feel Larina's tiny heart thumping against mine.

"It *can* be, and it is," he said. "Kalyll is a fool. He assumes there's loyalty where there's only greed. More than half of the council members are mine. That means that their men—the guards that you see around the palace and elsewhere and who belong to those council members' houses—also answer to me."

Kalyll was surrounded by traitors.

"You see," he went on, "while Kalyll went on battles and

charity missions around the realm, I garnered the favor of the people who truly matter. I didn't ignore them as he did. I promised them they would get their due when the time came. Loyalty is a mirage. Everyone has a *price* in the end. Wouldn't you agree?" His question was suggestive, and the way he emphasized the word *price* made me pause to ponder his exact meaning.

I bit down on my tongue to contain the urge to curse him and tell him exactly what I thought of his philosophy and where he could shove it. Instead, I held his gaze, wondering how much he knew about me.

Unless his spies had provided him with better information, he thought I was the daughter of a Jovinian dignitary and a scheming opportunist who had ingratiated herself with the new king. Likely, he also thought I was Kalyll's lover—not that he was wrong. In all, it wasn't a far-fetched theory, especially since, as far as he knew, Kalyll and I had just met.

He had no idea who I really was.

Cardian didn't know that Kalyll and I had been through hell and back and that something deep had developed between us during the hardships we'd endured together. Adversities have a way of bringing people together—not that we wouldn't have fallen in love if we'd met in line at the DMV. We were mates, after all.

Still holding Cardian's gaze, I pressed my lips together. Did I have a price? That was what he wanted to know. I let my silence be its own answer, an answer left to his sole interpretation.

He narrowed his eyes and hummed, taking a few steps to one side and regarding me from head to toe. "You have a very interesting skill, Lady Fenmenor. You went against Varamede Elis, the most powerful thunderlord in the realm, and you nearly beat him. He was hard-pressed to admit it, but I was there. I saw what happened. Try as he might, he couldn't lie to me. For a moment there, he thought you would win."

If I had killed and sucked dry someone else, I would have won. The thought came from Dark Dani, and though I hated the ease with which it pushed through my mind, I couldn't deny its veracity.

"I don't know if you realize this," he went on, "but there are few people in this realm or any other who have that kind of power."

A frown cut across my forehead involuntarily.

"Ah, I see you had no idea."

There were plenty of powerful people in Elf-hame and my realm, so Cardian's assertion sounded ridiculous to my ears. There was no way I was more powerful than the many midnight mages and witches that roamed the human world. Or the mighty sorcerers and sorceresses of Elf-hame.

As if he'd read my thoughts, he said, "You might think others are more powerful because they can perform many different tricks, while you only have one."

Cardian inclined his head to one side. He was asking if I could do more than blast pure energy. What if he knew my real power was healing? Would he be so interested in me? On the other hand, my ability to shoot beams of light clearly interested him. I hated to think of his fascination if he ever learned I had to murder someone with my bare hands in order to charge my batteries and shoot.

I gave him no answer other than a chagrined sniffle to let him think I had no other skills.

"Oh, you shouldn't be embarrassed, Lady Fenmenor. What you can do is outstanding. Don't ever think otherwise." He frowned. "Do you mind if I do away with formalities and call you Ylannea?"

I shrugged like it made no difference to me.

"Good. So . . . why don't you explain to me the nature of your relationship with Kalyll? Why would you risk your life for him?"

"What does it matter to you, *Cardian*?"

He raised his nose in the air, clearly bothered by what he considered irreverence. What did he want me to call him? King Cardian? I wouldn't even call him prince at this point. I could, however, offer him a list of alternatives he might not be familiar with: prick, douchebag, dickwad, asswipe.

Eyes narrowed, he considered me, then decided to let it go. He had been the one wishing to do away with formalities, anyway.

"It matters to me because you could become a valuable weapon in my arsenal." He raised an eyebrow, wearing an expression that seemed to say *you could profit from this too if you're smart*.

As difficult as it was, I feigned intrigue. Leisurely, I strolled around the room, picked the most comfortable-looking arm-chair, sat down, and crossed my legs.

"I'm listening."

Cardian smiled with satisfaction. He took the chair across from mine, then tapped his ear. "I'm listening first."

"Fine." I waved a hand in the air and tried to think of

something that would explain why I would jump in front of Kalyll to save his life. "He promised to . . . make it worth my while when he became king."

"Meaning what exactly?"

"He said he would help my family."

"How?"

"The Fenmenors would get preferential treatment in the wool trade."

"And you risked your life for *that*?" Cardian scoffed. He cared nothing for family, so of course, this reason sounded like a lie to him.

I pushed to the edge of the chair and looked him straight in the eye. "That is my inheritance we're talking about. Of course I would risk my life for it."

His eyes sparkled. Now, here was something he fully comprehended. Everything he'd done so far had been for what he considered to be his due.

He placed an elbow on the armrest and tapped his jaw with an index finger. "Unfortunately for you *and* your family," he chuckled at this, "Kalyll will never be king."

Of their own accord, my teeth ground, and a muscle jumped in my jaw. Fortunately, this natural reaction served me well because Cardian thought I was frustrated that my plans had been foiled.

"But maybe there is no reason for you to fret," he said. "Maybe you can still be friends with the Seelie King." His satisfied smirk stretched for a mile.

This time, I stopped my true feelings from revealing themselves. Instead, I lowered my eyes to the floor and let them wander as if I were deep in thought, considering all the ramifications of this new and unexpected boon.

Before I opened my mouth to speak, I considered the type of things a ruthless person might say in a situation like this. Would they express relief? Would they make demands? Would they appear suspicious?

I settled on the latter, snapping my gaze to his and holding it. "How can I trust someone who so easily stabs his brother in the back?"

His hands took hold of the armrests and squeezed them hard. "He is *not* my brother."

Holding my breath, I hardened my expression, trying not to appear intimidated by his sudden anger, letting Dark Dani tighten her grip on the reins.

There was so much hatred in his eyes, a clear desire to hurt anyone who dared link him to Kalyll, that I worried he might take it out on me. Obviously, he didn't care that they *did* share blood, shared the same mother. Denial made it easier for him to justify his actions, and he would cling to it if it was the last thing he did.

There was a knock at the door. Cardian looked annoyed but gave Cedric an indication to answer. The neutralizer opened the door cautiously. He peered out and after confirming that whoever was on the other side was an ally, he moved out of the way.

Varamede stepped into the room. Hands restless at his side, he gave me a wary once-over. I did the same.

Blinding light flashed before my eyes, conjured by my memories. This male had nearly killed me.

"What is it?" Cardian asked, irritated.

"They escaped."

"What?! They were outnumbered."

"Transfer token," Varamede informed him.

Cardian growled and pounded the armrest.

"Go." He dismissed Varamede. "I'll find you soon."

The thunderlord backed out of the room, never taking his eyes off me, and left.

Cardian seethed for a long moment, then took a deep breath, gathered his wits, and returned his attention to me. "Where were we?"

"I asked you a question," I said. "It still stands. How can I trust you?" I was grateful for the steadiness in my words. Perhaps, some months ago, and without my darker side at the helm, I would've melted from fear, but this cruel, dark court had taught me many lessons, and maybe, just maybe, I was learning to play the game.

"Moreover," I glanced toward Cedric, "*you* don't trust *me*. Not exactly the basis for a productive alliance."

"Trust is earned," he said. "So first, why don't you earn mine? Why don't you tell me where Kalyll's cronies went?"

I answered without hesitation because a better situation couldn't have fallen on my lap. The alliance Cardian was offering me was the best way to find and free Kalyll.

"If they kept to the plan, they went to Nerethien."

There was a small tremor in his expression, which let me know we were on the right track. Kalyll was in the Unseelie capital.

"We discovered your mole in my chamber. The crystal bird." I was playing a dangerous game telling him the truth, but it was the best way to earn his trust. "We used it to make you think we were going to Imbermore."

"Why Nerethien?" he asked.

"Because the Envoy said he was there," I lied.

"That's not possible."

I frowned and did my best to sound skeptical. "You mean the Envoy is wrong?" I huffed. "I always thought she was some sort of charlatan. I guess I was right."

"Not exactly a charlatan, but . . ." He rubbed his knuckles.

"But what?"

He waved a hand in the air. Of course, he would not share any details, especially when they highlighted a failure in his schemes. He had probably transferred Kalyll out of Nerethien during the time we were with the Envoy.

"Anything else you can tell me?" Cardian asked.

I shook my head. "No. That's all they know. Their plan was to find an inn, then go from there. They think he's being kept somewhere in Highmire."

This time, even though I watched him closely, I detected nothing in his expression to assert or contradict that this was actually Kalyll's location.

"I told you what I know," I said. "How will you earn *my* trust now?"

Cardian rose to his feet and looked down at me with cold blue eyes. I wanted to stand and hold my own as he glared at me, but instead, I relaxed further into the chair, acting the way a person who could shoot laser beams—nullifier or not—should act.

He thought for a moment, then turned to Cedric. "You may leave."

"Are you sure, my king?" Cedric asked.

"Of course I'm sure. Don't question me again."

"My apologies." The man bowed and retired from the room.

I blinked as a feeling of well-being flooded me, and suddenly I realized that the sick feeling that came over me when I first spotted Cardian and his guards had been due to Cedric.

"Feel better?" Cardian asked.

I stood up very slowly, my legs firmer than they'd felt a moment ago. A tingling sensation began in my hands. All I had to do was leap forward, wrap my hands around his neck, and drain every bit of life out of him. Except I couldn't do that, not when Kalyll was still a prisoner in Nerethien, not when Cardian was the one who could take me to my mate.

"I do feel better." I smiled in a crooked way that wasn't me at all.

"Good." Cardian matched my smile, and I had to admit I was surprised he hadn't shown even an iota of fear after Cedric left.

He really was certain I wouldn't hurt him. That was how blinded he was by his poor assessment of people. He measured everyone using his own standards. He was a slimeball, so therefore, everyone else must be a slimeball too.

"What now?" I said.

"You can return to your chamber. I will call you when I need you."

The chamber with the crystal bird that he could use to spy on me.

Without a backward glance, he hurried to the door to find Varamede, I assumed. There, he paused, his hand on the knob.

Over his shoulder, he asked, "Why did my brother have you up on a pedestal while you lay there frozen?"

Oh yes, a strange thing to do for someone Kalyll barely knew.

My thoughts raced at a million miles per hour, trying to figure out the appropriate response to this question. I snatched the first one that seemed reasonable and delivered a Hollywood-worthy performance.

"The fool fancies himself in love with me." I struck a femme fatale pose that made me feel absolutely ridiculous.

At first, he didn't appear to buy it, then he said, "Ah, the female guiles. You have plenty of them, Lady Fenmenor, and Kalyll can be such a trusting fool. Our alliance might be even better than I thought."

He left the room and closed the door behind him. I stood frozen for a long moment, then collapsed on the chair, a wave of exhausted relief washing over me.

CHAPTER 12
DANIELLA

When Larina wiggled herself out of my breast pocket, I nearly jumped. She had been so still, and I had been so focused on not being discovered that I'd forgotten she was there.

She shook herself, her entire body wiggling like that of a wet dog. Her wings gave a little snap and appeared behind her back. She jumped into the air and started hovering around.

I did a double-take.

"Where did you put your wings?" I asked.

"I can stash them away," she said as if that was the most obvious of things, and I should've known. Maybe I'd been wearing these pointy ears way too long, and she'd forgotten I was human and was still clueless about most things concerning Elf-hame and its people.

"I must say, you had him fanning your fire."

"I did what?"

"I mean you handled him."

"Oh, we have a similar saying." I stared at the pattern on the rug, still feeling addled by the rush of emotion and release of stress.

"Well, what is it?" she asked when I didn't elaborate.

"What is what?"

"Your similar saying."

I had to concentrate and think back and figure out what she meant. "It's . . . um . . . *to have someone eating out of the palm of your hand.*"

She nodded appreciatively. "I like it."

"Though I don't think I had anyone eating out of the palm of my hand."

"Yes, you did. After that performance, he'll believe anything you say."

"What do we do now, Larina?" I felt at a loss.

"We wait?" She sounded as uncertain as I felt.

I nodded thoughtfully. "Cardian's my best chance to find Kalyll, but what if I can't get the information out of him? What if we wait, and it's a waste of time?"

"It's definitely a possibility."

"The others could go on to search for him, I suppose."

"Yes, that's a good idea," Larina said.

"I need a way to communicate with them, though. Do you think they're all right?"

"It sounds like they got away."

"I hope so. Any idea how I can get in touch with them in Nerethien? Oh, God, I hope no one finds them."

"It's a big place," Larina said reassuringly, "and they're used to this kind of thing. They know what to do, so I don't think we should worry about them." She paused and thought for a long moment. "Maybe Shadow can help."

"But can we trust her? I know she was right about Kalyll's location, but—"

"I think we can trust her. When I was in your room,

retrieving the brooch, she came to warn us about Cardian being here."

I pulled at my hair. "The brooch." I had forgotten about it. "If I hadn't tried to go back for it, this wouldn't have happened. I would be with the others."

The brooch suddenly appeared in front of Larina. It floated with a layer of pixie dust and slowly descended to my hand. I tightened my fingers around it.

"Thank you," I said so quietly I barely heard myself.

"I . . . I think you could still go with the others," Larina said. "But . . ."

I looked up and met her eyes. "But that may not be the smartest choice."

"Yes. Now you have another path that can help you find the king, whereas before you only had one, a very unlikely one."

I couldn't argue with that, but the thought of being here and playing this game with Cardian, of all people . . . I wasn't sure I could do it.

You have to do it, that other voice spoke inside my head. *You have no other choice.*

I took a deep breath, finding enough strength inside me to face my situation in its entirety. Maybe I didn't grow up expecting to be stabbed in the back at every turn, but I was made of stronger stuff than I gave myself credit for. All of my siblings were fighters, and even though they would bet on me last because I'd always been the nurturing kind, I had Sunder steel in me. If I didn't, I wouldn't have survived Mount Ruin or an attack from the most powerful thunderlord in the realm.

Never doubt yourself, Dani. Those days are over.

"Can I ask you for a favor, Larina?" I said.

"Anything."

"If I ever doubt myself, remind me that I'm a Sunder."

She frowned, looking confused, but in the end, she just shrugged and gave me a strong nod. "I shall."

"Thank you." I paused and considered. "Do you think you can find Shadow?"

"Of course."

"Okay. I'll go back to my chamber since that's what Cardian expects. That crystal bird is there, so I'm sure he'll be watching me. When you find Shadow, bring her over if it seems safe. Warn her not to say anything, though. We'll find somewhere to talk."

"Very well." She started to fly away.

I put a hand out. "Larina."

She glanced back.

"Be safe?"

She nodded. "I doubt Cardian has noticed me. I'm just a servant, after all."

"I think when it's all said and done, he will know exactly who you are." I don't know what made me say that, but it sounded right. Someone like Larina should never be ignored. People like Cardian, on the other hand, no one should ever listen to them.

Larina disappeared through one of those tiny doors located close to the ceiling. The palace had them everywhere, it seemed, a convenient way for small, winged servants to go in and out between rooms, but also a callous custom that made it easier for those in power to ignore some of the minor folk.

Keep ignoring us, Cardian, and when you least expect it, we'll be your downfall.

I'd only been in my chamber for about ten minutes when Larina and Shadow floated through the small hole above the main door. They hovered in midair, waiting expectantly.

I pressed a finger to my mouth and went into the closet, humming tunelessly as if I didn't have a care in the world. I changed clothes quickly, selecting one of the flowing Jovinian dresses Cardian would expect me to wear. I much preferred the tunics and leggings, but I needed to play my part to perfection.

When I was done, I rejoined the pixie and the sprite, and we left the chamber together. Once in the corridor, I glanced longingly toward the garden exit, wishing we could leave that way. I wanted to get out of this godforsaken palace at least for a moment, but I was sure the exit would be locked.

I started to turn in the opposite direction, but Larina waved a hand, urging us to take the stairs to the left.

Once we had descended a few steps, she whispered, "King Kalyll had the door fitted to your touch?"

"He did? When? Why?"

"When you were asleep. He said you liked the garden, said he saw you heal a trampled flower once. It's the same reason he had me keep them fresh by your side."

I had done that for Valeriana, the sweet little druid girl

we'd found in Mid Crosswood what felt like a lifetime ago. I had no idea he'd seen me do that. From that simple act, he'd realized I liked flowers and unwittingly saved me from an eternity of frozen rest.

My heart constricted at the thought of Kalyll's pain while I lay there immobile. He must have felt so hopeless. What must he be going through right now not knowing I was awake? But in the same way he'd afforded me a way out of my death-like prison, I would do the same for him.

When we reached the large wooden door, I pressed a hand to the handle. A little shock of awareness went up my fingers, as if the metal recognized me, and the lock gave. I pulled and let us out into the beautiful Eastside garden.

It was a relief to feel fresh air on my face and stand under the open sky. I was starting to hate the Vine Tower—same as Silver—and if it was to be my home in the near future, maybe I needed to spend more time in the gardens rather than inside.

My future home, I mused. What an impossibility!

I walked to a bush replete with red roses. I cradled one in my hand. The silk-soft petals caressed my fingers. A sweetness that unleashed a thousand memories filled my nostrils. I recalled the rose Kalyll had given me in Imbermore, the one I'd left behind when Valeriana freaked out because I wasn't there when she woke up. I still wished I had kept it and pressed it between the pages of a beloved book. At least I had the brooch; my desire to keep it had caused me to get separated from the others, but in the end, it might be the thing that would lead me to Kalyll.

Slowly, I turned to face Larina and Shadow. They had respected my thoughtful silence, and I was grateful for that.

"Thank you for coming, Shadow," I said. "I know we weren't very nice earlier, and I apologize once more."

"No need for that," she said dryly, stopping me short.

She was stoic and off-putting, but I had no way of telling if this was her regular personality, or if we'd brought it out with our rudeness. Only time would tell.

"Very well," I said, inclining my head.

"You should know, *Lady Fenmenor*, that I am being dismissed," Shadow said. "Me and others who were faithful to King Beathan, Queen Eithne, and King Kalyll, are being sent away. We have an hour to vacate the premises."

"How dare he?!" Anger burned in my chest. "What a horrible, horrible male." I stretched my fingers, trying to dispel that tingling feeling gathering at the tips. Oh, how I would enjoy turning Cardian into a lifeless husk.

"It shouldn't be a problem," Larina interjected. "Cardian doesn't know about *me*. I can move in and out of the palace without constraint or care from anyone, so I can be your go-between, if need be."

"Thank you, Larina." I turned to Shadow. "Are you still willing to help us find King Kalyll?"

She nodded once. "Queen Eithne wanted nothing more than for him to ascend to the throne. I will endeavor to make her wishes come true. But you should know, *my* biggest desire is revenge against her murderer. In fact, just before I came to you, I tried to find Cardian, but the milksop is more heavily guarded than the gates to The Blessed Fields, and what is more, he has a nullifier with him."

I fully understood what she was saying, that even if Kalyll didn't wish to see his half-brother dead, her goal would remain. She would *not* respect Kalyll's wishes even if he was the king, even if there were consequences. She wouldn't rest until Cardian was six feet under. I was strangely touched by her murdering tendencies. They seemed to align with mine at my worst moments, like this one. Clearly, she had really loved the queen.

"I understand," I said. "But can you please hold off until Cardian leads us to the king?"

"Do you have a plan?" Shadow asked.

"A plan? Not really," I admitted. "Um . . . First, I guess the Sub Rosa needs to know that I'm all right and that I've infiltrated the traitor's ranks. Then I'll try to get Cardian to trust me further."

Infiltrated. I almost rolled my eyes at the word. What had my life turned into? I looked from the pixie to the sprite wondering if they were about to burst out laughing, but they looked as serious as two soldiers ready for orders.

Encouraged by this, I went on. "I think we should also contact Naesala Roka."

"Naesala Roka?!" they both exclaimed.

Now, they were looking at me as if I was crazy. I quickly explained how the sorceress had helped us hide when we escaped the Vine Tower the first time Cardian took over. For now, I left out the part about Naesala being a human spy. I had no idea how that would go over with them, so it was best to keep things simple.

Shadow looked baffled. "We never suspected her of being anything but loyal to Cardian."

By *we*, I assumed she meant she and Queen Eithne. It was starting to sound as if the two had been friends and not just a monarch and a subject.

"We can trust the sorceress," I said. "You can be sure of that. We need to enlist her. She can help us find Kalyll and fight Cardian. It wouldn't hurt to have a powerful ally like her. Then we can go at Cardian from two different sides. Here and Nerethien."

They both nodded, approving of my idea. At least I wasn't a complete fool when it came to espionage. Who would've figured?

Dani the healer spy slash human life-sucker slash future queen of the Seelie Fae. What a mind job!

"Larina, I trust you would be able to contact the sorceress," I said.

"Most definitely." She pressed a fist to her chest and inclined her head, a zealous expression on her face.

I nearly teared up, grateful that I had her help. She was as devoted to finding Kalyll as I was, and that was no small matter.

I faced Shadow next. "Could you get a message out to the Sub Rosa through your network?"

"Consider it done," the sprite assured me. "They will be informed before nightfall."

I had no idea how she would accomplish it, but I didn't question it. My gratitude extended to her as well. She seemed fiercely loyal to the late queen as well as her plans for her son, and I had a feeling Shadow would do everything in her power to reinstate him to the throne.

"Anything else you can think of?" I asked.

They both seemed slightly taken aback. I assumed it was because they weren't used to being asked their opinion.

"Look," I said, "I need all the help I can get. This court is a new beast to me. I don't know its etiquette. I don't know its rules, spoken or unspoken. For that, I'm going to need to rely on you two."

I waited expectantly as they thought for a moment.

"You . . ." Shadow began hesitantly, "should make sure that Cardian invites you to his nightly gatherings. He loves nothing more than to lounge with good wine and food while others parade in front of him, making fools of themselves as they try to impress him. Deep down, he knows no one respects him, so he constantly needs validation."

I listened intently, a picture of the exact type of person I would need to be around him quickly taking shape inside my head.

"Sometimes, when he gets drunk," Shadow went on, "he talks too much. Mind you, he knows this about himself, so he has learned to make an exit when things get out of hand. That thunderlord of his makes sure to intercede if Cardian fails to realize he's beyond his cups. Varamede Elis is the only person he fully trusts."

"That is great information, Shadow," I said. "I will take it to heart and do my best to get invited to his gatherings."

I glanced around the garden, feeling slightly better about our prospects. We had a plan, or the outline of one, at least. Now, I just had to let Dark Dani keep the reins.

Before this was over, her ruthlessness might be needed.

CHAPTER 13
DANIELLA

Shadow informed me that Cardian's revelries started shortly after dinner most nights. Dinner was normally served at 7 PM, so a few minutes before that, I made my way to the dining room in the west wing, the one he seemed to prefer because it was closer to his quarters.

But not only that, apparently, he wanted to change everything about the way his father, mother, and brother used to do things. The dining room in the east wing, the one I was familiar with, was considered the main one for a long time, so he was planning to convert it into a waiting room for petitioners. Larina heard the gossip in the kitchen and shared it with me after she helped me with my makeup.

"I'm glad to see he has his priorities straight," I said to the pixie as she pointed to the veil lying on Cylea's vanity. We came here to avoid Cardian's mole.

"That one matches your dress perfectly," Larina said.

I wrinkled my nose at the thing. I hated wearing a veil, but it was supposed to be a custom that single Jovinian females upheld proudly.

"He already saw me without it," I protested. "Won't he

think it's weird that I'm suddenly wearing it again? Besides, how am I supposed to eat?"

"You're not. That's why I got dinner for you." She pointed toward a small table in the middle of the room, and a light dinner of soup and bread appeared there.

"Are you serious?"

"Jovinian females eat in private."

"For God's sake, why? Is eating considered unladylike in Jovinia or something?"

"It's just a matter of keeping their faces covered. That is all."

"Does it matter that he saw my face? That he knows the Sub Rosa did too?" I hadn't stopped to consider this.

"It does. If he says anything, you could casually tell him you're against the custom, but you're trying to keep appearances for your family's sake. A growing number of Jovinian females feel that way."

"I could also not wear it, and tell Cardian that no one has to know who I am. That it would be best if no one realizes I'm the same female that Kalyll was involved with. That should spare his ego, wouldn't you say?"

"From what I know about him, he will want everyone to know that King Kalyll's lady is now with him. He wants everything of his brother, not only his throne."

"I see."

I took the veil with me as I walked to the table and made myself eat a few spoonfuls of soup. In the end, as I made my way to Cardian's gathering, I was grateful I wouldn't be expected to eat anything else. My stomach was in knots. I had no idea what awaited me, and if I would be able to hold my own.

When I took the last turn into the corridor Larina had indicated, I encountered a couple of Cardian's guards standing in front of the double door. They wore orange padded tunics to indicate they were loyal to him. As they noticed my approach, they wasted no time letting me know with their harsh glares that I wasn't welcome.

"Move along," one of them barked down the hook of his nose.

I stopped instead, Dark Dani pushing to the forefront.

"King Cardian," I almost choked at having to call him that, "will not mind my presence. Please inform him that Lady Fenmenor is here."

"He is not expecting you, so like I said, move along."

I tried to think of what to say that might convince them to let me in, but I had no authority here, and the only power I possessed would turn him into a husk—not exactly the best first step. Except Dark Dani didn't share that thought. In fact, she had me taking a step forward, one hand slowly reaching for the guard's bare arm.

A frown started to cross his features as I approached, but the sound of steps made me pause and glance back.

Varamede Elis, wearing a blue jacket embroidered with orange thread, had just turned the corner and was walking in our direction. He slowed his pace when he noticed me. His dark eyes narrowed, and his entire demeanor became guarded, as if he was ready to spring an electrical attack at any moment.

It seemed I had left quite the impression on him. Good.

Smiling, allowing my eyes to crinkle, I stepped away from the guard.

"Lord Elis," the guards said in unison, bowing.

"I'm glad you're here," I said, my voice chipper as if he were a long-lost friend. "They won't let me in, and as you well know, they should."

I had no idea if this was true. For all I knew, Cardian had no intention of letting me into his inner circle, but if he believed me as powerful as Varamede, I had to trust he would rather keep an eye on me. The *friends close and enemies closer* philosophy still applied in Elf-hame, didn't it?

"Open the doors and let us in," Varamede ordered after a moment's thought, as if he were the king himself.

The guards didn't hesitate, which made me realize the level of influence his friendship with Cardian afforded him. It was more than I'd suspected.

As they threw the doors open and I walked in, I *tsked*, *tsked* at the guards, gave them a once-over, and said in a haughty tone, "Let that be the last time you disrespect me."

Damn. Dark Dani was a bitch, and I wasn't sure I'd want her as my friend. Though that meant she was the perfect type of person for the likes of Cardian and Varamede.

What stretched before us was nothing like I'd imagined. This wasn't a simple gathering, but more like a grand opera after-party for a bunch of prima donnas. People milled about in expensive suits, gowns, and jewelry, their hair styled in elaborate and gaudy ways—too much gold and pixie dust creating ridiculously tall beehives, even on some of the males. They all had a certain air of superiority about them and looked down their noses at everyone else.

The walls were lined with tapestries depicting scenes of royal life, and the floor was covered in a thick, red carpet. Tables strewn all around the large space held plenty of food and drink.

"Just my kind of gathering," I found myself saying, as I sashayed, hips gyrating like some sort of out-of-control top-toy.

What the hell?!

Dark Dani seemed to find it very easy to act like a prima donna herself. *Witchlights*, I was possessed by Liberace or worse . . . Madonna.

Varamede gave me a sidelong glance as he made his way toward Cardian. I followed him since that was exactly where *I* needed to be, and if Varamede didn't look happy about it, I didn't give a shit.

As I moved further in, I took in the large area, which was abuzz with activity. Court members gathered deep in gossip or watched one of the many entertainment acts that would give a human state fair a run for its money. In one corner, a bard told stories. In another, a female with green skin juggled three torches. And in a third, a jester made a fool of himself while a group of people laughed with disdain. In the center of the room was a raised stage with a band of musicians playing a lively tune.

Some guests laughed, others danced, but their demeanor was barely festive. There was too much animosity here for true camaraderie.

As my gaze swept over those who accompanied Cardian at the center of a lavish narrow table from where he surveyed the crowd, I nearly choked.

Naesala Roka was there, talking to a young female with small fawn horns and a strange face. The sorceress noticed me out of the corner of her pale eyes but pretended not to recognize me. Larina had gotten the word out to her, and Naesala had lost no time making a reappearance amongst Cardian's acquaintances.

When we reached the table, Varamede walked around it and took a chair right next to Cardian. The thunderlord acted as if I wasn't even there, neither offering me a chair nor announcing my presence.

"You have the manners of an oaf," I told him, then bit my tongue, silently scolding Dark Dani.

Varamede had collapsed into a slouch, but as soon as the words were out of my mouth, he sat up straighter, shooting a menacing glare in my direction.

I felt my insides turn to water. If he decided to strike me with one of his electrical attacks, I'd have nothing to fight him with, and I would end up as a small piece of charcoal on the floor, all my hopes and long brown hair up in stinky smoke.

"Lady Fenmenor is right, my dear friend." Cardian slapped Varamede's shoulder. "You do have the manners of an oaf. Get up. Give her your seat."

Varamede sneered, and for a moment, I thought he would refuse, but in the end, he gave the person to his right a nasty glare—though not nastier than the one he threw my way. The male jumped to his feet and vacated the seat in an instant, not a sign of hostility or embarrassment in his manner. Honestly, he simply looked relieved to escape.

Great! Now I had to sit between the two assholes, the same ones that others were glad to abandon in a hurry.

I did my best to look pleased and plastered a smile on my face, as the hip gyration continued, and I tried to convince myself I really wasn't possessed by someone—maybe Shakira?—though I was starting to have my doubts. I figured I would know for sure if I broke into a full belly dance.

"I'm afraid oafish manners are contagious," Cardian said as I sat down and static electricity zapped my arm from Varamede's side.

My small hairs stood on end, but my expression revealed no discomfort. I had to give it to Dark Dani, she was kickass.

"Is that so?" I made a show of dusting off whatever cooties Varamede might have infected me with.

Cardian smiled, amused by my antics. "Yes," he replied, "I forgot to send you a dinner invitation. Unforgivable."

"Truly."

"You are amusing, Ylannea. I like that."

Crap, if I didn't want the crown jester post, I needed to watch myself.

"Delighted to please," I said, despite my reservations at being expected to entertain him with jokes.

He brandished a hand around, carelessly pointing toward my veil. "Why this again?"

I had been expecting the question, but when I leaned closer to whisper an answer, it wasn't the one I'd discussed with Larina. "I wouldn't want just *anyone* to see my face."

He narrowed his eyes distrustfully. "You allowed Kalyll's goons to see it."

Petty, petty, weren't we?

I shrugged. "As of this morning, they were important. Not anymore."

My answer seemed to satisfy him because there was a glint in his eyes as he let it sink in. No doubt, he was growing more confident by the second that I was a classic gold digger.

"So, what do you think of my little gathering?" he asked.

I let my eyes wander around the room, crinkling them as if I were smiling when in reality my mouth was suppressed into a thin line.

From what I'd observed so far, the display that stretched in front of me could only be called banal. I imagined this was how a political party at the White House would feel, or the Oscars ceremony. Everyone acting self-important while at the same time trying to see whose favor they could win or whose back they could stab in order to move up the food chain. It was a den of hyenas, and I was sitting next to the biggest, fattest one of them all.

And while the doglike creatures sniffed each other's butts, those who could later serve as fodder did their best to amuse them, like a crazy-looking Fae with the turquoise mane, wildly swinging his arms in front of the musicians, acting like their conductor.

"It is everything I imagined," I said, my words holding no lie.

I'd heard the others talk about Cardian's debauchery, and I wasn't disappointed in the least.

"I am extremely glad to hear that. How about a little food and wine?"

"No, thank you."

The food looked delicious, but there was the veil and the fact that I couldn't help but think of the poor people slaving away in the kitchens, hustling to feed a bunch of freeloaders. And nothing to say of the phenomenal waste.

The more I got to know Cardian and his tendencies, the more I understood why it was imperative for Kalyll to return. True, by their laws, he wasn't the rightful king, but there was nothing *right* about replacing him with this loathsome male, not even if his blood went back hundreds of years in a line of many Adanorin kings.

When he was done eating, Cardian stood and offered me his hand. Doing my best not to look as if I was about to throw up the moment I took his hand, I rose to my feet. The struggle not to draw out every bit of his life force was real. There was skin-to-skin contact now. Nothing any of his guards or his precious Varamede could do to stop me from turning him into a wilted dick, but I couldn't do that. Not until I found out where he was keeping Kalyll.

Parading around like some sort of peacock, he guided me around the edges of the rooms, stopping here and there to look at the performers who overexerted themselves to please him, and then exhaled in relief when we moved on.

I found it difficult to understand how such a weak-looking male could cause such fear. He was about my height and build, and had no magical powers. He also didn't possess Kalyll's commanding presence, and nothing about him inspired anything but a desire to give him a wide berth.

Frowning, I glanced back toward the table. The thunderlord was looking disinterested as he sipped from his wine glass. His gaze met mine, and I inclined my head in acknowledgment, refusing to be intimidated by his clear desire to turn me into a piece of burnt toast. Was all the fear Cardian produced due to his association with Varamede? Or was there another reason?

No, there wasn't.

He used others to instill fear in his subjects, which was why he wanted me.

"Did you see the prestidigitator?" he asked as we continued walking.

"Prestidigitator?" I asked, feigning a mixture of ignorance and confusion. Hearing the word here surprised me. I wasn't aware that such charades existed in Elf-hame.

"Yes, it's a human thing really. Manual dexterity, sleight of hand to fool the eye."

"Seems like a waste of time when so many things are possible with magic."

His expression tightened. "It requires more agility than you may think."

"Really?"

Why did he sound offended by my comment? Maybe because prestidigitation was very similar to what he was doing here . . . pretending to be something he was not.

"Really," he replied dryly.

"Then I would love to see this trickery," I put in, filling my voice with excitement.

Cardian's expression grew satisfied again, and he whirled back the way we'd come. "This way."

A female had just risen from a nearby chair, and unfortunately for her, she found herself in Cardian's path. They crashed. Her glass of wine flew from her hand and spilled its contents all over Cardian's cream-colored jacket.

He let out a frustrated growl and threw his hands to the sides, shaking wine off his sleeves.

The female's face disfigured in horror, and she immediately started apologizing. She was left with an empty glass in one hand and an odd little creature in the other. The animal was small and furry with what appeared to be the body of a dog and the tail and ears of a squirrel. It had a friendly demeanor and soulful eyes like a golden retriever. It was adorable.

She repeated her apologies effusively. "I am so sorry. I am so sorry. I am so clumsy. This is all my fault."

"Of course it's your fault, you vacuous trollop," he shouted, his face growing red with rage.

Before I could even begin to process what he planned to do, he reached out and grabbed the little creature by the scruff of his neck.

"Lord Snuffles, no!" The female's eyes went so wide I thought they would pop out of their sockets. She reached a trembling hand toward her little pet, fright disfiguring her face.

In an instant, the poor animal flew across the room and smashed into a nearby wall with a shriek and a stomach-turning crunch. It slid and hit the floor, where it collapsed in a heap and didn't move.

The female pressed a trembling hand to her mouth as she stared at what I suspected was now a corpse.

"Lord Snuffles," she whispered.

As if responding to her voice, the animal twitched. Its owner let out a squeak of relief. When Cardian noticed the slight movement, he started moving toward the discarded mound of bones to finish the job.

"What a bore!" I exclaimed, looping my arm through his and trying to sound like an unfeeling, spoiled brat. "Where is this prestidigitator you were telling me about?"

Cardian blinked at me as if he'd completely forgotten

about me. He composed himself with some effort. He appeared slightly chagrined, but I doubted it was due to his actions. I suspected he was only bothered by the fact that I'd been a witness to his outburst.

"Perhaps you can find him by yourself," he answered in a controlled tone. "I'm afraid I have to go." He looked down at his jacket and then at the female, who hadn't dared move despite the repeated twitching of her pet's little legs and tail.

"What a shame," I said. "But of course, I understand, you can't go around looking like that."

His upper lip twitched. He hadn't liked that comment. He was clearly one of those people who liked to pretend nothing could ever be wrong with them—not even an accidental wine spill.

After inclining his head, he took a step toward the female and said, "I don't ever want to see you here again." And with that, he made his exit, guards, and his dear friend Varamede quick on his heels. For a moment, I thought that perhaps I should follow too, but I'd had enough of Cardian for one night. Besides, I wanted to talk to Naesala and find out what sort of help she could provide us.

Time was running out on Kalyll. His brother had a very-easy-to-trigger temper.

CHAPTER 14
DANIELLA

As soon as Cardian left, the female rushed to her crushed pet and picked it up, keeping her desperate little sobs as quiet as possible.

"Oh, my poor little Lord Snuffles."

I tried to let Dark Dani lead me away from them, but in the end, it was impossible for my true self to ignore the poor creature's whimpers.

Hiding my concern under a layer of irritation, I stomped toward the woman.

"I think you should leave now." I grabbed her by the arm and led her toward the same door Cardian had used to exit.

She didn't oppose me. She only clenched her little friend to her chest and allowed me to guide her outside. Once out in the hall, I was glad to find that Cardian and his retinue had disappeared.

I let go of the female's arm, and she began to retreat.

"Wait a moment," I said, my tone a million times warmer than it had been a moment ago. "Let me see what is wrong with your pet. I hate to see animals suffer. People, on the other hand . . ." I shrugged one shoulder and winked, hoping that if

Cardian heard I had a compassionate side, it didn't extend to bipedal creatures.

She looked up in surprise and searched my eyes.

I placed a hand on her pet's tiny body. I immediately surveyed the damage and detected several broken ribs and deep contusions. Letting my healing magic flow, I repaired each injury. When I was done, Lord Snuffles' body gave a shudder, then a long exhalation of relief. Looking lively, the animal lifted its head and snuffled, doing honor to its name.

The female looked surprised again. Though, this time, gratitude also mingled in her expression.

"Thank you," she mouthed as if it were a crime to undo the awful things Cardian did.

Her joy at seeing her little friend restored to health warmed my heart, but I couldn't let it show, so I batted a hand in the air.

"It's nothing. It was either heal it or kill it. This was far less messy."

Her gratefulness disfigured into horror. Slowly, she took two steps away from me, then whirled and ran down the hall, casting fearful glances over her shoulder as if she expected me to pull out a bow and arrow to shoot her in the back.

Her reaction both pleased me and made me feel like shit. It was great for my mission that I could convince people I was as awful as Cardian, but it was sobering to realize I had that ability in me.

I went back to the party, sliding past the door I'd left cracked open. Before making my way toward Naesala, I spent some time meandering through the room, giving everyone haughty looks that matched Cardian's and Varamede's. In turn, I received jealous glances as people gossiped behind their hands, probably asking each other how I'd earned Cardian's favor so quickly, especially when I was supposed to be Kalyll's ally.

But why were they so surprised? They should've recognized a backstabber when they saw one. Takes one to know one, after all.

As I got closer, Naesala moved away from the female she was speaking with and meandered my way. Her raven hair fell straight to frame her pale face, and her matching gown flowed like dark water around her. She wore bright red lipstick and nail polish just as vivid.

"Hello, Dani," she said.

I gasped, my eyes going around the room, trying to see if anyone had heard her call me that.

"Oh, don't worry. I'm using a little spell that will make them hear some dribble about how much we love Cardian."

My panic eased immediately. "Nice."

"Right? It's my specialty. So, what do you think of this bed of vipers? I was afraid you would be out of your depth, but you fit right in. Don't take me wrong, I mean that as a compliment. Did you ever think of becoming a spy?"

"No, but I'm not quite the same person I was before I came to Elf-hame."

"The shadowdrifter energy?"

I nodded. When we stayed at her house waiting for King Beathan's send-off to The Blessed Fields, we told the sorceress everything. She knew every dirty little secret that pertained to Kalyll. She could easily ruin everything if she decided to switch sides. Not a comforting thought. Not at all.

"Then you should be grateful you have it," Naesala said.

"Oh, believe me, I am."

We were quiet for a moment, observing Cardian's syco-phants.

"How can you stand it?" I asked.

"I focus on the little pleasures." She held up her wine glass.

"They do have good food." A pause. "But I need to get out of here. I need Cardian to go to Nerethien, so I can find Kalyll. Do you have any idea how long Cardian plans to stay here?"

"I'm afraid he's not going anywhere, at least not for an extended period of time. He has some work to do in order to bend all the generals to his will. He and Mythorne want to attack and take over the smaller courts, but he can't do that unless all the leaders agree. He'll use fear, bribery, murder, imprisonment, or whatever means at his disposal, so it'll take some time."

I shook my head, desperation mounting. "We can't allow that, and we can't allow Kalyll to remain in the Unseelie cap-ital. What do we do?"

"I have been thinking about that since your pixie friend came to visit me and explained everything, and I have an idea."

My heart lifted, if only a little. "I'm all ears."

"We will need a loyal male of about Kalyll's build and height. I suggest his half-brother, Kryn."

"Okay." I didn't know where she was going with this, but I hoped Shadow would be able to get in touch with the Sub Rosa through her network sooner rather than later.

I waited for the sorceress to explain further, but she just stood straight, her chin held high as she surveyed the guests, looking more regal than Cardian ever could.

"So what's this plan?" I pressed her.

"Let's sit." She pointed toward a couple of chairs in a secluded corner. We sat down, and after she reassured me that her spell was still obscuring our conversation, she explained what she had in mind.

When she was done, I had to admit her idea was very clever and made my hopes soar even higher.

CHAPTER 15
DANIELLA

It took two days, but Shadow came through. Her network had been able to deliver a message to the Sub Rosa, and in a few minutes, I was going to meet Kryn. It worried me that Cardian's spies could find my friends too, but Shadow assured me it hadn't been easy and Cardian had his hands full with trying to wrangle everyone to go to war against the minor courts.

I left the Vine Tower through a service door with Larina. She was standing on my collarbone and hiding behind the ruffles of my veil. She'd been whispering instructions in my ear, guiding me out of the palace. Once more, I was glad to have her with me.

"Walk straight ahead for two squares, then turn right."

"Squares?" I figured she meant blocks, so I peered ahead and then asked, "take a right at . . ." I squinted to read a hand-painted sign, "Floxen's Apothecary?"

"Precisely."

We made a few more turns, and the further we went, the faster my heart beat.

"Are we almost there?" I asked.

"You sound like a child. *Are we there yet?*" she asked in a high-pitched voice.

I smiled. It sounded like that was the universal question children asked, no matter the realm.

Suddenly, Larina's voice acquired an urgent tone. "Wait! Stop!"

My feet immediately came to a halt. I was paralyzed, adrenaline punching me right under the breastbone.

"Turn and face the window," Larina urged. "Pretend to look at the pretty baubles."

I did as she instructed, feeling robotic in my movements. "What's the matter?" I whispered under my breath.

"We're being followed."

"Shit."

"It's Varamede Elis."

"Double shit." All the baubles on display blurred in my vision. "What do we do?"

"I . . . I . . ." Larina sounded more nervous than I felt.

Words began pouring out of my mouth of their own accord. "Can you fly ahead without being noticed?"

"Yes, I think so. Why?"

"We need to warn Kryn. Go and tell him I can't meet him in the tavern. Tell him to . . ." I glanced around at the different stores that lined the path, trying to look as casual as possible. Then I spotted just the place a few stores across the street. "Tell him to go into that dress shop instead. I'll meet him when I shake Varamede off."

As someone walked behind me, Larina jumped off my shoulder and took a ride on a stack of boxes the person was carrying. Taking a deep breath, I walked into the shop and spent a few minutes looking at expertly designed bracelets, earrings, and necklaces.

I had no money, however, so my charade of shopping wasn't quite going to work, was it? As I left the shop, I surreptitiously glanced about, trying to spot Varamede, but I saw no sign of him. Clearly, he was a better spy than me.

Meandering slowly, I only allowed myself to look at the dress shop out of the corner of my eye. When I perceived a male hooded figure slipping through its door, I knew it had to be Kryn. That or a very burly lady who needed a gown for an upcoming ball. My vote was on the former.

I took my time making my way there, appearing like someone who had all the time in the world. I saw no sign of Varamede, and I had no idea if I'd shaken him off. Probably not, but I had to talk to Kryn.

Seeing no other choice, I went into the shop, my eyes roving all around. I spotted the hooded figure in the back of the room. I started walking in his direction. His back was turned to me, and for an instant, I feared I'd made a mistake, then the figure turned slightly, and I caught a lock of bright red hair just Kryn's shade.

Stopping near a shelf with an assortment of embroidered bodices, I spoke in a low whisper. "I'm so glad you're here."

"Not the most likely place for a meeting," he said in one of his usual grumpy tones.

I noticed he was standing in front of a basket full of what looked like intimate garments. Larina was standing next to it, quiet as a mouse.

"I think the crimson-colored one with the lace would look good on you." I pointed at a pair of underpants.

"Ha-ha," was his only dry response.

"Is everyone all right?"

He nodded once. "We tried to come back for you, but we couldn't transfer into the palace—not even with Kalyll's token."

"Thanks for trying. Naesala said Cardian had her put a blocking spell on the entire Vine Tower. She decided it was okay to do it since it served my plan."

"Are you sure you can do this, Dani? Are you sure you're safe? Kalyll will kill us if something happens to you."

"I'm all right. I promise."

"We were surprised to hear from a puck that you wanted to see us. We thought it might be a trap set by Cardian, but then he showed us the brooch. Here." He offered it back.

I snatched it and quickly slipped it under the folds of my dress. It had been hard parting with it, but I'd suspected the Sub Rosa might need proof that the message truly came from me. I was glad to have the brooch back, though.

"So what is this all about?" Kryn asked.

We hadn't dared send more than a brief message through Shadow's network. The sprite had said she trusted her people, but one never knew who might be captured and tortured for information.

I reached into one of the many pockets of my dress and surreptitiously placed a small drawstring bag on the shelf with the bodices.

"This is a potion Naesala made," I said. "Drink it. It will change your appearance for a day or so."

"Why in the name of Erilena would I need to change my appearance?"

"Because it will make you look like Kalyll."

Slowly, Kryn lifted a hand and reached for the tiny bag. I could only see his profile, but I could tell his thoughts were racing to the right conclusion.

"The plan was for you to show up at the palace door and cause a ruckus, be seen so that Cardian thinks Kalyll escaped, so that—"

"Cardian goes back to Nerethien to see if Kalyll is still where he left him."

"Exactly!"

"Why did you say *was*? What changed?"

"Varamede is following me."

Kryn's emerald eyes cut toward the window. Where he stood, no one could see him from the outside—not unless they came very close and cupped their face against the window.

"But now you want *him* to see me," he said slowly.

I nodded. "Cardian will be more likely to believe that someone saw Kalyll if that someone is his trusted thunderlord."

"Good idea."

"But I also need him not to suspect me, so this is what I propose. I'll go back outside and take Varamede to that tavern where I was supposed to meet you. If I can find him, that is. Larina saw him, but I haven't caught a glimpse of him. Anyway, if I get him to the tavern, I'll sit somewhere near a window. Then all you need to do is walk by. If he doesn't notice you himself, I'll point you out to Varamede."

He frowned. "That's a weak plan."

"What? Why?"

"He might still suspect you."

"Well, I guess I'll just have to risk it."

"No. This is what we'll do. I'll go into the tavern and rough you up."

"Rough me up? What are you talking about? You shouldn't go anywhere near Varamede. He'll kill you."

"It's the only way you'll earn their full trust. I'll act jilted, hurt that you're with Cardian now."

"No." I refused. "That risk is far greater for you. I promise you I'll be fine. All we need to do is instill a little doubt in Cardian's mind, then he'll go to Nerethien, and I'll find a way for him to take me along."

"If he doesn't trust you fully, he will leave you behind, and all of this will be for naught."

"Please, Kryn. He'll kill you, and then Arabis will kill me for allowing it."

His expression tightened. "Arabis? Has she said anything to you about . . .?"

"Don't be an idiot. Of course she hasn't, but it's not like I'm blind."

"You think . . . she cares about me?"

"God, Kryn. I guess you're the one who's blind."

"But she—"

"We don't have time for this. Now, just do as I said. And if this doesn't work, we go to the original plan, and you show up at the palace gates and make a ruckus." I whirled and left him behind. Larina caught up with me before I exited and hid behind my veil again.

As I went past the peeved-looking attendant, I crinkled my eyes and said, "I will be back for one of those beautiful bodices."

She remained just as serious. Clearly, she didn't believe me.

A bell sounded above the door as I exited. Once on the cobbled path, I twirled a lock of hair around my finger, putting on a bored air. After a moment pretending to consider my options, I started walking as Larina whispered directions toward the tavern.

"Do you see him?" I asked.

"Not yet. Oh, wait. I see him now. He just went under the awning of the bakery we just passed."

"Perfect. Now, make yourself scarce."

"What?"

"I mean . . . hide."

As soon as she was out of sight, I dashed across the street and headed straight for the bakery. I only slowed my pace when I noticed Varamede's shoulder. He was attempting to make himself smaller, pressing his back to the closed door. As luck would have it someone pushed the door open, causing the thunderlord to stagger forward.

The smell of freshly baked bread and a comfortable warmth rushed out the door along with a stout woman with skin the color of a Granny Smith apple. She gave Varamede a disapproving look. He took a step to the side, looking as if he was trying hard not to unleash his power on her for daring to glare at him.

I put on a pleasant expression, making sure it carried to my eyes. "Varamede, what a surprise to see you here."

He huffed and said nothing.

"I feel like we got off on the wrong foot. Don't you think so?" It was an understatement. We had tried to kill each other, and he'd almost succeeded. Not only that, I was certain he was pissed at himself for failing.

He only answered with another huff.

"Why don't we try again over a tankard of ale?" I gestured toward the tavern.

His sneer told me he would rather get impaled. The tips of my fingers tingled.

Get rid of him, Dark Dani whispered.

But I couldn't do that. The realm, the universe, would be better off without him, but it would have to wait. I needed him to raise the alarm to Cardian, so he could lead us to Kalyll.

Varamede's head turned to one side. He glanced down the street, clearly finding an exit more appealing than sharing anything with the likes of me.

I decided to try a different approach. "Keep your friends close and your enemies closer."

His gaze snapped back to mine.

"Isn't that what humans say?" I asked, hoping to dispel the suspicion that seemed to have risen to the surface.

"It is," he said, some mistrust leaving his expression. "It is a great saying, isn't it?"

"I'm glad you like it as much as I do."

"Let's have that tankard then." He gestured toward the tavern, a small, dark building with a tiled roof and a sign that swung creakily.

I went in first and quickly snatched a small table by the window. The place was filled with smoke and the smell of ale. The walls were decorated with faded tapestries and old weapons. It seemed a popular enough spot for travelers and locals alike, a place to hear the latest news and gossip.

A boy of about fifteen—that was my guess, with the Fae it

was hard to know exact ages—came to take our order. He was small and agile, with the nimble limbs of a deer and the curious eyes of a fawn. As he left us, we sat uncomfortably, looking at everything but each other. The boy was back quickly, and I occupied myself with my drink as I riffled through my mind trying to find the best topic of conversation. Finally, I settled on the only thing we had in common.

"How long have you known . . . King Cardian?" I asked.

"Forever. I don't remember *not* knowing him." Varamede pushed a very straight, very silky strand of black hair away from his forehead. It plopped right back almost immediately.

I glanced out the window, pretending to take an interest in the people walking by. "I see. No wonder you are such good friends."

"We are more than friends. We are brothers."

"Literally?" I asked, unable to help the question from jumping out of my mouth since he'd sounded so adamant about it.

"We may not be related by blood, but we certainly are by choice."

"Oh."

"So you should know that no matter how much you squirm and how much you slither, you won't be able to get between us. He'll get tired of you. It's nothing new."

If he thought that was a threat, he needed to try harder. I was already tired of Cardian and Varamede. They were nothing but scum, unhappy people who took joy in spreading their misery. I just needed Cardian to remain interested until he led me to Kalyll.

Outside, a familiar figure appeared. Across the street, the hood pulled over his head, Kryn stood, his shoulders squared with the tavern, his head moving right and left as if he were looking for danger.

My heart clenched at the sight of him, and I had to remind myself that it wasn't Kalyll, that it was just a trick, a spell from a very talented sorceress. Those weren't his midnight blue eyes and matching hair. That wasn't his supple mouth, which I longed to kiss again. That wasn't his usual intensity and poise. It was only his half-brother, someone who clearly knew Kalyll's mannerisms. Only an illusion.

I willed Varamede to glance out the window, but he was intent on the contents of his tankard. The asshole. Was he good for anything other than blasting people? Well, someone needed to get this ball rolling.

"Well, I think that—" I cut my sentence short, widened my eyes, and jumped to my feet, causing the table to rattle and the ale to spill. "It's him!" I exclaimed. "He's here."

In an instant, Varamede was on his feet, lightning crackling between his fingers. He followed my gaze and it landed squarely on Kryn.

CHAPTER 16
DANIELLA

Varamede wasted no time shooting out the door. I nearly screamed for Kryn to run, but I managed to bite my tongue as I rushed after the thunderlord, wanting to trip him or slow him down somehow.

When I burst out the door a few steps behind Varamede, I was glad to see that Kryn was already marching down the street, the bottom of his cloak swaying from side to side.

Varamede went after him, dodging people, electric power growing brighter in his hands. I struggled to keep up as the thunderlord got closer to his quarry, without divulging his presence. Except Kryn knew we were after him, so why wasn't he running?

"Hurry up," I urged Kryn through clenched teeth.

At the corner ahead, Kryn stopped. Then, he glanced over his shoulder and pretended to finally notice his pursuers.

Varamede jerked an arm forward and lightning flew from his fingers, heading straight for Kryn. Not an instant too soon, he took off at full pelt, swiftly disappearing around the bend. The thunderlord's attack struck the road, sending cobblestones flying in every direction. People screamed and dashed out of the way, running into adjacent businesses, whose doors and shutters quickly slammed shut.

As he reached the corner, hand ready with another attack, Varamede put on the brakes and carefully peered around the wall.

My heart hammered at the same rate that my feet struck the street. "Kryn, you idiot!" He was going to get himself killed.

Just as I got there, Varamede turned the corner and disappeared. I followed, just to run straight into his back as he came to a sudden stop. He staggered forward, cursing.

"Dammit," I cursed too, and quickly backed away from him, rubbing my left boob, which had gotten squished during the collision.

"Where did he go?!" Varamede demanded. He whirled on me and repeated his question. "Where the fuck did he go?"

"How should I know? You lost him. How do you expect me to run with these shoes?" I tried to appear as irritated and frivolous as the vapid women in Cardian's gathering last night.

"What good are you? You didn't even launch an attack to stop him."

"Well, I could have, but you were in the way, and I suspect you wouldn't be happy if I'd given you a haircut."

God, my levels of bluff were epic. I couldn't have damaged one precious hair on his head even if I'd busted a blood vessel trying. I was dry.

He huffed in displeasure but didn't argue with my logic. He liked his hair *and* head right where they were.

"That was . . . him? Wasn't it?" I asked. "We didn't just imagine that?"

He gave me a look that suggested he thought I had no more than two neurons to rub together.

I smiled inwardly. He'd bought it.

"I need to warn Cardian." He took off in the direction of the palace.

"Wait." I went after him, trusting that Larina was keeping up but staying out of sight. "I was the one who spotted him. I should be the one to tell Cardian." Maybe I was laying it on a bit too thickly, but if he thought I was trying to gain favor with Cardian, he might mistake that pettiness for loyalty.

Of course, Varamede didn't wait for me, so I took off my uncomfortable shoes and rushed over the meandering cobbled streets, barely keeping the thunderlord in sight.

When I arrived at the palace's gates, I bent over, breathing hard. The guards eyed me with amused expressions.

"What's so funny?" I straightened and stomped by. They composed their expressions and went back to looking blank. "Assholes," I mumbled under my breath.

As I entered the palace, I searched for a sign of Varamede but found none.

"Which way did that thunderlord go?" I asked the guards stationed there.

"Toward the throne room, my lady," one of them answered.

"Thank you."

He raised his eyebrows at my good manners, something I'd come to realize most people in the upper echelons didn't waste on those they considered beneath them.

I burst into the throne room, considering for the first time that none of Cardian's appointed guards had tried to stop me. It was a good sign. He must have told them I was one of his crew. But now came the real test.

Eyes roving all around as Varamede stood in front of the dais, I was glad to see that Cardian wasn't there. Panting, I joined the thunderlord's side.

"Where is he?" I asked.

Varamede gave me a sidelong glance and didn't bother answering my question. My answer came in the form of a page boy, who entered through a side door and announced that the king would arrive shortly.

Good, it would give me a moment to compose myself. I was finger-combing my hair back, when Cardian marched through the door, looking peeved.

"What is so important that you had to interrupt me?"

Interrupt what? His nap? He was known to enjoy daytime leisure as his nights ran late almost every day of the week. But maybe he was finding out that being king and mounting a war wasn't at all compatible with sleeping until noon.

"You are—" Varamede started, but I jumped right in, not giving him a chance to finish.

"I spotted Kalyll in town."

Varamede glowered, bits of an electric storm crackling in the whites of his eyes. *Witchlights!* What if his looks could actually kill?

Cardian considered me for a moment, examining my disheveled hair, then focusing on my bare feet and the shoes I carried in my right hand. I resisted the urge to hide my dirty toes under my dress and stood straighter instead.

I thought he would judge my appearance harshly, but to my surprise, a smile stretched his thin lips.

"You are a wild one, aren't you?" he asked.

What? Was that what he chose to focus on after what I'd just said? This time I did hide my toes under my dress. I didn't like the lecherous expression on his face as he looked at them. Disgusting!

"Cardian?" Varamede said the name like a question that, had he spoken at liberty, would have probably been *What the fuck, Cardian?*

Very slowly, Cardian swiveled his head to look at the thunderlord. "She must be mistaken. There is no way that—"

"I saw him too," Varamede interrupted.

For the first time, Cardian appeared concerned. "Are you sure?"

"Certain."

The false king's shoulders seemed to shrink as he started pacing the length of the dais. "Were the others with him?"

"I didn't see them," Varamede and I answered in unison.

We swapped mean glowers. Maybe I could kill him now. He had served his purpose and had delivered a convincing message to Cardian. I looked down at his hands. All I had to do was reach over and . . .

Stop!

I slammed Dark Dani back. She was a real murderer, that one. How could she make killing someone seem pleasurable? I had sworn an oath to protect and save lives. I couldn't go around killing everyone who looked at me the wrong way.

He would kill you *if he thought he could get away with it.*

Very true. In fact, I had no doubt that as soon as Cardian got tired of me, Varamede would release the mother of all thunderstorms on me.

"There's no way he escaped," Cardian said, sticking his hand in the right pocket of his trousers. "He's well guarded. Isolated."

"What if someone helped him?" Varamede asked.

Cardian's blue eyes snapped to his pet thunderlord. "No one would want to. No one would dare." He paused, seemed conflicted for a short moment, then made a snap decision. "I need to make sure."

As I noticed the change in his expression, I made a snap decision of my own. Following my instincts, I took a step forward and grabbed Cardian's arm. I knew my hunch had paid off when I felt the throne room dissolve around me, its walls melting down to the floor like candle wax. A familiar dizzying feeling took hold of me, and I fought to stay upright as my stomach flipped.

In the next instant, we re-materialized and, for a short instant, I had the glimpse of a peaceful meadow carpeted with thousands of dandelions. I knew instantly I was in my realm, passing through. The land seemed to pull on my blood and whisper *you belong here*. The sensation only lasted for one precious second, and then we were dissolving again, and when we reappeared, we were in a drab room with gray, sooty walls and only the glow of a dozen half-spent candles illuminating the space.

It all happened in under a second, too fast to keep my head on straight and answer Cardian when he whirled on me and shook his arm out of my grip.

"What do you think you're doing?"

"I . . . I . . . what happened?" I glanced around, feigning surprise and ignorance. "Did you transfer? Oh, no. I hate transferring." I pressed a hand to my stomach, letting my face show how sick I felt. I didn't have to fake that. My heart was hammering, and my nerves were making me feel nauseous. It really didn't pay to slam Dark Dani down. I let her out again.

My surprise and confusion served me well, however. Cardian batted a hand in my direction, then walked toward a dilapidated wooden door.

"Stay here," he ordered me. "It won't take me but a minute, and we'll go back to Elyndell right away."

"Thank Erilena." I invoked the goddess they all do even though I know nothing about this deity, then wrinkled my nose and glanced around the room. "I don't think I like it here."

"What is there not to like?" Cardian managed to sound amused despite his obvious tension. "Take a seat on that lovely chair while you wait." He pointed at a dusty rickety thing with a moth-eaten seat cushion, which would probably collapse under the weight of a newborn.

I rolled my eyes, and he finally left the room, smiling, as if pleased with his own wit.

As soon as he disappeared through the door, I discarded my shoes on the decrepit chair—sending a cloud of dust flying into the air—and went after him. As an afterthought, I also tore the veil off my face and threw it to the stone floor.

CHAPTER 17
DANIELLA

I peered carefully out the door and into a dark corridor. Sparse fairy lights illuminated the area. From the dank smell of things, we were in some sort of subterranean place, somewhere beneath a major structure, I decided.

The sounds of steps and an elongated shadow in the distance let me know Cardian had gone right. I took several silent, tentative steps, and when I was certain I could move stealthily, I hurried after him, leaving a safe enough distance between us. I passed many closed doors and could only hope no poor souls were locked behind them. The air hung thick with what felt like fear and despair.

The passages wound intricately. I prayed no one would see me and was glad for the apparent seclusion and gloominess. Of course, they would keep Kalyll in the bowels of some derelict quarters no one wanted to visit, some depressing place that would slowly steal his hope.

As I started to go around a corner, I perceived Cardian's head swiveling to check over his shoulder. I jumped back and hid, holding my breath, back pressed tightly against the wall. I waited a long minute, then carefully peered again.

He was gone. No sight of him.

"Dammit," I cursed under my breath and tiptoed forward.

I walked the entire length of this new hall without signs of Cardian. Where had he gone? He must have entered one of the many rooms.

Retracing my steps, I stopped to listen at every door. Through the third one, I heard Cardian's muffled voice. I couldn't make out what he was saying, but he was definitely in there. Gathering my courage, I flexed my fingers and made up my mind. It was now or never. I would not get another opportunity to free Kalyll.

I pushed the door open, willing it to glide silently, but I might as well have wished for a cell signal in my portable thumb-and-pinky make-believe phone.

Hello, Toni, guess where I am?

No luck. The hinges screeched like giant rats, alerting Cardian. He whirled on his heels to face me, and something about my expression must have told him that I meant no good because he jumped backward, pulling out a jeweled dagger from his belt and brandishing it in front of my face.

"I told you to stay put," he spat.

Despite the danger, I couldn't stop my attention from wandering toward a giant sphere floating a few inches off the floor. It crackled with light and static, transparent enough to reveal a crumpled figure at its base.

Kalyll sat slumped, his spine curving over the back of the sphere, his face battered, his long midnight hair chopped unevenly. His fingers and naked toes were blue and blistered. He appeared to be unconscious.

"So this is where you're keeping him," I said, taking a step closer to the magical prison. "I guess he didn't escape, after all."

At the sound of my voice, one of Kalyll's eyes opened. He seemed to have trouble focusing, and though he appeared to recognize my voice, his battered face showed little awareness of anything else.

My chest squeezed. What had they done to him? I tried not to let my heartache show on my face. He was alive, and I'd found him. But . . . now what? Even if I was able to get rid of Cardian, how would I get Kalyll out of that damn sphere?

There's only one thing you can try, Dark Dani whispered inside my head.

I turned away from Kalyll and faced Cardian. He was still holding the dagger and had started making his way toward the door, taking small sideways steps, eyes fixed on me.

"You're a clever fox, aren't you?" he said.

I frowned. "What are you talking about?"

"This was what you wanted. You tricked Varamede somehow so that I would lead you here."

"That's nonsense. I was just curious. That's all. It's pretty impressive, I must admit. Unlike any prison I've ever seen."

I took a casual step in his direction, which he counteracted with two of his own. Now he was at arm's length from the door. I couldn't allow him to leave. I had to get my hands on him. I had to—

Unable to control the panic and desperation surging through my body, I leaped in Cardian's direction, hands outstretched to grab his arm. He could stab me, if that would get him close enough to touch. But he was fast, and before I could reach him, he slammed the door shut behind him, leaving me trapped inside.

I pounded on the door. There was no response.

After a few beats, Cardian asked, "Why not use your power against this obstacle?"

Freezing with my fist up in the air, I realized he'd been waiting for me to blow the door to smithereens, except I was on empty.

"I . . . I don't want to hurt you," I said, feeling proud of my duplicitous answer. "C'mon, Cardian. I know it's not easy to trust anyone in your position, but this is ridiculous."

"Daniella," a raspy voice said behind me.

I whirled and faced Kalyll, who was now kneeling toward the front of the sphere, one bloody hand propped against its surface for support.

Panicked, I ran to him and pressed a finger to my lips.

"No, not Daniella," I whispered. "Ylannea. Just be quiet, okay?" I ran back to the door. "It seems like a fresh round of torture is due. He's awake."

Nothing.

"What is . . .?" Kalyll tried to ask in a hoarse voice, but he trailed off, too weak to even speak.

"Cardian," I called. "Let me out. I'm starting to get mad." Maybe that would do it, a sort of threat.

Still nothing.

Was he still waiting for me to blast the door? Was he questioning my ability to shoot laser beams? I shook my head. No. That was my own insecurity talking. Cardian had seen me go against Varamede. He knew what I could do. He just didn't know I needed a live charge.

I pounded on the door some more, but it seemed he had left.

Unable to ignore Kalyll any further, I walked back to him.

I kneeled in front of the sphere. Tentatively, I raised a hand and slowly moved it toward the crackling surface of Kalyll's prison, unsure of whether or not it would hurt me. But he was touching it from the inside, so I was hoping it wouldn't light me up like a Christmas tree.

My hand lined up perfectly with his as I laid it on the force field. A strange prickly sensation went up my arm, but that was the extent of its effect. My hand looked tiny against his large one, almost like a child's.

"Kalyll," I whispered in a trembling voice. "What have they done to you?"

"You're . . . here. You're awake. How?" He managed a broken smile. His lower lip was swollen and cracked. Dry blood was caked on his chin, trailing down his neck.

"It doesn't matter how. I can explain later. Now we have to get you out of here." I glanced around. "Any idea how?"

He shook his head, and his expression changed, the smile turning into a frown. "It was stupid to come."

I pulled away from the sphere and stretched to my full height to look at him better. "You're welcome."

His legs trembling visibly, he also rose. He towered over me thanks to his broad shoulders and added height from the floating sphere.

"Now we're both . . . trapped," he said.

"Not for long," I boasted. I had no idea where my confidence was coming from, but doom and gloom weren't going to help, were they?

Kalyll glanced toward the locked door. "Did you come alone?"

I shrugged one shoulder. "Yes."

His upper lip curled up. "Whose idea was it to send you? It should have been Jeondar or Silver."

"Do you realize you're digging yourself into a big hole?" I asked. "Watch yourself, or I might start shoveling dirt into it."

To my surprise, the smile returned. "This is why I love you. You always put me in my place." His knees gave out then, and he collapsed to the bottom of the sphere.

I kneeled once more. His body was molded to the shape of the sphere, and I could look at him eye to eye.

"That bastard will pay for this." I pressed a hand to the force field as if to cradle his cheek. I needed to heal him.

Praying the sphere didn't block my attempt, I released a burst of healing power. As it hit, the force field buzzed and wavered like a television with static. At first, nothing happened, but then Kalyll lifted his head and blinked in surprise, his cobalt eyes locking with mine as he exhaled in relief.

"I didn't think it would work." I pressed my other hand to the sphere. "Touch here, too."

Kalyll started to lift his hand, then put it back down. "It's designed that way to let the sorcerer's spells in."

"What sorcerer?" I asked.

Kalyll didn't respond.

But there was only one answer. Cardian couldn't even do his own torturing. He had a sorcerer in charge of Kalyll's torment. Bastard!

"Touch your hand here," I urged him.

"No. Save your energy. You might need it." Already his voice sounded stronger, and a little bit of color had returned to his cheeks. He needed this.

"And you'll need yours, so we can run out of here, so c'mon," I insisted.

He remained stubborn. Regardless, I pushed more healing energy from my other hand. When he felt it, he stood up with a jolt.

"Stop it, Dani." This time his voice had a rumbling quality as he commanded me. This was Wölfe, through and through. He'd even called me Dani.

I wanted to give him a bit more, but he was standing straight in the very center of the sphere, keeping away from me.

"Hardhead." I scowled. At least he looked better. It would have to do, for now.

The handle rattled at the door, then it whined open, revealing two gray-skinned males wearing identical black uniforms. They had no hair, and small horns protruded from the top of their bald heads. Several ridges like exposed bone lined up beneath their cheekbones.

"Lady Fenmenor," one of them said, eyeing me with distrust, "King Cardian requests your presence."

A derisive laugh burst out of Kalyll. "King Cardian? What a joke."

The guards ignored him, showing no reaction to the jab. Clearly, they didn't give a shit about Cardian. They were loyal to Mythorne, I had to assume.

Contemplating my next move, I pondered the possibility

of draining the energy from these two guards and using it to free Kalyll from the sphere. But then what? What would be our means of escape without a transfer token? I'd been counting on stealing Cardian's token before he got away. That meant I had to go to him and hope I could still take it from him.

My decision made, I heaved an irritated sigh. "It's about time. I was starting to get very bored in here. It was so rude of Cardian to . . ." I waved a hand in the air. "Never mind, I guess I understand his reasons. Let's go."

"Da— Ylannea, don't go with them, with Cardian," Kalyll said, looking terrified to let me out of his sight.

"As much as I enjoyed your company," I said, acting as vapid as possible, "this place is repellent." I sashayed toward the guards and waved over my shoulder. "It was nice knowing you, King For-a-day Kalyll."

It killed me not to look back, but I walked straight toward the guards, past them, and left Kalyll behind. My heart twisted in my chest.

I'll come back for you, Kalyll. I'll come back. I sent the thought out, hoping it would reach him, hoping he knew I wasn't abandoning him. *Don't worry about me. I'll be fine.*

I knew he would fret for me even more than he'd been fretting already. Even if I'd been frozen and nearly lifeless before, I hadn't been in the bed of vipers the Unseelie Court was famed to be.

And I hadn't been alone.

Whatever confidence I'd possessed the moment I decided to walk out with the guards, it vanished when I stepped out into the hall and found myself face to face with a hooded figure. The cloak and hood were woven with threads of silver and gold, and it seemed to shimmer as if enchanted with spells. The garment was long and flowing, and it changed colors as if to blend in with its surroundings.

Even if I couldn't distinguish a single feature in the depths of his hooded cloak, I sensed piercing eyes drilling into my own. My spine seemed to shiver, sending tremors to the rest of my body. Of course, Cardian hadn't trusted two lame guards to fetch me and deliver me to him. He'd send someone else, someone with a terrible aura of power hanging around them. Was this the sorcerer who had been torturing Kalyll? Something told me that he was.

"Friend of Cardian?" I said, shaking myself in an attempt to pass my fear as surprise.

He said nothing.

"My mistake, not the friendly sort, then." I was acting like a total idiot, but I felt oddly protected by the shallowness I attempted to portray.

The guards marched ahead, and I ended up sandwiched between them and the hooded freak. I tried to sashay along, but the swishing of the male walking behind me forced my back into a stiff line. Layers upon layers of whispering voices seemed to sound inside my head, all of them seeming to pray to a god they knew wasn't listening.

I shook my head, trying to clear it. Was it a past echo that lingered in these empty, dank corridors? Or was it something else? A spell from the male stalking behind me? I dared a glance back to quickly snap my eyes forward once more. There had been two glowing embers inside of that hood.

For the first time, I wondered if they were marching me to my death and not to Cardian.

"Are we almost there? I'm famished," I asked the guards.

"Just a little bit further, my lady," the taller one responded. He sounded reasonable, not like a murderer.

I hurried my step a little, getting closer to the guards in the front. If that creep behind me tried anything, I could jump the guards, steal their life force, and at least have a hope of defending myself.

Gradually, the floor beneath us grew steeper, and we moved upward as if climbing from the bowels of some hell. A bright light shone ahead of us, and I prayed it was the exit. In my mind, I quickly retraced my steps back to Kalyll. I went over the passages and turns we'd taken to ensure I wouldn't forget how to find him.

I'll get back to you, Kalyll.

I chanted the phrase inside my head over and over, aware that I was doing it to reassure myself, to reassure myself I would not die today, and that somehow, I would live to rescue Kalyll.

I squinted as we reached the exit. For a moment, I was blinded, thinking that maybe we'd come up to an open field, where the sun shone brightly, but as my eyes adjusted, I realized we were in a large room hung with hundreds of fairy light chandeliers. Moreover, gilded mirrors reclined against the walls, multiplying each light by the thousand.

Why such a display of light? It was dizzying.

I placed a hand over my brow to shade my eyes.

"Did she try anything?" Cardian asked behind me.

Putting on a pout, I turned to face him. "Like what? Cry myself to sleep? Why would you leave me in such a horrible place? I think my bones have caught a chill." I rubbed my arms for effect.

I held his gaze as he scrutinized me. He certainly wasn't one to trust easily.

"If you try anything, Runik here," he gestured towards the hooded figure, "will make sure you don't live another day."

I eyed the male distrustfully. "What is he? Some sort of sorcerer? Could he be more powerful than your precious Varamede?"

"You don't want to find out," Cardian assured me.

Rolling my eyes, I nodded. "Yes, I guess you're right about that, but I must insist, you have nothing to worry about. Now, where are we? Interesting place. Why so many mirrors?"

"Do you ever stop asking questions?"

Do you ever take the stick out of your butt? I almost let that question slip out, but I bit my tongue just in time. It wouldn't help to overdo my blasé act.

When I didn't say anything, Cardian huffed. Yet, he seemed satisfied. He liked to feel in control.

"As my task here is done," he reached into his pocket, "it's time to leave."

Leave? Now?

No! I wouldn't go. Not without Kalyll.

Cardian crooked an elbow, inviting me to join him. As I approached, he pulled out the token and weaved it skillfully between his fingers like some sort of poker player.

The moment I looped my arm through his, he would wish us away from here, and I couldn't have that. I hadn't gone through all of this just to go back without the male I loved.

If I'd been able to stop and consider the consequences of my actions, I might've acted differently, but I wasn't fully in control. Dark Dani was.

With her at the helm, I jumped forward to seize Cardian's wrist.

CHAPTER 18
DANIELLA

As I took hold of Cardian's wrist, the transfer token flew out of his hand, hit the floor, and rolled out of sight. I barely had the sense to regret its loss. There were more pressing matters to deal with.

Still holding on, I whirled and hid behind him.

He tried to get free, and he might have succeeded had my siphoning powers been slow, but they were instantaneous, and in one beat, his body went limp against mine, his life force channeling into my body. A drawn-out moan issued from his lips, something I was sure was meant to be a cry for help. His energy filled my chest, expanding my ribs, building that pressure I once mistook for guilt.

But even though my powers worked quickly, the sorcerer, Runik, and the Fae guards were quick as well.

A spell flew in our direction and enveloped our bodies. A crackling force wedged itself between Cardian and me and pried us apart. I flew backward, landing on my ass, and he collapsed to the floor, his joints completely unhinged, his skin a putty shade of gray. He twitched, his eyelids fluttering.

A few paces from Cardian, the sorcerer weaved his hands in the air, and I knew that another attack was coming. I scrambled to my hands and knees and crawled backward. A blast of energy hit the spot I'd just vacated.

Pieces of splintered wood flew in every direction, several of them embedding themselves in my exposed skin. I clenched my teeth to stifle the pain and kept moving.

The guards rushed to Cardian, took his arms, and dragged him out of the way.

Moving as fast as I could on all fours, I lunged behind one of the mirrors just as Runik unleashed a second attack. I braced myself for an explosion of glass and shards to join the splinters already embedded in my body.

Instead, I heard a muffled cry, followed by a *thud*. I dared peek from behind the gilded mirror to find the sorcerer lying on the floor, his voluminous robes pooling around him. His own spell had bounced off the mirror and hit him.

The guards stood, Cardian on the floor between them, and stared at Runik in confusion, as if seeing him defeated was something they could have never predicted.

In unison, their gazes abandoned the sorcerer to look for me. They found me peeking from behind the mirror and drew their swords with a *zing*, but there was something in their expressions that told me they were afraid. Had they not seen what happened? Did they think I was the one who fell Runik? They had been dragging Cardian away, so maybe they'd missed the split-second result of the sorcerer's miscalculation.

Their scared expressions and that pressure pushing against my ribs drove me to my feet and out of my hiding place. As I stepped out, a small object hiding behind a second mirror caught my eye.

The transfer token!

It seemed luck was on my side today.

Moving casually, acting as if my heart weren't trying to pound its way out of my chest, I picked up the token and palmed it.

"Go on. Leave." I made a sweeping motion with my hand, trying to sound generous. "Unless you don't value your lives and want to end up like a husk." I stared pointedly at Cardian.

They took a step closer, brandishing their swords. Even though they looked scared of me and my threat seemed to have some effect on them, there was clearly someone else they feared more.

Out of the corner of my eye, I glanced toward the door we'd used to enter this peculiar room. Flinging my hair behind my shoulder, I started walking in that direction.

"As much as I would like to stay and find out why you would rather take your chances with me than whoever would skin you alive for letting me escape, I have to go."

Moving with the grace and speed of the Fae, the guards rushed forward and blocked the exit.

"You're not going anywhere," one of them said.

I put a hand up and willed the energy in my chest to manifest. For a second, nothing happened, and I started to fear that the attack I'd unleashed on Varamede had been a fluke, but then a ball of light appeared there, powerful and threatening. I stared at it in awe. It was beautiful, really, and it threatened to hypnotize me with its dancing quality. It was nearly blinding, like a million diamonds reflecting sunlight and bouncing back and forth.

"I don't want to shoot your hearts out of your chest, but if

I must, I will do it." As I said the last word, I peeled my eyes away from the beautiful display and stared at the guards with murderous intent.

Part of me wanted to pretend I only wished to intimidate them, but another part of me knew I was capable of delivering on my promises.

One of the guards inhaled deeply and the other one sniffled. They were afraid, all right, but still, I was promising them a swift death, which was likely much better than what they would receive from . . . whom? Cardian, if he survived? No. I had a feeling it wasn't Cardian.

I had a feeling it was Kellam Mythorne that terrified them so.

They pressed forward, pointing their swords straight at my chest.

"I warned you." I jerked both hands forward and released the blazing heat of my light power.

As time slowed, I imagined them limp on the floor, gaping holes in their chests. It was a horrific tableau, and in the last instant, I prevailed over the darker side of me, and I held back, quickly changing the direction and intensity of my attack and aiming it at their faces.

A weaker beam of light hit them. They screamed. Their swords clattered to the floor as they pressed their hands to their faces and stumbled around drunkenly.

Oh, God! Had I blinded them for life? The thought horrified me, but I couldn't linger on it. I had to get out of here, and at least I had spared their lives.

I started to run back toward Kalyll, then stopped short. The pressure around my chest wasn't strong, and I feared the energy left in me wouldn't be enough to pierce the sphere. Whirling around, I looked at the guards. They were screaming, palms pressed to their eyes. One of them was on his knees, speaking words in a language I didn't understand. The other one was weeping and shaking his head.

My hands tingled. I needed more energy. I would have to kill one of them, after all. Then I noticed something, something moving under Runik's robes. He wasn't dead. Heedlessly, I ran to him. Peeling his hood back I nearly screamed at the sight of his face. It was twisted and contorted, the mouth a slash with no lips that revealed a rictus grin. Hundreds of small scars like slashes from a razor marred his weathered skin, and wisps of hair clung to a pale scalp.

"You tortured Kalyll," I said, wrapping my hands around his neck.

His eyes sprang open. They were clouded and small specks of black moved inside them like ants. I resisted the urge to vomit and started drawing his energy just as he attempted to fight back. In an instant, I was done. His face was even more hideous than before, dried out and cracked.

"You'll never hurt anyone again," I spat.

There was someone else in this room who deserved the same fate. I let go of the sorcerer, stretched to my full height, and turned toward Cardian. I took two steps toward him, determined to end him.

The sound of voices made my head snap up toward the source. I froze, then knew I had to get out of there before I was spotted. Turning on my heel, I ran at full pelt, my bare feet slapping on the floor. I didn't look back. I just ran, but a cry of alarm let me know that I'd been spotted.

I ran faster, arms pumping, that map I had created in my mind jumping to the forefront. I took one left and then a right. The sound of stomping boots and insistent cries to hurry up followed close behind me. I ran past a wide corridor, then skidded to a stop and retraced my steps. Left, I had to go left again. I kept going, and for a moment, I thought I'd made a mistake, then, a few steps ahead, I spotted Kalyll's door and breathed a sigh of relief.

I'm almost there. Almost there.

The voices and the racket behind me were closer now. The Fae were so much faster than me. My human legs were failing me. For an instant, I considered blasting a beam of light over my shoulder to blind my pursuers, but I couldn't risk it. I needed all the power I'd drained from Runik to break Kalyll's prison. I couldn't fail. If I did, I didn't want to imagine what would happen. Cardian, whom I'd failed to kill, would make sure we paid dearly.

"Stop!" someone shouted.

There was a whistling sound, and as I rounded another corner, an arrow whizzed by.

"Oh, God."

I needed to dig deeper. The next arrow would kill me.

"C'mon," I urged myself, clenching my teeth.

Suddenly, I was moving faster, much faster than I ever had. Doors zoomed by right and left. I watched everything as if detached or caught in one of those dreams where you're capable of impossible things. But it wasn't a dream, I was really moving as fast or faster than Fae.

"Shit!" I exclaimed as I ran past Kalyll's door.

Grabbing the doorjamb, I jerked myself to a stop, kicked

the door open, and busted in. Kalyll was on his feet, expectant. No doubt his Fae sharpened senses had warned him we were coming.

"Daniella!"

"Stand back," I ordered him, without stopping to consider the risks.

"What?"

I blasted the sphere, letting all the light pour out of me in one shot. My energy crashed against the prison. A horrible screeching sound pierced my ears as the two magical forces combined in a blinding flash.

I wrapped my arms around my head and ducked, bracing for an explosion, for death. But the sound quickly died out, and I opened my eyes to a diminishing glow that consumed itself, growing weaker until it disappeared with a soft pop.

For a nanosecond, Kalyll seemed suspended in the air, then the sphere completely vanished and he dropped to the floor. He landed on his feet and glanced around with wide eyes as he faced his freedom.

He barely had time to recover from his surprise when I crashed into him, wrapping my arms around his waist. Just as he held me back, the door burst open, and a host of guards rushed in. All along, the transfer token had been clenched tightly in my fist, so I wasted no time wishing us away to the first place that jumped into my mind.

As the guards reached out to grab us, we dissolved and left that awful place behind.

CHAPTER 19
KALYLL

I held her tightly, not caring that the guards were here to pull us apart. In my despair, I'd been sure I would never lay eyes on her again, and now, here I was, my arms wrapped around her, her warmth and delicious scent seeping into me.

I could die now, and I wouldn't care.

But I would die defending her, killing every bastard who dared touch a hair on her head.

I started to pull away, but then the dank room that had served as a prison started dissolving around us. A familiar feeling washed over me.

Daniella had a transfer token.

Great Erilena! She'd done it. All by herself, she had freed me. I always knew she was extraordinary, but this went beyond my imaginings. She was a force, a creature to be reckoned with. I held her tighter. Even as we materialized in a different place, I pressed my mouth to the top of her head and inhaled her scent. Her heart pounded against me, her desperate embrace a lifeline that gave me back the desire to keep going. I had nearly given up. I thought her gone in eternal sleep, and I'd seen no reason to go on.

"We're safe. We're safe. We're safe," she repeated over and over as if to convince herself that it was true.

I opened my eyes to see where she had taken us. The place was familiar, a patch of forest with supple ground covered in soft moss. A circle of trees surrounded us, creating our own private space. The scent of wild flowers floated in the air and triggered a host of blissful memories. We were at the clearing near Mount Ruin, where we'd mated for the first time.

Reluctantly, I pulled away and held her at arm's length. I scanned her face, drinking in each and every one of her features.

Gods, she was beautiful, even in her altered Fae state, which still remained.

Suddenly, she regarded me with a determined expression. With stern focus, she began examining me. She grabbed my chin and turned my face left and right. Her tender hands slid down my neck, palpating me, prodding my pectoral muscles and my abdomen. Then she took my hands in hers and examined each digit carefully.

"They're swollen," she said.

The healing energy she'd poured into me when she first arrived in my prison had healed most of my injuries, leaving only remnants that I could easily disregard. I'd been through worse pain than Runik and Mythorne put me through. I had learned to compartmentalize, to detach myself and go elsewhere, even as my body was ravaged by pain.

But none of that mattered right now. Only Daniella did.

"What happened to your fingers?" she demanded.

"Nothing," I lied and batted her hand away.

She frowned, her mouth twisting to one side in disapproval.

"I'm fine, woman. I'm only worried about you. How? How are you here? How did you wake up? I thought . . . I thought . . ." I couldn't finish. Instead, I pulled her to me and crushed her against my chest.

She remained stiff but only for a second, then her body molded to mine.

"I thought the same," she said. "Thought I'd never see you again."

Slowly, I sat down on the moss-covered ground, pulling her down with me. "You must tell me everything."

"You first."

I shook my head. "There's nothing worth telling."

"They . . . tortured you." Her eyes wavered with unshed tears.

"Don't fret about it. I'm fine."

She reached over and pressed a hand to my cheek. "Your body, yes, but what about your mind? Your spirit?"

My heart swelled with love for her. Though young, she was wise beyond her years. "I promise I'm fine. You're not only the salve for my bruises. You are the light that shines through all the darkness."

She bit her lower lip, a sign that she didn't quite believe me.

"Wölfe was with me," I added. "The beast is strong. It made things easier." It wasn't a lie.

She seemed doubtful still, but her misgivings seemed to ease, if only a little.

"Now, will you tell me everything?" I insisted.

And she did. She explained how she'd slowly siphoned energy from the flowers Larina kept at her bedside, gaining strength little by little. She'd awakened the very day Cardian took me, and since then, she and the Sub Rosa hadn't stopped looking for me. She explained how Cardian had, once more, installed himself as the Seelie King, a post I would gladly let him have if he weren't so bent on destruction. When she was done explaining, I stared at her in awe.

"You have changed a lot, melynthi," I said.

She pondered for a moment, then said, "I have. I hope that's not a problem."

I blew air through my nose. "Not at all. I always knew you were fierce. A trait I admire. You have only grown fiercer. The way I always imagined my queen would be."

One of her eyes twitched at the word *queen*. She had faced Runik and a host of guards without flinching, but the mention of wearing the Seelie crown was enough to cause the tic.

"Destitute queen, perhaps," she said. "Because your court is full of traitors. I have a feeling they have outnumbered those loyal to you. And with your mother . . . gone, without her support, I have a feeling going back wouldn't work the way it did last time, would it?"

"I'm afraid you are correct."

"It's prejudice, isn't it? Because you're a shadowdrifter."

Despite the fact that Daniella was new to my realm, she had a good understanding of how things worked.

Once more, she pressed her hand to my cheek. "I'm sorry. It's so stupid. If they can't see that you are the right choice, they don't deserve you."

I narrowed my eyes. "What about Wölfe? Is he the right choice?"

She seemed at a loss for words at the question.

Her lack of response rattled me somehow, provoking anger and bringing the interloper forth.

WÖLFE

"What is it?" I demanded. "Don't you like me anymore?"

She pulled her hand away from my cheek, her dark eyebrows drawing together and her gaze roving over my face.

"Wölfe." My name escaped her lips as if of its own accord.

"Yes, melynthi."

"I thought . . ."

"What? That I was gone?"

She shook her head, looking uncertain. "The last time we were together, you, Kalyll . . ."

I said nothing, hoping she would finish, but her words dried out. The last time we were together was at Naesala's house. Then, Kalyll had managed to subdue me. No. Subdue was the wrong word. I hated to admit it, but it had seemed as if we both found a way to be present, to be one. Even if he had remained mostly Kalyll, I had felt satisfied.

A growl escaped me at the traitorous thoughts. If anyone should take backstage, it was him, not me. Dani watched me closely, not in the least intimidated by the guttural sound. Well, it seemed I had to set things right.

"The last time we were together," I sneered, "you hadn't nearly died, and I hadn't nearly given up. He couldn't have survived without me. If you ask me, that means he doesn't deserve to live alongside me."

"Oh." A single exclamation left her lips, then unexpectedly, she was climbing onto my lap and wrapping her arms around my neck.

At first, I didn't know what to do with my hands. She had surprised me. I'd thought she would push me away and be riddled with uncertainty the way she had been in the past. Instead, she was clinging to me as if . . . as if she had missed me.

Reluctantly, I pushed her away to look into her face and read her expression. Was she lying? Trying to manipulate me somehow? No. It didn't seem that way. Her relief seemed genuine, and the tenderness in her gaze told me she cared about me.

"I'm right here," she said. "I fought my way back, and I'm not going anywhere."

"What are you doing?" I demanded. "You've never been this way with me. You're trying to bring him back, aren't you?" The realization dawned on me, cleaving me in half like an ax straight to the chest.

I stood up, and she spilled onto the ground. As I stretched to my full height, she looked up with wide eyes, her mouth hanging open, though her surprise lasted only a moment. In the next instant, she was on her feet, planting her hands on my chest and shoving me.

"You infuriating bastard," she snapped, then she whirled and turned her back on me. "What made me think you had gained any sense? You're the same jerk you've always been."

Now, that was more like it. This was the vitriol I was used to.

She whirled back to face me. "You don't deserve—"

I took a step toward her. Her hand was up, index finger posed to denounce me. I seized her wrist, wrapping my hand around it. She fought, trying to extricate herself, but I laced my other hand around her hip and tugged her to me.

My cock was instantly hard, and the rest of my body just as full of want. She set my blood on fire and made me yearn for the sweltering feel between her legs.

I leaned down to kiss her lips. She turned her head to one side to avoid me, but I wasn't deterred. I liked her like this: fiery and wild. So I kissed her jaw, then trailed a path with my tongue down the column of her neck. She pushed, her hands flat against my bare chest, but her attempt was feeble. She was right where she wanted to be.

My fangs slid into place, and I nibbled her shoulder, making her shiver and practically melt in my arms. She abandoned all pretense of resistance and slid her hands over my torso, her fingernails raking over my taut muscles, payback for the scrape of my fangs.

In one swift motion, I swept her off her feet and cradled her to my chest. Finding the softest patch of moss, I laid her down, and knowing I had her full permission, I proceeded to thoroughly fuck her.

CHAPTER 20
DANIELLA

I'd taken in the sharper quality of his cheekbones and jaw, and the way his dark blue eyes seemed to glow from within, and I'd known Wölfe had taken over.

But the truth was, I was beyond caring and attempting to make a distinction between Kalyll and Wölfe. That was what had driven me to climb on his lap and throw my arms around his neck in an attempt to make him feel better.

"The last time we were together, you hadn't nearly died, and I hadn't nearly given up."

He'd thought everything lost, and the idea of his utter despair chiseled my heart in two. Then, of course, he'd grown paranoid, the way he always did. For all his bravado, he surely was insecure. Though there was nothing uncertain about him when he swept me off my feet, laid me down on the moss-covered ground, and pressed his body to mine.

The same part of me that had called him a bastard wanted to fight and tell him to stop, but there really was no point. I was done beating myself up about who I loved.

Kalyll . . . Wölfe . . . it didn't make any difference.

When he fucked me, I liked it both tender and rough, and

166

I knew what I was about to get right now. And it was exactly what I needed. Any other way, and I would cry. In the last few days, I'd also thought I lost him, thought I would never see him again. In that, we suffered equally.

So I didn't want his tender kisses and caresses. I didn't want whispered words of comfort in my ears. I wanted him to pound me, to fill all the hollows that pain had left behind with his rough growls and dirty talk.

"Open for me, melynthi," he purred as he kissed his way along my thigh and hiked my dress to my waist.

I obliged, even as he pushed my knees apart, spreading me to an aching point. As he reached the hem of my panties, he pulled away, and in the next instant, I felt them snap, the rake of his claws up my belly letting me know he'd cut my underwear open.

With no regard for subtleties, he made a hungry sound and descended on me, his lips circling that aching nub at my peak, his tongue flicking it with force.

He sucked and licked, then slipped a finger into me, making me gasp as he pumped in and out. The finger curled and rubbed that raw spot inside me every time it came back in. His tongue and finger worked in unison. His free hand slipped under my butt, and he lifted me a bit higher for better access.

The sounds in the back of his throat would leave no doubt to anyone that he was feasting, enjoying something utterly delicious.

His rhythm was intense, making me feel the world was ending in the best way possible. He took my clit into his mouth and sucked harder. Pure ecstasy flowed through my veins like lava. My fingers dug into the dirt as pressure built inside me. I teetered at the edge of a precipice wanting more of this, but also wanting to jump and soar.

As if sensing where I stood, Wölfe slipped a second finger in and thrust harder. I plummeted. The moan that escaped me was release and want all at once. All my built-up tension was released, and I screamed as waves of pleasure washed over me. I writhed under him, surge after surge assaulting my body and leaving me completely at his mercy.

As I climaxed, his hands slid up and down my body. They cupped my breasts and pinched my peaked nipples, they caressed my spasming belly and graced my mound, making me aware of every ecstatic corner of my body and intensifying my pleasure, wringing out all I had to give.

When I was almost spent, he placed both hands on my hips and turned me over. Pulling me to my knees, he sheathed himself and unapologetically started pounding in and out. With each thrust, he reached deep, bringing tears of pleasure to my eyes.

He moaned and growled with abandon, his girth and length filling me to burst, reaching untouched places and pushing me to the edge once more.

Wölfe's skin slapped against mine, and his fingers dug possessively into my flesh. He thrust violently and recklessly, eliciting cries of delicious pain and rapture from me. We both came at the same time, our cries of release sending a flock of birds flying off the branches above.

Spent, we collapsed to the ground, Wölfe's weight resting reassuringly on top of me.

We slept like two abandoned kittens, curled up against each other, heads pillowed on the soft moss. At some point, the morning light peeking through the trees and the soft chirping of birds woke me up.

Kalyll—I knew it was him because his features weren't as sharp as Wölfe's—was already awake. His deep ocean eyes regarded me with an intensity that made my heart squeeze as if to take hold of this moment to never let it go.

I wanted to always remember this expression, this unshakable certainty of his love for me.

He licked his lips and said, "I can still taste you."

I felt a blush climb up my neck and bloom on my cheeks. I was beyond caring whom I loved, but was he? He had said so once, but it was at a time when he'd seemed better able to control his wilder side.

"I do believe it is my turn," he said, slowly climbing on top of me.

Well, it seemed that answered my question. He didn't care.

And what a lucky girl I was to have two adoring males ready to satisfy my every need and mix things up to keep it interesting.

I succumbed to his kisses and caresses and the tender and attentive way of his love-making. While Wölfe possessed me, Kalyll worshiped me, every inch of my body an altar for his devotion and undivided attention.

Kalyll held the transfer token in the palm of his hand and regarded it with sadness.

"I almost killed Cardian," I blurted out, for the first time experiencing the guilt I should've been feeling all along. "But I think he's fine."

I didn't want to kill his brother. I had siblings, and I couldn't imagine a situation where Kalyll killing one of them would ever be all right, even if they became as evil as Cardian. I could only be glad Runik had attacked just in time to prevent me from draining Cardian completely.

Kalyll's azure eyes met mine as shame burned on my face.

"Do not feel bad, Daniella," he said, reading my emotions without fault. "I know of your realm's commandment of *an eye for an eye*, and I would not fault you for applying it. His pet thunderlord nearly killed you on Cardian's orders."

I shook my head. "It's not like that. He—"

". . . was trying to kill you," he finished for me. "That would also justify your actions. In fact, I wouldn't blame anyone for outright killing him based on the fear of who he might become, and what he'd be willing to do to get there. Cardian was always . . . different, troubled somehow. He is twelve years younger than me and was always treated differently. Mother and Father placed no expectations on him. None. Up until recently, I thought they'd only managed to turn him into a careless, spoiled brat. But now I know the damage runs much deeper."

He paused to consider as if he were trying to puzzle

something out. I could almost hear him thinking and had to fight the urge to smooth the crease between his eyebrows with my finger.

"Cardian grew up to resent us, to hate us even. In sparing him the rigors of a strict upbringing, they failed to teach him an appreciation for his privileged situation, and he now operates under the misconception that he's entitled to more, despite the fact that he already has more than he deserves."

And wasn't that the mistake of all parents who wished to spare their children every difficulty and who gave exaggerated praise for the slightest accomplishment? They thought they were doing their kids a favor when they were only setting them up for mediocrity.

I laid my hand on his. "He's still your brother, and I know his death would bring you no satisfaction."

"I'm not so sure."

"You can't mean that."

"A lifetime of imprisonment might be worse."

"Perhaps there's another option."

He searched my face, seeming at a loss.

"Exile?" I asked. "Is that possible?"

"It might be too dangerous to allow him to go free. But we may be wasting our time with this conversation. He is the king now. The rightful one. Perhaps it is I who should be exiled."

There was a strange longing in his expression, as if the idea of being exempt from the duties he was raised to shoulder was highly tempting. But I knew the temptation of a much simpler life would never be enough to pull him away from his responsibilities. He was not a quitter.

"Perhaps," I said, "but Elf-hame needs you, and I know you won't abandon it."

He sighed. "I often feel that I've . . . ruined your life."

"What? Are you serious?"

"I am. Before I so rudely intruded, you had a calm, safe existence. But ever since, you've been tied up, terrorized by a decayana, turned into something you're not." He waved a hand in front of me to demonstrate my Fae features. "You've been nearly killed. Twice. I have brought you nothing but distress."

"That is not true."

He frowned.

"If I'm being honest, my life was pretty boring before coming here. I mean . . . I loved my job. I found satisfaction in giving sick children a second chance, but now that I have you, I understand that something crucial was missing. You've given me the most important thing of all. Love. I love you, and I would give everything up to be with you."

His expression fell, which was the exact opposite of what I intended. "I don't want you to give up anything for me. It's wrong. It should be me. I should leave with you, go to your realm, start a new life. Just the two of us."

"That sounds wonderful. I'm not going to lie. I think we could be happy if we did that, at least for some time."

"Forever."

"No, Kalyll. Not forever. If you fail your people, things would sour eventually. You would have many regrets."

"But what about you?" he asked. "Won't the same thing happen to you? Won't your life with me turn sour when my love becomes quotidian?"

"Wow, chill it with the fancy words, King Adanorin."

He smirked. "It means something that occurs daily."

I swatted his arm. "I know what it means, and to answer your question . . . no, things won't turn *quotidian*. There is a huge difference between me giving up my calm, safe life, and you giving up yours. When this is all said and done, I can go back to healing, to helping people who need me. But if you walk away now, there's no going back for you."

"But what if we don't make it?" he demanded, a blue glow flashing across his eyes, a clear sign that Wölfe was trying to push forward.

Kalyll fought back and got himself under control, for which I was grateful. His thoughts of leaving Elf-hame to live a quiet life with me were real enough. They stemmed from the side of him that cared nothing about duty. They stemmed from Wölfe.

I took both his hands in mine and looked him straight in the eyes. "Then we don't make it, but we'll fight together side by side. Promise me that."

He opened his mouth to protest. I knew it would be his desire to keep me safe, but I couldn't have that.

"Promise me," I insisted, "that you won't leave me behind while you and the others fight."

A deep frown parted his forehead. Clearly, he'd already been planning to leave me somewhere safe while he went around slaying his enemies.

"If you don't promise, I'll make you a promise of my own, Kalyll Adanorin, and you won't like it," I said, my voice firm and commanding.

He seemed to reappraise me, his gaze roving over my face with surprise.

"What?" I asked, feeling self-conscious.

"Nothing, just that you got me properly scared, and that you're not a queen yet, but you certainly sound like one."

"Don't think flattery will make me forget what you owe me." I put out a hand and tapped my palm with my index finger. "Where is my promise?"

He placed his large hand under mine and deposited a tantalizing kiss right in the middle of my palm.

"I promise, my queen." He straightened back up as a delicious shiver ran up my arm.

I narrowed my eyes skeptically.

He cleared his throat, and sensing that his slightly sensual promise hadn't fully satisfied me, he said, "Do not think I make this promise in vain. You have proven that you can take care of yourself. You single-handedly rescued me from the very jaws of the Unseelie Court. The Daniella I first met wouldn't have been capable of that. So I mean what I said."

Satisfied, I nodded. "Thank you." After a moment's pause, I asked, "What do we do now?"

"It was the question that first assailed me when I woke up this morning. I thought about it, and I think our only option at the moment is to go back to Elyndell."

I'd been afraid he was going to say that. "If they spot you . . ."

"We won't let that happen. We will go at night, find refuge at Naesala's home since she still seems amicable to our cause."

"She is."

"Then it's decided. We go there. Ask Larina and Shadow to contact the Sub Rosa, and we'll make our plans."

We had to wait the entire day in the forest before using the transfer token to go back to Elyndell. I couldn't say I minded it, though. Kalyll was very hungry and thirsty. They had barely fed him while he was imprisoned, but that patch of forest proved so affable that we had no trouble finding a gurgling stream and bushes replete with fat raspberries, three times the size of those back home. After eating our fill, we made love right by the stream, our mouths and teeth purple from the fruit, our movements languid, unhurried.

We'd never had time to enjoy each other like this, and I was sad when the sun went down, and it was time to go.

As we stood in front of each other, the transfer token held tightly in my hand, Kalyll said, "I promise you one more thing. We will return here to this magical clearing so full of the best memories I have."

"I would love that," I said as I wished us back to Elyndell, back to the lion's den.

CHAPTER 21
DANIELLA

We appeared in an alley only a block from the sorceress's home. The night was quiet, and if I was honest, the loudest thing was the pounding of my heart. I had halfway expected the city to be in disarray as Cardian sent guards in search of Kalyll, but the night was quiet. Placid, even.

Kalyll made a rumbling sound in the back of his throat as he scanned the alley. It seemed he didn't trust the quiet, so maybe my unrest was not misplaced.

"What is it?" I whispered so softly that I knew only his Fae ears would pick up my question.

He shook himself. "Nothing. I think it's safe to go on."

That surprised me because I'd been expecting him to say that a full battalion was waiting around the corner.

He interlaced his fingers with mine and walked out of the alley, his back ramrod straight and his steps confident. I mimicked him. It wouldn't do for anyone nearby to see us skulking around. That would only raise their suspicions.

When we arrived at the front of Naesala Roka's place, we stood in front of a massive wooden gate—one that didn't allow a glimpse inside the residence.

"Do we knock?" I asked.

It seemed unlikely that she would be able to hear us all the way from where the house sat. Her estate was of a considerable size with the stables close to this entrance, and the house set further down from here. Moreover, she didn't seem to have any servants—not unless one counted the bespelled brooms and shovels I'd seen come out of the stables the first time we were here.

Kalyll shrugged, raised his fist, and rapped softly.

She would definitely *not* hear that.

"She's a sorceress. She likely has a spell that lets her know when someone is at her door," Kalyll said as if reading my mind.

He was right, of course, and I should've thought of that.

We waited. No response. Kalyll knocked again, but after a few minutes, I felt pretty certain no one was coming.

"Maybe she's not home," I said.

"Maybe," Kalyll repeated as he examined the gate and the surrounding wall. "We shouldn't stay out here too long. Someone will notice us."

"What are you thinking?" I knew what he was thinking, but sneaking in hardly seemed like the brightest idea. Surely it wouldn't be as easy as just climbing the wall. For all we knew, she had demonic Rottweilers—or better yet, demonic raptors—stashed somewhere, and they would attack as soon as we started climbing.

Sure enough, Kalyll made a beeline for the wall and tested it for footholds. I rolled my eyes. Really?! Were all males this senseless in all the realms? I rushed to his side and pulled him down by his torn pants.

"What are you doing?"

"Obviously, she's not here, so we just go in and wait until she arrives."

"That's if you survive her raptors."

"What raptors?"

"You know, the ones that will tear you to shreds the moment you reach the other side."

"Why would she have raptors?"

"For intruders such as yourself."

He frowned. "Elyndell is a safe place. No one has a need for *raptors*."

"Not so safe when you have the king himself scaling walls to break in."

"I'm not breaking in."

"Oh, you're not?"

"No. That's ridiculous. I'm just . . . I'm just . . ."

I lifted an eyebrow, waiting for his answer.

He gave me none. Instead, he proceeded to climb up the wall.

"Don't come crying to me when a raptor snaps your head off."

"I hardly think I would be crying without my head."

"You'd be surprised." I had seen some weird stuff in the ER while I was doing my residency. You could count on any number of strange things happening whenever Skews were involved.

As he climbed up the wall, I glanced all around, fearing someone would see him. There were a few houses across the street, but everything seemed quiet. Their doors were shuttered and no lights seeped through any of their windows.

I was squinting into the darkness when, suddenly, several knocking sounds reverberated through the night, followed by Kalyll yelping and falling on his ass right at my feet.

"Fucking Erilena!" he exclaimed, rubbing the side of his head. "Ouch."

Kneeling next to him, I grabbed his wrist and pulled his hand away. "What happened?"

I squinted at his forehead. There appeared to be a bump forming right next to one of his tattoos. "A raptor?"

"It was no raptor," he said. "It was a damn broom."

Pressing my lips together, I did my best to stifle a laugh, but it was no use. It came out, a full belly cackle that nearly dropped me on my ass.

"Would you not?" He glared at me, stood, and dusted the back of his trousers.

I continued laughing, unable to help myself.

Kalyll opened his mouth to say something, but a clanking sound had us whirling in its direction. The wooden gate was open a crack. We exchanged a wary glance, then slowly approached.

I peered inside through the gap but saw nothing. Kalyll pressed a hand to one side of the gate and widened the crack. Now we could see the sorceress standing on the other side, her arms crossed over her chest as she glared at us.

We hurried inside, and the gate closed behind us of its own accord.

"You *are* here," I said. "We thought you were out for the night."

"So you decided to break in?"

Kalyll huffed. "I was *not* breaking in."

We both gave him raised eyebrows.

"For Erilena's sake!" he exclaimed. "All right, I was breaking in. I wanted one of your enchanted brooms so badly that I figured I could steal one." He rubbed the bruised spot on his forehead and rolled his eyes.

"You're lucky you only had to face one of my brooms and not the raptors," the sorceress said, giving me a quick wink that let me know she'd been listening to our conversation while Kalyll and I had been bickering.

Kalyll looked from the sorceress to me, then back again. He was judging us with narrowed eyes, suspecting that we were ganging up on him.

"Raptors, huh?" He thumped his chest with one fist. "Send them in, and I shall teach them a lesson."

"Just like you taught that broom a lesson." I gestured toward the retreating offender, which was sweeping its way back to the stables.

"Did you miss the part where I said I wanted one of the brooms?" he asked. "They're a fantastic and easy way to keep things clean."

"Cute, you two." Naesala whirled on her heels and headed toward the house. "You have disrupted my beauty sleep, but I guess I'm glad to see you are all right. You know your way around the house. Make yourself comfortable."

We made our way to the bedroom we'd shared the last time we were here. The first order of business was to take a hot shower, which quickly devolved into an intense session of kissing and groping and . . .

It seemed we couldn't keep our hands off each other. Once clean and refreshed, we fell asleep on the large bed, arms and legs tangled together, impossible to say where Kalyll began and I ended.

CHAPTER 22
KALYLL

O nce more, I awoke before Daniella. It was a treat to watch her sleep, and a relief to find her by my side safe and sound after the woeful time I spent fretting and mourning over her. At every moment, I wanted to keep my eyes on her to ensure she was all right. How she had coerced a promise out of me to let her fight, I still didn't know.

I did believe she could take care of herself. She had gained a couple of very dangerous skills, after all. Yet, I didn't think I would ever stop worrying about her well-being.

But a promise was a promise, and I would not use my worry to stifle her.

Her eyes fluttered open, and it was like sunshine warming my face as they appraised me with tenderness.

"Good morning," she said, covering her mouth with one hand.

I pulled it away and planted a kiss on her lips. "Good morning, my queen."

Immediately aroused, I started sliding a hand down her side, ready to make her wriggle under me, but my plans were destroyed when the door burst open. Shirtless, wearing only a pair of loose trousers, I jumped to my feet, expecting guards to pour in and arrest us. Instead, Kryn stomped into the room, wearing a huge smile.

"We've been waiting too long. This is an indecent hour to still be in bed." He marched straight in my direction, wrapped me in a tight embrace, and thumped on my back. "Brother."

I thumped back, my chest swelling with a myriad of feelings.

Awkwardly, Kryn pulled away, avoiding eye contact, for which I was glad. It seemed he'd marched in here on impulse alone and was embarrassed by his display of affection. I was chagrined as well. This was highly unusual. Still, I couldn't be anything but grateful to call him my brother.

The rest of the Sub Rosa entered the room. They were all smiling and looking relieved. Daniella, for her part, was sitting up against the headboard, the sheets pulled tightly around her.

"I see you've been making up for lost time," Cylea said, wiggling an eyebrow.

A fierce blush colored Daniella's cheeks. She opened her mouth to say something, then her gaze flicked to the door. "Larina. Shadow. Please, come in."

The pixie and the sprite hesitated for a moment but eventually flew into the chamber. They both inclined their heads in a respectful salute.

"King Kalyll," they said in unison.

Abandoning all shyness, Daniella flung the sheets aside and got out of bed. "Larina, I'm so happy to see you."

The pixie zoomed to Daniella's shoulder and hugged a lock of her hair. It was the strangest thing I'd ever seen. Pixies were distrustful of the big folk, as they called us. True, Daniella was not Fae, but I wasn't the only one who seemed surprised by the gesture.

Larina batted her wings and backed away from Daniella.

"Are you all right?" Daniella asked. "I was worried about you."

"Worried about me? You were the one who disappeared without telling anyone. We thought . . ." She couldn't finish. She only appeared distraught.

I regarded Daniella with pride. She had made a friend of the pixie, had broken through untold species and social barriers with her warmth and kindness. She would make a better queen than anyone my parents could have chosen and would help me fulfill my plans for equality and progress in Elf-hame.

"Dani, you have to tell us how you freed him," Silver said. "The sorceress couldn't give us any details. You think she would've at least found out the barest minimum last night."

"Perhaps we can discuss it over breakfast," Jeondar said. "I'm sure they're hungry."

Arabis approached Daniella and took her hand, shaking her head in disapproval. "You were reckless, weren't you?"

Daniella shrugged one shoulder.

"You were simply supposed to find out where Cardian was keeping him so we could all rescue him. You could've been killed."

"I know," Daniella admitted, "but things didn't go exactly as planned. As soon as Cardian heard, he started to transfer by himself. I couldn't let the opportunity slip away."

"And then you got infinitely lucky, it seems." Kryn looked me up and down as if I were the resulting miracle of Daniella's recklessness.

"There was no luck involved, I assure you." I had to make this clear. No one should think of Daniella as anything but capable. "But let's do as Jeondar suggested. We'll tell you everything over breakfast."

I started trying to usher them out of the chamber so that Daniella and I could change into proper attire when Shadow—who had remained quiet but for the whir of her wings—cleared her throat.

"Is Cardian Adanorin dead?" she asked without a preamble of any sort.

Her question made me bristle, especially because she seemed terribly eager for an answer.

"Shadow of Sunnar," I said, pressing a fist to my chest and bowing my head. "I find your inquiry inappropriate."

To my right, Kryn shuffled from foot to foot, finding the rug very interesting. The sprite showed no signs of chagrin, however. Instead, she raised her chin higher, unapologetic.

"I have made no pretense that I want him dead," she said. "He murdered my queen. For that, I wish death upon him, preferably at my hand. Am I too late?"

The reaction that assailed me was unexpected. I couldn't believe she would dare to ask such a thing. That was my little brother she was talking about. I still remembered him crawling at Mother's feet, still recalled the way he looked up to me when he began his sword-fighting lessons and promised me he would be as good as me. Despite the horrors he had put me through in Nerethien, why did I want to spare him?

Despite everything, this reaction showed me I didn't wish him dead. Mother and Father would not want that either.

I took a step forward, an involuntary growl rumbling deep in my throat.

"Kalyll." Daniella placed a hand on my elbow. "Shadow

and her network of friends were instrumental in your rescue, as I've already explained." Her voice was soothing and diplomatic as she, once more, demonstrated the qualities of a true leader.

Inhaling deeply, I relaxed my shoulders and regarded Shadow with ill-gotten composure. "I will beg you to refrain from expressing yourself in that manner in front of me. In fact, I wish for all of you to do so. I can understand your reasons for wishing Cardian dead. By the gods, until this moment, I thought I wished the same. But despite everything, I do not find solace in the prospect of his demise."

"Apologies, my king." Shadow inclined her head. "It will not happen again."

The sprite had always been direct and a creature of very few words. I knew I could trust her to refrain from ever discussing this matter in front of me again. "Thank you, Shadow, and I also thank you for your help to my friends and to me."

Another curt bow from her.

"Well, now that that's out of the way," Silver said, "Naesala mentioned something about a full delicious breakfast. I'm quite looking forward to it, even if I don't know what it is. The food here is always interesting."

The tension leaked out of the room. It was Silver's specialty to diffuse a situation with some nonsense or another, and in this instance, I could only be grateful to him.

CHAPTER 23
DANIELLA

Fifteen minutes later, we were sitting at the dinner table in front of a lavish breakfast of eggs, bacon, sausage, hash browns, biscuits, gravy, pancakes, and more. Larina and Shadow also sat at the table, literally, legs crossed in front of tiny pieces of diced fruit.

"What is this called?" Silver dangled a square of bread from the tip of his fork.

"French toast," I said, buttering a piece of toast.

"French? I thought this was supposed to be an American breakfast."

"I think the creator's last name was French, but he was American."

"So shouldn't it be French's Toast?"

I shrugged. "It beats me."

Silver shoveled the toast into his mouth, and I started to relate what happened in Nerethien. The others listened, pushing food around their plates, never interrupting me. It wasn't easy reliving those moments, but it was my second telling of the events, and I found that my heart didn't pound as hard and fast as when I'd told Kalyll the first time.

"As you can see, nothing but capable," Kalyll said when I was done explaining how I'd transferred us to the forest near Mount Ruin.

"Indeed," Kryn said, sounding impressed.

"Runik was legendary, Dani," Naesala said, her pale eyes narrowed. "Many feared him."

"It was luck, really," I said.

"I doubt that. I think your powers are off the charts."

Silver paused mid-sausage. "Off the charts?"

He had such a liking for human idioms and sayings, he always perked up when he heard one.

Cylea, who had spent more time in my realm, always took it upon herself to educate him. "It means that something is outside the normal range, which makes it hard to measure."

"Got it." Silver brandished his fork, then stabbed a pancake with it.

"Cardian," I started hesitantly, "said that I must be as powerful as Varamede and that he . . ." I trailed off. This felt too much like bragging, but it wasn't. I was just puzzled by the idea and actually wanted someone to say it wasn't true.

Except no one said anything. They just looked at me with frowns and cocked heads, even Kalyll seemed to be reevaluating me.

"Never mind." I broke a piece of toast and poked my sunny-side-up egg with it, making the yolk run all over the plate. "You don't have any ketchup, do you?" I asked Naesala as a way to distract everyone from this uncomfortable conversation.

A squeezey bottle materialized in front of me.

"Thank you." I proceeded to squirt a generous amount on my egg.

"What in the name of Erilena is that?!" Silver asked in a combination of awe and excitement at this new item.

"Only the most hideous condiment ever created," Kalyll said.

I narrowed my eyes at him. "How dare you? If I had known, I would have never . . ." I sighed with exaggeration. "I believe I'll have to reevaluate our relationship."

He smirked. "I will endeavor to like ketchup for you. Anything to keep you happy."

"Honestly." Cylea's fork clattered to her plate. "Do we have to endure your sickeningly sweet love affair?"

"Yes, do we?" Kryn asked.

"Oh, c'mon," Silver mumbled through a full mouth, "like you don't wish for the return of your own sickeningly sweet love affair?" His clear eyes cut to Arabis.

Kryn sank in his chair, going uncharacteristically quiet. Had something happened while they'd been away in Nerethien? Arabis also seemed mollified. Hmm, it seemed something *had* occurred.

"I think it is our turn to relate our side of things," she said, swiftly changing the topic the same way I had. "We were stationed in the Unseelie capital for a few days, after all, and we noticed some things worth mentioning. Also, we need to discuss what to do next. We can't allow Cardian to remain in power. I'm sure we can all agree on that much."

"Certainly." Kalyll steepled his hands over his plate. "Tell me, are Cardian and Mythorne proceeding with their preparations for war?"

"They are," Arabis said. "In fact, troops have already been dispatched to the Winter Court. Though I'm sure the Winter

King is already planning his unconditional loyalty and alliance speech. I doubt he will fight Mythorne's army."

"I disagree," Silver put in.

Arabis waved a hand in the air. "I know you do."

"And as a member of the Winter Court, shouldn't my opinion weigh more?"

She rolled her eyes and conceded nothing.

Silver went on. "King Naeduin's wife might be ready to write that speech to Mythorne, but the king is a proud bastard. He has gone along with a traditional alliance with the Unseelie Court because he has autonomy and full control of the land and its resources. Now, Mythorne wants more, and Naeduin would become nothing more than a figurehead. If he's allowed to stay, that is. No," he shook his head, "I have a feeling he will choose to fight."

"Fighting will only squander those precious resources you're talking about," Arabis said.

"I don't disagree with that. I just think that Naeduin would rather squander them than let Mythorne have them."

It seemed that Arabis could not argue with that comment. Instead, she sighed and stared at her plate in defeat.

Kalyll's hands remained steepled as he listened without interruption. His eyes were narrowed, and behind their darkened quality, I could see a million thoughts speeding by.

"We have been in touch with your uncle," Jeondar said, taking over.

Captain Loraerris was in a precarious position, and it was a wonder Cardian hadn't thrown him in a dungeon. The male had to be artful at diplomacy to be able to convince Cardian he accepted him as king.

Jeondar continued. "Of course, he remains loyal to you as do others, and they are doing their best to delay things. Cardian's orders were to send troops to the Summer and Spring Courts as soon as they were ready. Clearly, there have been delays due to conflicting commands from you and Cardian, which is fortunate, I suppose. They will not be ready to depart for another week. We have dispatched news to my father as well as the Spring Court king and queen, so they can be ready. I know for a fact that my father will fight."

He appeared conflicted on the matter, which I could not blame him for.

"For him," he went on, "it's not a matter of resources and power. He fears what would become of our realm if people like Mythorne and Cardian are allowed to take control without opposition. I fear for our people, for the inevitable loss of life and the horrors war will bring, but on most days, I agree with my father. In Nerethien, you can feel the people's fear in the air. They walk with their heads bowed and swallow their words when they see injustice. They are beaten down by their rulers' evil, by the threat of retaliation should they speak against those in command. That is no way to live."

I swallowed thickly, fighting the tears that rose to my eyes. In our history books, we had enough stories of such things and the horrors that came with allowing egotistical, evil people to rule.

"The Spring Court will also fight," Cylea said.

Kalyll turned slowly to Kryn, a questioning look in his eyes. "Why have we not heard of the Fall Court?"

Kryn sighed heavily. "Because our father is an asshole." His face lit up bright red, and he appeared both angry and embarrassed.

Leaning back on his chair, Kalyll waited patiently, giving Kryn ample time to formulate an answer. When he next spoke, he ripped off the bandage with a bombshell.

"Earl Qierlan, finding that he couldn't marry his daughter to a prince, will now marry her to a king."

I let out a gasp. Mylendra was going to marry Mythorne?

Kalyll formed a fist and his jaw tightened. "I assume he is forcing her."

"He is," Kryn confirmed. "She would have gladly married you, but Mythorne? For all her faults, she is not crazy. I tried to talk sense into him. I used your transfer token to go to Thellanora last night, but his mind is made up. He has struck a pact with the Fall King. They think Mythorne will look at them favorably and let them go on as they have, but they're deluded. Father plans to visit Nerethien and make his proposal tomorrow."

"You see," Arabis told Silver, "the Winter King is hoping to prevent a war."

Silver turned his mouth upside down. "If Mythorne thinks nothing of this proposal, King Naeduin will fight. Mark my words."

"Is Mythorne looking for a bride?" I asked. "Or is throwing females around to see if they stick to some jerk a thing here?"

Naesala laughed as she daintily wiped her mouth with a cloth napkin. "That would be entertaining to watch. Demeaning, but entertaining."

I ignored her and so did the others. "Is it even safe for them to go there?"

Kryn huffed. "I warned him they could end up in a

dungeon, but he's so stubborn and thinks so much of him-self, he can't conceive the possibility."

A grunt came from Kalyll. Something in his expression as well as a spark in his eyes told me he'd had an idea.

"What is it?" Jeondar asked, noticing the same thing I had.

Kalyll slowly turned to the sorceress and asked, "That elixir of yours—the one that helped Kryn impersonate me—tell me all about its attributes."

"No! Absolutely not," I protested for the hundredth time. "I just got you out of there. You're not going back." I pointed a finger at him as he paced in front of the large wooden desk.

"Once more, I agree with Dani," Arabis said.

We had left the breakfast table and were now in Naesala's study. She had left us to argue, saying we were giving her a headache. I didn't blame her. We'd been in here for an hour, trying to dissuade Kalyll.

"You can't take such a risk." Jeondar stood next to a tall bookcase and spoke with his usual composure. "You need to stay in Elyndell and get back on the throne. You can stop the deployment of the Seelie troops and keep the Summer and Spring Courts from war."

"Only for the moment," Kalyll replied. "War will still come to them. To all of us. This isn't an opportunity we should squander."

"No one said anything about squandering the opportunity," Kryn said.

Rubbing his forehead, Kalyll sighed and took a seat in one of the empty armchairs. "For the last time, I'm not letting anyone take my place. It's too dangerous, and I would never ask you to—"

"You're not asking. I'm offering," Kryn said, nearly shouting.

In one swift, abrupt motion, Kalyll rose to his feet and actually shouted his next words. "I am your king, and you will obey." His voice was so deep, several octaves lower than his natural tone, that for a moment, I expected Wölfe to make an appearance. But, though his eyes flashed for an instant, his features didn't turn razor-sharp.

No one dared speak, not even me.

"I will pose as Mylendra, then," Cylea said.

Arabis shook her head. "No. I will. No offense, but my power might prove more useful."

Cylea threw her hands up in the air. She resented her simple power of plant healing. She would've likely preferred being able to turn people into empty husks.

"Yes, Arabis can—" Kalyll started, but I interrupted him mid-sentence.

"I will go with you."

Kalyll's head whipped in my direction, and I could almost see the protest hanging from his lips. But he bit it back, and though he clearly didn't want me to join him on this mission, it seemed he remembered the promise he'd made me.

"You two are insane," Silver said. "But I respect it."

The others gave him a dirty look.

"What?" he said. "I do. I like knowing that my king and

future queen are honorable, that they are willing to make sac-
rifices, and don't only expect others to *take the bullet*." He
winked at me, proud of the use of another human phrase.

It was easy to see the others holding back their protests.
They were not only frustrated. They were angry, and I understood why. If Kalyll died doing this, his death would bring
about everything he was trying to avoid. Cardian would
remain king. The Seelie troops would march to the Summer
and Spring Courts while the Unseelie Court threatened the
Fall and Winter Courts from the north. The war that would
ensue would likely destroy Elf-hame, and whoever survived
the atrocities of the conflict would end up living under a
reign of terror.

But if Kalyll didn't do this, the outcome might very well
be the same. Mythorne wasn't backing down now, even if
Kalyll retook the throne. War would still come. Elf-hame
would still suffer.

So yes, I understood why Kalyll wanted to take this chance,
why he wanted to infiltrate the Unseelie Court while pretending to be his father, Earl Qierlan.

And if I had to change my appearance once more, this
time to that of the woman who almost became Kalyll's wife,
I would do it because nothing and no one would keep me
away from him.

CHAPTER 24
DANIELLA

There was no time to waste. The Earl would be taking Mylendra to Nerethien tomorrow, so we transferred to the vicinity of the Qierlan castle immediately. We couldn't appear inside due to blocking spells, but Kryn knew how to get us in unnoticed.

The entire group, except for Shadow—Kalyll had ordered her to stay behind despite, or perhaps due to, her eagerness to accompany us—materialized in a patch of woods behind a tall stone wall.

As Kryn made his way toward the front entrance, where he could waltz in unbothered, the rest of us skulked behind the tree trunks until he appeared at a small private gate and let us in. Once inside, he guided us down several winding passages until we arrived at his chamber, and he locked the door behind us.

Exhaling in relief, I set down my messenger bag on a tall, round table adorned with a vase full of roses. Their scent brought back panicked memories of my time trying to climb out of the depth of my frozen sleep, and I had to step away in order to think clearly.

Kalyll walked up to me and rubbed my arms for warmth. "Are you all right?"

I had no idea how he always knew when I needed him. "I'm fine now." I wrapped my arms around his waist and rested my head on his wide chest.

He pressed his nose to the top of my head and inhaled as if I were an infusion from an aromatherapy machine, and he was drawing peace and calm from me, which was exactly how I felt about him.

We pulled away from each other and smiled. I felt a thousand times better, and he looked as if he did as well. My arm wrapped around his waist and his around my back, we turned together to face the others. Arabis was looking around the room with wide eyes, eagerly drinking everything in.

I noticed Kryn rush toward the night table on the left side of his bed and swiftly set a picture frame face down. I had enough time to notice it was a portrait of Arabis herself. A quick flick of my eyes in her direction told me she hadn't noticed. She was too taken by a tapestry hanging above a small fireplace in the corner.

I caught Kryn's eye and raised an eyebrow. He huffed and crossed his arms over his chest, closing himself off. He tried so hard to appear tough and aloof, and yet . . .

Curious, I decided to ask Cylea if something had happened between Kryn and Arabis in Nerethien. I was never one to play matchmaker, but these two were killing me. They'd been pining over each other for so long, and it was time they let go of their past and started living in the now.

"So now we wait until dinner time," Kalyll said, checking

the clock on the wall, a small elaborate piece with a pendulum that hung freely at the bottom.

"Dinner is served at seven," Kryn said. "Father and Mylendra should be in their rooms getting ready at least a half hour before that. We'll make our move then as we planned. Now, I'll go and make sure there are no changes to the regular routine."

"Get us a bottle of wine while you're at it, will you?" Silver said, throwing himself on the bed and resting his head on the embroidered pillows.

Kryn ignored him as he walked out, and I seriously doubted there would be any wine on his return. For the next twenty minutes, we took turns sitting and pacing. We didn't talk much. In Naesala's house, we had discussed ad nauseam what needed to be done. Now, we just needed the plan to work. If it did, we would prevent the potential destruction of the entire realm, and that made the risk worthwhile.

At some point, Kalyll reclined against the frame of the window and looked out at a dreary afternoon. I joined him and let my eyes sweep over the forest that surrounded the castle. Evergreens seemed to compete against each other for height. Some seemed to even tickle the bottoms of the gray clouds that threatened heavy rain but only managed a slow drizzle.

Absent-mindedly, I interlaced my fingers with Kalyll's, and we regarded the scenery in silence.

"I spent a summer here once when I was a child," Kalyll said at last. "In retrospect, I remember feeling very awkward around Earl Qierlan. I wonder if, deep down, I knew he was my father. Do you think that's possible?"

I thought for a spell, recalling everything that had happened and everything I had learned in the books from his library. Finally, I said, "I believe so. Shadowdrifter blood is very strong. You already know that his blood calls to yours. It was how we hoped to . . ." I trailed off.

". . . kill Wölfe," he finished for me.

I simply nodded.

"But you didn't manage it," he said in a deep rumble as he wrapped an arm around my waist and pulled me to him.

My back ended up flush against his chest, and pushing my hair aside he performed a quick nibble on my neck as if he meant to eat me.

"I want to rip off your clothes and fuck you," Wölfe said, sending a shiver down my spine and a jolt of electricity to my core. Immediately, my panties were wet and images of his tongue on me flashed through my mind.

For a moment, I didn't care that the others were there, and I nearly whirled around and started ripping my clothes off myself. I glanced over and was relieved when I noticed that Silver was asleep on the bed, Cylea and Arabis seemed lost in their own conversation, and Larina sat on the mantle, a place she seemed to prefer everywhere we went.

Wölfe turned me around to face him and possessively pressed me to him. He flashed his pointed canines, releasing an ache between my legs that made my knees wobble. I feared the male could make me climax if he just kept looking at me with such hunger and ferocity.

"Missed me?" he asked.

We had each other in the clearing only the other night, but I *had* missed him. "Yes."

He smiled a crooked smile of satisfaction. "I won't let anything happen to you, melynthi."

He smoothed my hair tenderly and gradually his features lost some of their sharpness, and Kalyll was back. He continued almost in the same breath, the line that separated his dual personalities blurring even more every day.

"I will be glad to have you by my side," he added, surprising me.

I thought he was mad for making him take me with him, but he sounded genuine enough. "Will you really?"

"Yes." He caressed my cheek with the back of his fingers. "I'll be able to keep a good eye on you." He winked.

"Oh, is that why?"

"Mm-hmm."

I mock-punched him in the shoulder.

"I only jest. I'll be glad of your company. You're powerful. If you get close enough to Mythorne, he is *done for*, as you say in your realm. Though we have to be careful. We don't know what his power is, and it's rumored to be notable."

My hands itched at the thought of draining Mythorne dry—not to mention Cardian. The feelings were strong, but they came from that dark side of me, the one that was a perfect match for Wölfe. I wanted those two to pay for what they'd done to Kalyll. Whatever torture they'd put him through, I could tell it had affected him. He didn't want to talk about it and tried to hide it, but at times, he went still and quiet, his gaze lost in a faraway place.

On a previous occasion, Kalyll had asked me if I would kill someone if the situation demanded it. I said *yes*. Dark Dani had helped me come to terms with the awful and dire need to sometimes end a life. But there was something else I needed to come to terms with: the possibility of having to kill Cardian.

I didn't want to kill him. I didn't want to kill anyone. But if it came down to it, I would do what I had to do to protect Kalyll. In the end, I knew he would understand. He would know that I had done it for him. But still, it was a hard thing to contemplate. I hoped it would never come to that. But if it did, I would be ready.

Kalyll tapped my nose, pulling me back from my gloomy thoughts.

"What are you thinking about?"

My words came tumbling down without my permission. "Would you forgive me if I killed your brother? I wouldn't just—"

He cut me off, this time placing his finger across my lips. "We talked about this. Please don't worry. It may sound terrible to say this, but my love for you is greater than any love I have left for Cardian or anything else. If Wölfe destroyed the universe to save you, I would not only forgive him, I would applaud him."

Wow. Once more, he left me speechless. It took me a few seconds to recover.

I wanted to say something equally romantic but what came out was, "But if the universe was destroyed, where would we live?"

He leaned closer and whispered in my ear. "In the void, where we could fuck in any position without the need to worry about gravity or much else."

"With you, everything comes down to fucking?"

"Oh, most certainly."

Smirking, he leaned down to kiss me, except Kryn came back into the room and the moment was broken.

"No changes," he announced. "Everything shall continue as planned."

CHAPTER 25
DANIELLA

Sometime before dinnertime, Kryn guided Kalyll and me out of his chamber, while the others stayed. We avoided areas with high traffic and made it toward his sister's room, which was on the opposite end of the castle. Apparently, it was an area reserved for the chambers of the single women in the earl's family.

A few times, we ran into people, but Kalyll's shadow-drifter powers wrapped us protectively, while Kryn kept walking as if he owned the place, which he did—or would soon, at least.

When we arrived at Mylendra's door, he knocked three times, loudly and firmly. A young chambermaid answered, peeking out with one eye as if she expected trouble.

"I need to see my sister," Kryn said, while we faded into Kalyll's shadow, unseen by the young girl.

"Lady Goren is—" the chambermaid began, but Kryn pushed his way in without waiting for her to finish, sending the girl stumbling backward as she issued a little cry of alarm.

"In Erilena's name, what is the meaning of this intrusion?" Mylendra exclaimed, her eyes flashing with anger.

"I need to talk to you," Kryn said, as Kalyll and I slipped

through the door, unseen by the chambermaid, who was distracted by the rude intruder.

Mylendra stood in front of a large mirror trimmed in silver, half-dressed, her corset unlaced, which didn't seem to bother her in Kryn's presence. Her hair was a mass of red curls that tumbled down her back in an unruly cascade, held in place by a few scattered pins. Her cheeks were flushed from the exertion of dressing and from half-applied rouge.

Despite her undone appearance, there was something undeniably alluring about her. Her skin was smooth and creamy, the perfect canvas for the delicate lace of her corset that pushed up her bosom.

"What do you want?" she asked, facing the mirror and pinning a few locks.

Kryn glanced sideways at the maid.

Mylendra rolled her eyes in a tired way, reminding me of my younger sister, Lucia. "Leave. I'll finish getting ready myself."

The girl curtsied and left, never noticing the deeper shadows that had scurried to a corner that the light from the sconces didn't touch.

Mylendra picked up a brush and used it to gather her hair together. She applied a few more pins, accomplishing a look that appeared almost careless but was anything but.

"If you've come to tell me you haven't been able to talk Father out of his evil scheme," she set the brush down, "don't waste your breath. I already know. He scolded me for sending you to intercede on my behalf."

"No, that's not why I'm here."

"Then don't waste my time." She sighed, frustration

evident in the way she tugged at the laces of her corset. "I need to get ready for dinner where I'm sure he'll inform me exactly how to behave tomorrow. I'm supposed to smile and keep my mouth shut." She sniffled. "He has lost his mind, Kryn. Mythorne will not take kindly to Father's betrayal. He crafted an alliance with the Seelie King and Queen, and now he expects the Unseelie King to play second best. Honestly, I don't think his mind is sound."

"I agree. That's why I'm here with a proposition for you."

She hesitated for a moment, but then curiosity got the best of her. Looking down her nose, she plumped her cheeks and faced her brother.

"I'm all ears." She waved a hand. "But be quick about it. I don't have all night."

"I propose that you don't go to Nerethien."

"Oh, brother, you're a genius!" Sarcasm dripped from her voice in a way that seemed universal to younger siblings. "I already tried to escape. It got me *this* bruise and a horrible threat." She held up her wrist to show the imprint of a hand wrapped around it. "The threat also extends to our mother—not that she tried very hard to go against his wishes."

"You know she's utterly beaten down by him."

"Just like I will be when he marries me off to that monster." Mylendra pressed a hand to her mouth, and I feared she would start crying, but she blinked rapidly and took a deep breath, effectively reining in her emotions.

"You will not marry him. All you have to do is stay in my chamber tonight and act like you're not here."

"They'll go looking for me," she protested.

"They won't because someone else will take your place."

She blinked her big green eyes. "W-who? How?"

"Don't get scared." Kryn put a hand up as if pacifying a horse, then nodded toward the corner where we were hiding.

Slowly, Kalyll pulled the shadows back to reveal our presence.

Mylendra gasped, covered her bosom needlessly—she was overdressed by any modern human standards—and took a step back. Her gaze jumped back and forth from Kalyll to me several times before she found her words. "Prince Kalyll."

"My lady," he bowed his head.

"King Kalyll," Kryn corrected.

"I'm sorry." Mylendra curtsied, a very slight bend of her knees and a bob of her head. She seemed to forget all about her outfit.

Kalyll waved a hand. "It is of no consequence, especially since I have no kingdom at the moment."

"You're here to . . . rescue me." Mylendra touched a hand to the bare top of her bosom, looking as if this was what she'd been expecting all along.

I took a step forward and interlaced my fingers with Kalyll's, staking my claim.

Her satisfaction turned into sour incredulity.

"My lady, this is Daniella Sunder, my . . ." Kalyll turned to look at me, "My betrothed." He smiled and cocked his head to one side.

I nodded once, letting him know I had no trouble with that title. He could call me whatever he wanted as long as it meant we would always be together.

"Betrothed?" Mylendra glared at me. "Beware, lady, that title means nothing to this male."

"Sister," Kryn scolded her.

"What?"

Kalyll interjected. "I mean no disrespect, Lady Goren. I simply wish to make things as clear as possible to avoid confusion. Our engagement was one of convenience, established under circumstances much different than the ones we face now. Your father withdrew his offer as soon as I fell out of favor, which set me free to pursue the female I truly love. Now, my only intention is to avoid a war and, in the process, save you from a fate worse than death. If we succeed, I hope you will then be free to do as I did and find someone you truly love."

Mylendra's mouth opened and closed a few times, but in the end, nothing came out. For what could she say when Kalyll had disarmed her so utterly with honesty? And not only that but with hope for something better.

At least, I expected her to see it that way. For all I knew, her only goal was to marry a royal male—just not one as despicable as Mythorne. But if status was all she wanted from a relationship, then good luck to her.

"So what?" she said to Kryn, her words biting. "You said someone would take my place. You don't mean this . . . person." She made it sound as if a gnat might have a better chance of impersonating an eagle.

"Watch how you talk about her," Kalyll growled, his voice nearly that of Wölfe.

I patted his arm. "I can take care of this."

Letting Dark Dani loose, I stuck my chin up and strolled in a semicircle in front of Mylendra, scanning her from head to toe with as much disdain as she'd shown me.

Take the high road, Sensible Dani was saying.

Nope. Not today. I really didn't feel like it. I was here to save this spoiled brat from a nightmare, she could at least be civil.

"You're a bit pale and bony, but I think I can manage it." I pointed at my face. "I can sneer just as well, you don't have an exclusive license on making horrid faces. Doing so will give you wrinkles, by the way, so you'd better try to smile once in a while."

"How dare you come to my home and insult me?"

"If Mythorne gets his way, this may not be your home for long. So it would be wise of you to treat those who are willing to help you with decency. Unless you . . . don't want my help." I raised my eyebrows as if I'd just realized something. "Oh, perhaps that's it. You *want* to marry that awful male."

"I do not."

"The lady doth protest too much." I nearly cheered. I had just quoted Shakespeare, and I couldn't have done it at a better time. I didn't even sound like a geek out of place and time. My eleventh-grade teacher would be so proud of me.

"Shakespeare?" Kalyll said. "Really?"

I rounded on him and glowered. How dare he try to spoil my moment? He put both hands up, holding back a smirk.

"What are you two about?" Mylendra asked.

I shrugged dismissively. "You wouldn't understand, dear."

"Don't *dear* me and don't pretend that you're doing this for me. You want your throne back." She pointed at Kalyll. "And you," her finger moved in my direction, "you're likely just some fortune seeker who wants to become queen."

"Not everyone shares your same motives, *dear*, but we're wasting time. If you want to marry Mythorne, by all means, don't let us get in the way." I walked back to Kalyll's side and waited for her answer, a bland smile stretching my lips.

Kryn glanced at me disapprovingly. It wasn't as if we had a choice, and we could allow his sister to decide what to do. If she said she wanted to go to Nerethien with her father, we would have to knock her out and supplant her anyway. He had wanted to avoid doing that, but to me, it was a win either way. Of course, I would rather her eat humble pie than render her unconscious.

Or would I? That was a tough one.

After a loaded moment, Mylendra swallowed thickly, stared fixedly at the ceiling, and said, "Do what you need to do. I will go along with your scheme."

"Excellent." I clapped my hands together, reached into a hidden pocket of my dress, and pulled out one of the many vials Naesala had made for us.

"What is that?" Mylendra asked, looking panicked.

"Not to worry," I said. "I'm the one who has to drink this. All you have to do is hold my hand."

Since the sorceress had only seen Mylendra once and from afar, this potion was a little different. It contained an added spell that would scan Mylendra as she was and would turn me into her. I wasn't looking forward to it. The last time Naesala had altered my appearance, it had hurt like hell. Though she promised it wouldn't be nearly as bad this time, since the alteration was temporary and would slowly wear out unless I drank another dose once a day or so. She had given us a two-day supply, all she'd been able to brew on short notice.

I extended a hand in Mylendra's direction. One of her sneers nearly took shape, but she stopped it just in time. It seemed I'd succeeded in curbing what appeared to be a natural disdain for others. I vaguely wondered how much more difficult she would act if she knew I was human.

She placed her hand in mine, looking everywhere except into my eyes. Uncapping the small vial with my thumb—the cork tumbling to the floor—I downed its contents to the last drop.

CHAPTER 26
KALYLL

Daniella let go of Mylendra's hand and clutched her stomach, making a pained sound in the back of her throat. Her knees bent, and she started to fall. I rushed to her side, scooped her up, and laid her on the bed.

She immediately curled up into a tight ball, arms hugging her legs as she trembled and whined.

"I thought she said it wouldn't hurt much," I barked, knowing I would have torn that sorceress's head off if she was here.

"She said it wouldn't hurt as much as the time that you . . . well, you know," Kryn said. "But it *does* hurt."

I watched as Daniella's features changed. As I stood there, a slew of memories hit me like a landslide. I saw the sorceress walking into my chamber in Elyndell, accompanied by Wölfe. It was the day Daniella and Naesala met for the first time. I saw the sorceress lift a hand and release a spell that made Daniella scream and collapse. I saw my mate writhing for hours as Fae features replaced her much softer human ones.

I had done that to her. *I* had put her through all that pain. And now here she was again, enduring so much for me.

How could I ever repay her? How could I ever be worthy of her?

As was to be expected, Mylendra ran out of the room, disappearing through a side door.

I pushed her out of my mind and held Daniella's hand as her brown hair turned red, her beautiful features took the wrong shape, and her olive skin turned pale.

"Here." Mylendra came back and was offering me a cool wet cloth.

I took it, surprised by the gesture. "Thank you."

Watching anxiously, I pressed the cloth to Daniella's forehead. At last, she gave a shudder, and slowly her breathing went back to normal. She remained on the bed for a long moment while I dabbed her forehead. When she was ready, I helped her sit up. She took several deep breaths, then slid to the floor. She was a couple of inches taller and watched me with foreign green eyes.

I forced a smile to my face. It was unsettling to see my beloved's warmth in those calculating eyes. Still, I refused to show her anything but love, no matter what.

"By Erilena!" Mylendra exclaimed as she examined Daniella's matching appearance. "It is eerie to see you thus."

"I can imagine," Daniella responded in a tired tone that wasn't her own. She sounded exactly like Mylendra, who blinked, even more bewildered.

"Please forgive me, Daniella," Mylendra said.

Behind her, Kryn frowned, looking surprised, as if he'd never heard an apology from his younger sister.

"I . . . I was unfair to you. I . . ." She trailed off, clearly unaccustomed to putting her pride and haughtiness aside.

My mate, on the other hand, wore her virtues like a badge and said. "No ill feelings, Mylendra. We are all in a high-stress situation, trying to make the best of what we're offered. I can very well imagine how the thought of being forced to marry that awful male must have made you feel. But I can tell you're strong. Sometimes we females have to build a tough exterior to survive."

Mylendra's eyes silvered with a line of tears that she fought to keep at bay. Daniella's words seemed to touch Kryn as well because he reached for his sister's hand and gave it a squeeze. They exchanged a rare warm look, then she rushed into his arms.

"Oh, brother, thank you," she sobbed. "And thank you both," she added, without letting go of Kryn.

I was assaulted by the idea that she was my sister too. Perhaps one day we could tell her, and she would understand that the termination of our engagement was a blessing and not something to bemoan.

"Now, I need a gown and shoes." Daniella wiggled pale toes. "I need to visit your father." A cautious expression shaped her face, and she said no more.

Whether we could trust Mylendra with the exact details of our plan was irrelevant. We couldn't risk any of it being divulged purposely or otherwise.

Mylendra nodded and gestured toward a door that I assumed led to her closet. They went together, and ten minutes later, Daniella walked out, wearing a gown of the finest silk, its threads interwoven with the deepest green. The bodice was low-cut, and the sleeves were long and flowing. No question about it, Mylendra was beautiful in her own way, but not like Daniella. And though they shared fierce wills, Mylendra lacked the vivacity and aura of warmth and kindness that my mate possessed.

Wasting no time, we headed back the way we'd come, making our way toward the earl's chambers. On our way there, we dropped Mylendra off in Kryn's room and left her with the others.

Since Kryn had warned me of guards posted at different intervals leading to the earl's tower, I pulled back and blended into the shadows, letting Kryn and Daniella lead the way. She walked with a slight affectation that gave her that haughty air that seemed to emanate from Mylendra and made her a convincing replacement.

We passed several guards, who only bowed to the earl's son and daughter. It wasn't unusual for them to visit their father without an invitation, so they passed unmolested. When we reached the door to his chamber, the guard there seemed a bit surprised, but recognizing the visitors, he relaxed.

Kryn knocked on the door, while surreptitiously Daniella reached for the guard's hand. He jumped in surprise when her fingers brushed his. The immediate lascivious spark in his eyes had me on the brink of throttling him, but I was able to prevail over the impulse. Though only because I knew what was coming next.

Whatever immodest thoughts were crossing his mind quickly died out, turning to panic as Daniella drew his life force. She only held on for a couple of seconds, then the guard's knees gave out and he started to fall. Swiftly, I became corporeal and caught him before he hit the floor alerting others. I eased him down, pulling him out of sight around the bend, then waited as Kryn and Daniella walked into the earl's chamber and closed the door. I wasn't to go in, in case the earl could sense my presence. We didn't know enough about shadowdrifters' powers to understand all the possibilities, so we needed to be safe rather than sorry.

Besides, I had no doubt that Kryn and Daniella could handle Earl Qierlan without trouble.

CHAPTER 27
DANIELLA

When Kryn and I walked into the earl's chamber, we found him sitting on an armchair, legs crossed as he read a book. His blond hair was a bit of a mess, and he wore a somewhat crumpled brown jacket.

He looked up and bestowed a mean glare in Kryn's direction and a half smile in mine. "You're back," he told Kryn. "Please don't waste my time trying to talk me out of my decision. I already made myself clear."

"We're not here for that, Father," Kryn said.

"Then what?"

The earl seemed to relax and went back to perusing his book, lazily turning the pages. Kryn gave me an encouraging nod, and I meandered closer toward the earl, feigning curiosity over the book.

"I have," Kryn started, "just come from Elyndell."

"I wish you would stay there," the earl snapped. "I hate those damn transfer tokens. I yearn for the days before unwanted people gained the ability to come back too quickly."

Sheesh, what an asshole!

How could he talk to his son like that? Mom was always happy when we visited her. She invited us over constantly, luring us home with creamy tortellini, lasagna, or her signature spaghetti Bolognese. She made sure to let us know that she loved us. Often.

Poor Kryn. No wonder he had such a hard time expressing his feelings, and like his sister, hid behind an aloof mask.

"So what news from Elyndell," the earl demanded when Kryn said nothing else.

Kryn watched me get closer to his father. "I met with Kalyll."

"And what of the fallen king?"

I took one more step. The earl caught me in his peripheral vision. He looked up, surprised.

"What are you reading, Father?" I hurried to ask, leaning slightly forward as if to catch the words on the page.

He wrinkled his nose in a sneer, appearing confused, as if Mylendra wasn't the kind to care about his literary pursuits.

As he closed the book and turned it over to read the title, I took hold of his wrist. He startled, his eyes going wide with something like recognition, as if somehow he could tell that a bit of his shadowdrifter darkness lived inside me.

He was strong and tried to fight. He almost managed to free himself from my grip, but my powers worked too quickly, and in the next instant, his eyes rolled to white, and he slumped in the chair, the book thudding to the floor.

I let him go once his heart had slowed, and he turned a little pale. I was worried his shadowdrifter power would help him recover quickly and watched him warily for a long moment. He didn't move at all.

Kalyll approached, and I handed him the second small vial with the transformation potion. He got a hold of the earl's wrist and, without a moment's hesitation, downed the liquid till its last drop. I braced for the agony that would follow. It had been an intense, bone-splitting pain, accompanied by an infernal heat that seemed to melt my every cell. It had been almost as bad as my first transformation—except much quicker.

A shudder seemed to run up Kalyll's spine, and he shook his shoulders. He winced and clenched his teeth, a muscle feathering along his jaw. I wrapped my arms around his waist and thought to guide him backward, so he could settle in an armchair, but his feet seemed nailed to the floor, and he only held on to me.

His body shrank somewhat, his tattoo disappeared leaving behind a plain, uninteresting-looking face, his midnight blue hair faded to blond, and his features twisted in the earl's sour expression. At last, it was over, and he took a long, deep breath.

"Once more, I'm sorry you had to go through that," he said.

The slightly higher tone of his voice surprised me. I pulled away, feeling disgusted at the thought of hugging Kryn's father.

Logically, I knew this was Kalyll, but it still was weird as hell. For the first time, I realized it must be the same for him seeing me as Mylendra. But despite the change, the familiar understanding in the depths of his eyes helped my unease settle. He knew exactly how I felt, so I had nothing to worry about.

"I suppose now we should go to dinner," he said, turning to Kryn.

"Yes," he responded. "It'll be a good test and practice. You can put faces to each name I taught you."

On our way here, Kryn had given us a detailed account of

Earl Qierlan's and Mylendra's attendants. We would need to be acquainted with them, if we planned to make a successful trip to Nerethien in their company.

After lying the earl on his bed, we exited the chamber and headed to dinner. Ten minutes later, we found ourselves in a rustic room the size of a tennis court. The ceilings were high, and the walls covered in tapestries. The floor was made of stone and the furniture of heavy oak. The space was poorly lit, with only a few floor candelabra set around the long table.

A couple of males were already there, and the earl's wife. The males stood when we entered, "the earl" ahead of us, while Kryn and I walked a few steps behind him. The earl's wife remained seated. A grunt was all Kalyll gave them as a greeting as he took a seat at the head of the table. Kryn went to sit to his right but got a dirty look. He was taken aback until he seemed to remember that Kalyll was only doing his best to impersonate their father, and currently the prodigal son was out of favor.

Instead, Kalyll glanced in my direction and gestured toward the chair. Kryn did a good job of acting as if he both cared and didn't care where he took a seat. The earl's wife, seated to the left of her husband, gave Kryn a small smile as if it were a consolation prize for the ill-treatment.

"Is everything ready for our journey?" Kalyll demanded.

"Yes, my lord," one of the males responded, a lanky individual with a long beard.

Kalyll's eyes flicked to Kryn for an instant. Kryn quickly mouthed a name.

Dakian.

"Good, Dakian," Kalyll answered. "I don't want any

delays. And you, Orist," he addressed the second male, "what of the gifts for the Unseelie King?"

"The *Zylnala* sword has been carefully packaged, my lord, along with the jeweled gauntlet to match."

Kalyll grunted and stabbed a piece of meat, looking as pleasant as an angry walrus.

"Is this really how your father is?" I leaned to my right and whispered to Kryn.

"On his good days," he whispered back.

Witchlights, how miserable.

Dinnertime with my family had always been chaotic at the start, with mom nagging at us to hurry and set the table before the food got cold, but once we settled, we talked about our day, joking and offering encouraging comments or advice when someone was having a particularly bad time. Some of my fondest memories involved a meal with my family, enjoying mom's delicious Italian dishes.

Kryn's mother took little bites of her food and flinched every time Kalyll made a sudden movement, which he seemed to be doing a lot. His mannerisms were completely different from his usually composed, methodical way. In fact, he was behaving more like Wölfe, wiping his mouth with the back of his hand and audibly guzzling wine.

When he was done eating, he slammed his tankard down and pushed his plate aside. He picked up his steak knife, twirled it in his hand a couple of times, then stabbed it on the table, where it stood, its tip embedding in the wood.

What the hell? He seemed to be taking this impersonation affair a little too far. Though on second thought, as I noticed the many indents in the wood, I realized that table-stabbing might be a common occurrence.

After a disdainful glance around those gathered, "the earl" stood, huffed, and walked away, leaving everyone without a word. The entire room seemed to exhale in relief, even me, who knew there was nothing to fear from him.

What a tyrant!

More at ease, I ate a few bites of food to assuage my hunger. It had been a long day, and I'd barely had time to eat anything. My chest felt tight after taking some of the earl's life force, however, so I couldn't stomach much. A few times, I glanced toward Kryn's mother, but she pointedly avoided looking at me. She appeared embarrassed, probably at her inability to save her daughter from a marriage far worse than the one she'd endured.

Head down, Kryn pushed his food around. I watched him for a long moment thinking that, at last, I understood him: his cold and mean behavior toward me, his distrust. I saw the way he must have been mistreated as a child, the way his father taught him to be afraid of physical and emotional closeness. And yet, despite his cold exterior, he had let Kalyll and the others in, if only because they'd grown up together and they understood what he'd been through.

It didn't necessarily excuse the way he'd behaved toward me, but I got it now.

After several minutes, Kryn and I got up from the table and followed Kalyll. We were all to meet in the earl's chamber. In fact, the others must already be there, ensuring the awful male remained incapacitated. It wouldn't do for him to wake up, shift into a scary creature, and chase us around the castle to tear us to pieces.

"Your father is a gem, isn't he?" I said as we made our way back.

"A gem?"

"I mean . . . he's not very nice. Forgive me for saying that, if it offends you."

He barked a laugh. "Offend me? He's an asshole, and everyone knows it, especially those closest to him."

"It must've been terrible growing up with him," I said tentatively, afraid he would shut me down.

To my surprise, he seemed open to conversation tonight. "*Terrible* is an understatement. He was civil with my sister, but he never showed such consideration for me. Since I learned what he is, I've begun to suspect he's disappointed that I don't share his shadowdrifter gift. He likely suspects he fathered a child with another woman before I was born. Maybe he even suspects Kalyll is his son, despite Queen Eithne's lies. And yet, he insists on blaming my mother, going as far as to insinuate he didn't sire me when he knows perfectly well he has been no paragon of virtue."

A shadowdrifter's power was only bestowed to their first-born child, and Kalyll bore that title.

"But I think," he went on, "it was my relationship with Arabis that undid whatever love he might have felt for me."

"I'm sorry."

He shrugged. "I suffer not for the loss of a father. I only suffer for . . . her."

"If only you two could work things out. It's obvious you care for each other."

"I suppose I'm an open book, am I not? But Arabis . . . she holds no tenderness for me, not anymore."

I shook my head. "You're mistaken. She loves you."

"You are the one who is mistaken, Dani. You don't know Arabis well enough. What you mistake for love is nothing more than civility and respect for the Sub Rosa."

"That can't be right." I had seen Arabis's concern for Kryn whenever he was in danger and the furtive looks she sent his way whenever she thought no one was paying attention. There was way more than just civility in those blue eyes of hers.

Kryn smiled sadly. "Trust me. I know. I've been at the receiving end of her civility for a long time. It feels nothing like . . ." He trailed off. "Never mind."

Despite his gloomy words, I had a feeling he still held hope. "Did something happen between you two in Nerethien?"

His head snapped in my direction. "What makes you say that? Did she mention something?"

"No. I just thought I perceived . . . a change. Some tension between you."

He was quiet for so long that I thought he wasn't going to say anything, and when he finally did, I was surprised that he would confide in me.

"We shared a kiss," he said in a voice so gentle that it sounded nothing like the Kryn I knew. "But before you say that this means she loves me . . . It doesn't. She was . . . drunk, and she doesn't hold her liquor well. I took advantage of the situation, which she made abundantly clear."

"You do know that alcohol lowers our inhibitions, don't you?"

I wanted to say more, but we arrived at his father's chamber, and he immediately opened the door and entered.

As I'd expected, everyone was there already—except for Mylendra, who needed to remain in Kryn's chamber, since no servants bothered to go there.

"Has he stirred?" I approached the bed.

"No," Jeondar said, "but I think he has regained some of his color."

Quickly, I checked the pulse on his wrist. It was stronger than before, though not by much. Jeondar was right, though, his lips and cheeks were slightly pink—not ghost-white, like before. I checked the time. He had been out for nearly two hours.

"He should stay unconscious until morning, I hope," I said.

"What about this one?" Silver pointed to the guard that had been standing outside the earl's door. They had brought him in and laid him on a settee.

"Witchlights, I forgot about him." I rushed to his side and checked his vitals. His pulse wasn't as strong as the earl's, but it was within a safe range. "He'll sleep longer, but he'll be all right." His Fae healing ability would make sure of that.

Glancing around the room, I met Larina's gaze. She smiled and flew over from her place atop a pile of books on a side table.

"You look tired," she said.

"I am. You?"

"Restless." She pointed toward a spot at the foot of the bed. "I put your messenger bag there."

"Thank you." The batch of transformation potions

Naesala had made for us was in there. "Everything depends on that."

Larina shook her head. "No. Everything depends on you and the king."

"Gee, thanks, Larina. Way to ratchet up the pressure."

She put her small hands up. "Oh, I'm sorry."

"I'm just kidding."

"You're going to have to get used to her sense of humor," Kalyll said, coming up behind me.

"I *will*, my king." Larina inclined her head, turning serious.

Ah, maybe one day she would stop getting flustered when Kalyll was around. Hmm, I could think of one thing that might take her a step closer.

"Kalyll," I started, "while you were gone, I made Larina a member of the Sub Rosa, and I told her you would make it official upon your return."

The pixie's cheeks turned violet, and her wings whirred so fast I was afraid she would shoot up into the rafters.

A blond eyebrow went up in Kalyll's borrowed face.

"My king," Larina said, "it's not nece—"

"Everyone! Gather round." He waved everyone in.

The others abandoned what they were doing and came to form a circle with Larina in the middle. The violet on her cheeks quickly tended toward purple.

Suddenly, Kalyll pushed me into the middle of the circle, and it was my turn to blush.

"You need to become official, too."

I opened my mouth to protest, but he silenced me with a raised finger.

He cleared his throat. "For your loyalty, relentless desire to help, and friendship, we welcome you into the Sub Rosa." Kalyll put a hand up and inclined his head in encouragement.

Larina and I lifted our right hands.

"Repeat after me," Kalyll said. "I swear, by all that is sacred, that I will remain loyal and dedicated to the Sub Rosa and will never reveal its secrets to anyone."

The pixie and I solemnly repeated every word.

"Furthermore, I swear I will come to the aid of any Sub Rosa member, no matter their need."

Larina and I repeated again, and as soon as we were done, the others chanted in unison, "I SWEAR!" and thumped their chests with their closed fists.

Their voices echoed through the room, and for a moment, I was worried we might attract attention, but the earl's chamber was too secluded for that.

Larina and I exchanged a smile, and I was sure she felt as I did: literally and metaphorically in the middle of a protective circle of dear friends.

The others offered their congratulations, and Silver swiftly found a decanter and passed drinks around. We clinked our glasses and were merry for a while, joking and teasing.

It was what we needed, for tomorrow our journey to unknown dangers began.

CHAPTER 28
DANIELLA

The next morning, we got on the road early. As much as we would've liked, we weren't going to be traveling to Nerethien using our transfer token. It wouldn't do for a dignitary such as Earl Qierlan to simply appear when he hadn't been invited.

Mythorne hadn't reached out for an alliance, and though word had been sent to the Unseelie King, he hadn't replied, which apparently wasn't uncommon for the monarch. It seemed he enjoyed being an asshole and making himself feel important.

This was the reason Kalyll and I exited Qierlan's castle riding horses and being followed by a small retinue that would tend to our needs while on the road for the next day. Jeondar and Arabis were with us. They were in the guise of the earl's and Mylendra's attendants, respectively, also aided by Naesala's potion, the others—Kryn, Silver, Cylea, and Larina—had snuck out of the castle before sun up and were likely already waiting for us in the Unseelie capital. Lucky them.

The real earl and his daughter remained behind, the former asleep, and the latter stashed away in Kryn's bedroom.

I felt at ease as we departed, trusting that they would cause no trouble. Earl Qierlan hadn't awakened all night long, so I'd drained him again, then we transferred him, along with the guard and attendants, to the dungeon cell Kryn had prepared for them during the night.

I only regretted I would miss seeing his face when he woke up and found himself weighed down by heavy chains—nothing like the Qrorium ones we'd used on Kalyll in Imbermore, shadowdrifters were especially powerful when they first came into their abilities—but strong enough to hold him. And the bonus? Kryn told us, wearing a too-satisfied smile, that no one went to the dungeons. Ever. I was sure he would've also loved to see his father's expression when he realized he would not be selling his daughter to Mythorne.

In the end, three days of quiet travel ended up being better than I expected. Kalyll and I rode ahead of the group, and we had time to talk and be together like never before. We'd been through so much together, peril a constant shape looming at our backs. And though this time we were headed straight into danger, we were able to find some much-needed peace.

Every day, we kept our new appearances in place by drinking one of the potions, and I watched with concern as our supply dwindled.

Too soon, our journey was over, and after we crested a steep hill on the third day, we caught our first sight of Nerethien.

From this distance, the city appeared to be a dark and dirty place. The streets were narrow and winding, and the buildings squat and cramped, except for the large, blackstone palace that loomed at the north fringes.

My horse's hooves seemed to grow heavier as we started

our descent toward the city. I knew it was my imagination, but I felt as if even the animal feared the place.

As we reached a cobblestone road that led straight to the Unseelie palace, my first impression proved right. The city wasn't pleasant. The air was thick with the smell of sewage and smoke, and rats scurried through the gutters, bold and fat. I sensed an edge of desperation from the people and wondered at the levels of crime and disease in these unhealthy conditions. Their poverty was evident in their rags and sallow faces. Here, unlike Elyndell, the houses ran in rows and left no room for nature. There were no hanging bridges going from tree to tree, no dwellings that grew and morphed from thick trunks. No moss-carpeted paths, no flowers.

Everything and everyone appeared lackluster. Compared to the splendor of Elyndell and Imbermore, Nerethien seemed to belong to a different realm altogether.

A dirty-faced child stood on the side of the paths and held what appeared to be a doll made from scraps. She stared at us with big violet eyes, a pair of iridescent wings hanging limply behind her. Her insistent gaze seemed to pierce through me and made me squirm on my saddle and resent the fine dress and jewels I wore.

I thought I couldn't feel any worse until, gradually, the look of the place began to change, giving way to larger and better-looking homes. The changes happened at a steady rate until we arrived at a grand palace that was as opulent as the outer edge of the city was drab.

"I knew it was like this," Kalyll said. "But seeing it with my own eyes . . ." He couldn't finish and just shook his head, appearing troubled.

I never imagined that things could be this bad in Elf-hame. The disparity in wealth was staggering. How could anyone live with themselves when others suffered, and they were responsible for it? Mythorne was supposed to take care of these people. Instead, he only took advantage of them.

As we approached the guarded gate, my heart started pounding. At first, I tried to disguise my fear, but in the end, it was easier to allow my gaze to dart from side to side and my chest to move with agitation. Mylendra would've felt the same or worse, after all. So why not let it show?

It wasn't until Kalyll reached for my hand, and we rode into the castle after announcing who we were, that I managed to gather my strength. I had to usher Dark Dani forward, and it was all right. There was nothing wrong with fighting darkness with darkness.

The ancient castle loomed over the city, its massive dark walls casting shadows over the surrounding dwellings below.

We dismounted in front of a large arched entrance, flanked by two towers. The doorway was made of stone and covered in intricate carvings, the same as the towers and their battlements. The structure was a formidable sight, clearly built to withstand outside forces. It seemed a place of mystery and intrigue, somewhere I'd rather not visit.

A spindly man dressed in a long black tunic very similar to what human priests wore greeted us at the door.

He showed two rows of pointed teeth as he grimaced at us. I wondered if he thought he was smiling.

"Earl Qierlan Goren of the Fall Court, and his lovely daughter Mylendra Goren. Welcome to Highmire. Your visit is unexpected, to say the least, and I must immediately inquire as to its purpose." The male's smile/grimace died a slow death with each word, leaving only suspicion behind. If this was how they received their supposed allies, I didn't want to know how they treated their enemies.

Kalyll didn't bat an eye, however, and when he spoke there was nothing but surety in his voice. "I am here to talk to the Unseelie King, not one of his . . . subordinates."

I nearly choked. The animosity that hung in the air felt like a shroud descending over us. Did Kalyll know what he was doing? God, I really hoped so. Treating the Unseelie King's emissary badly didn't seem like a good idea, but then again, appearing weak probably wasn't one either. There was a balance, I supposed. A game that Kalyll had been raised to play. I had to trust this situation was in the best hands possible.

The *subordinate* as Kalyll had blatantly called him showed his teeth again, though this time the gesture could not be confused with a smile. Not even close.

"This subordinate has the authority to kick you out," he barked, spitting saliva.

This time it was Kalyll's turn to show razor-sharp teeth. I blinked in surprise. It wasn't known that Earl Qierlan was a shadowdrifter, and Kalyll had just made the decision to reveal it. I had no idea what consequences the earl would face once the secret was made public, but perhaps Kalyll believed that the male deserved whatever was coming to him.

"Go ahead and try," Kalyll growled. "I'm sure King Mythorne will have no difficulty finding someone to replace you. People like you are as common as dirt. I should know because when one displeases me, I simply find another one."

The male took a step back, his eyes narrowing with caution. Surely there were guards he could call to help him throw us out the door, but I had a feeling he sensed "the earl" would be done with him before he could utter a single word.

"So what shall it be?" Kalyll demanded.

"The king is busy. He can't abandon everything anytime a minor court member arrives unannounced."

"Now you are just being petty." Kalyll laughed. "But that is fine, we'll wait. I will, however, make sure the king hears about your behavior toward someone who comes to offer troops and alliance for the upcoming war. C'mon, darling, we will sit over there to wait. I know you're tired from your long journey, but just hold on a little longer. Meeting King Mythorne will be your recompense."

The male whirled on his heel and walked away, his long black robe sweeping behind him. As we sat on a velvet upholstered bench, Kalyll squeezed my hand and gave me a reassuring smile.

I wouldn't have been surprised if we'd had to wait for an hour, but within the span of ten minutes, a page boy came to fetch us and guide us deeper into the palace. As our steps resonated across the dark cavernous halls, my hands began sweating. We were willingly moving deeper into the devil's den.

The thought occurred to me that we might end up in the same dark cell from which I'd rescued Kalyll only days ago. If that happened, I feared no one would be able to find us ever again.

Pushing my worries aside, I matched Kalyll's firm steps and pushed my shoulders back, determined to portray nothing but strength.

After we entered a dimly lit area, the page boy paused, then made a sweeping gesture with his hand. After that, he exited and a set of double doors closed behind us with a *clank*. A few torches glowed from their high perches on the slick dark columns that lined the path ahead. At the end of the long corridor sat an empty throne lit from behind, two guards standing at either side. Someone had a flair for the overly dark and dramatic.

We walked forward, our steps echoing as they would in a mausoleum. We stopped a few steps from the dais, and I had to stop myself from gaping at the baleful throne, which seemed to be built from veined black marble and bones.

The Unseelie King entered from one side and sat down. He crossed one leg and propped an elbow on the armrest of his grotesque throne, one index finger tapping his sharp chin. He was a tall, thin male with pale skin, a hooked nose, and shoulder-length white hair. His demeanor was full of impatience and annoyance, as if the existence of others were a nuisance to him, as if it made him angry that others breathed the same air he did.

"My King," Kalyll said, after swallowing the bile that acting servile in front of this male must bring to his throat.

I paired his bow with a curtsy as I held Mythorne's inquisitive gaze. He was getting an eyeful of my boobs, which meant the revealing dress I'd chosen was doing its job.

Mythorne lifted an eyebrow, as if unsatisfied by the proffered respect. When Kalyll frowned, Mythorne's eyes lowered to the floor. Taking the hint, Kalyll bent a knee, teeth clenched. I did the same, bile burning in my throat. It was humiliating.

After the shortest bow in deference, we stood back up. Impatiently, Mythorne waved a hand and glanced to the side of the dais where he had entered. He waved again, inviting someone in. Footsteps sounded, and a person appeared beside Mythorne. I nearly choked and had to look to Kalyll for an example of how to remain composed. I honestly didn't know how he managed to look so calm at the sight of Cardian at the right hand of the Unseelie King. Or how he bowed when what he clearly wanted to do was chop their heads off.

"What do you think of this, Cardian," Mythorne said. "He comes to offer me troops that are *already* at my disposal."

"The gall of it." Cardian smirked.

Kalyll slowly glanced around the throne room as if searching for the *subordinate*. He seemed to ponder for a moment, then decided to go for shock value.

"Nonsense, I've come to offer you a wife." He took a step to the side and made a flourish in my direction.

CHAPTER 29
DANIELLA

"A wife?" Mythorne repeated, though not with surprise. Instead, he seemed to roll the word over in his mouth as if to taste it and learn whether he found it savory or not.

A chill assaulted me as he inclined his head and his eyes roved over my body.

Next to him, Cardian appeared ill at the news. His fists clenched, and his lower lip trembled, denouncing his anger. Why such a reaction? What did he care who Mylendra married?

"You've come to offer your king scraps?" he said.

Kalyll's head snapped in his brother's direction, his gaze alighting on Cardian for the first time. "How dare you call my daughter scraps? Come down here and say that again."

"Don't talk to me like that," Cardian barked. "I am the Seelie King."

Kalyll threw his head back and laughed. "Here, you are nothing. It is Kellam Mythorne who rules. Go back to romanticized life in your flowery tower."

Mythorne observed everything with a slight grin stretching his thin lips. Without abandoning his amused expression, he said, "But you seemed to have a different opinion mere days ago, *Qierlan*. You were quite willing to bestow your . . . *non-scraps* to that place you now disparage."

And wasn't that the crux of the matter? Earl Qierlan couldn't be trusted. He would side with whoever gave him the greatest advantage. But Kalyll didn't let this little inconvenient truth hinder his award-winning performance. Instead, he smoothly transitioned into the next scene of our little act, which we had planned carefully, knowing this particular subject would come up sooner or later.

Thumping a fist against his chest like a good Catholic, Kalyll said, "That is, of course, entirely my fault, as my clever daughter pointed out from the beginning. If only I had listened." He inclined his head in my direction, letting me know it was my time to shine, and by shining I meant using Mylendra's female guiles.

Okay, Dark Dani, ready?

Sashaying, I paced back and forth in front of the dais, one hand on my waist and the other one elegantly trailing behind me.

"From the start, Kalyll Adanorin was not to my liking. I always thought he was weak, and as it turned out, I was right."

I glanced in Cardian's direction for just a second, then let the breadth of my attention settle on Mythorne. My intention was to convey that I understood it was he and *not* the youngest Adanorin brother who had brought about Kalyll's dethronement.

"She *is* headstrong, so be advised." Kalyll chuckled.

"You lie," Cardian spat. "You were taken with him. Both of you."

I allowed my gaze to lazily go back to Cardian as I twisted my mouth in distaste. "With all due respect, *Seelie King*," I sounded respectful not at all, "I do know my way around politics, and I also know how to follow orders, even if I don't like them." I followed this with a cheeky wink toward my supposed father.

"A female who knows her place is the best kind of female," the Unseelie King said.

As we'd guessed, Mythorne wanted a dutiful wife. It was a balance to show a bit of attitude, and at the same time, paint the picture of a female who would not go against his wishes. I nearly rolled my eyes. Some males could be so predictable.

"You should not trust this," Cardian started, but Mythorne put a hand up to stop him. Cardian's lips sealed as if by magic.

Witchlights. If he really thought he was a King, why allow anyone to treat him this way? Immediately, I chided myself. Why ask myself such a stupid question when I already knew the answer? With Kalyll free, Cardian didn't feel like a king at all. He was scared that his older brother would soon return to tear him from the throne and shatter his ambitions to bits.

Mythorne rose from his throne and descended the dais. My hands started itching, eager to wrap around his neck, but he hadn't come close enough.

"Kalyll Adanorin isn't weak," he said, taking me aback.

His statement was true enough, I could feel my mate's latent strength radiating from him even now, but I didn't expect *this* male to admit it.

"Kalyll Adanorin killed my son," he continued. "Moreover, he survived a not-so-welcoming stay under our care." He stretched his arms upward and swept them to the sides as if introducing his humble abode to us. "So you are mistaken, my lady."

I drummed my fingers against my waist. "Perhaps not weak," I admitted. "But weaker." I lazily swept my eyes from the tips of his boots to the top of his head.

"That is yet to be seen," he responded.

"Never took you for a humble male," I said. "I must admit I am surprised."

"Don't be. I am anything but. That, however, does not mean I am stupid. Adanorin is at large and still poses a threat to my allies." He pointed vaguely toward Cardian. "And to me. Not to say that I am intimidated by that. I welcome a good challenge, and I have not had one in a very long time. I would like nothing more than to meet him face to face."

What a fucking liar! A good challenge, my ass. He had tortured Kalyll, keeping him behind a force field, while he stood safely on the other side. He was a coward.

Kalyll's right hand tightened into a fist, no doubt entertaining the same thoughts I was, wishing to smash his hooked nose with one swift punch.

"Oh, Father," I reached for Kalyll's fisted hand and gave it a squeeze, "isn't he just like I told you he would be?"

"Exactly so, my dear," he replied.

Mythorne examined us very carefully, his expression so severe that I feared he was seeing right through our charade. I almost exhaled in relief when he smiled genuinely enough and spoke with the charm befitting a king. "I am delighted you have come, Earl Qierlan and Lady Mylendra. I appreciate the offer of a more meaningful alliance between the Unseelie Court and the Fall Court. I don't take it lightly and feel I must seriously consider this opportunity. Obviously, dear Earl, the first order of business is for me to become acquainted with your lovely daughter. I must learn if we are compatible. More than her impressive beauty will guide my decision."

"This is already more consideration than the former Seelie King offered me," I said, lifting an eyebrow toward Kalyll.

"Will you ever cease pointing out how wrong I was," "the earl" chided playfully.

"Never, Father. Never." I laughed and shook a finger at him.

Mythorne clapped his hands, and two servants scurried in from a side door. They bowed low, their faces etched with servility and defeat. It was clear they knew what would happen to them if they did not obey their master's every command.

"We have guests," he announced. "Ensure their comfort." He turned to us. "For now, I have matters to attend to, but I will be delighted if you join me for dinner." He left, which seemed to carry an implied order for Cardian because he hurried after him, going so fast he barely had time to give us a dirty look as he exited.

The servants guided us to a separate wing of the palace that seemed to house guest chambers.

"I hope you will approve of your accommodations, Earl Qierlan." One of the servants threw a door open on the left side of the hall.

"Where is my daughter's chamber?" He demanded, treating him with as much civility as Mythorne had, which was to say none.

"Just over here." He ran ahead a few paces and pointed to another door on the opposite end of the hall.

Kalyll grunted. "You may leave now. Please ensure our servants know where to find us."

When they had disappeared, Kalyll took my hand and guided me to his room. Once inside, he locked the door behind us, pressed a finger to his lips, and walked around the chamber, examining everything closely, looking behind every door and curtain.

When he was satisfied no one was in the room, he said, "I hate to admit you were right, daughter."

"You should listen to me more often."

"Don't get a big head now."

"What shall I wear to dinner to impress the king?"

And that was how our conversation went on until our "servants" arrived with our luggage.

Acting swiftly, Jeondar pulled a wand from one of the suitcases and proceeded to sweep the room, waving it about like an incense stick. It only took him a couple of minutes to discover a magical listening device, which turned out to be the only one in the room. Quickly, he laid a bespelled piece of cloth over it, which would turn all sounds, no matter how damning, into innocuous ones, like casual words, coughs, furniture taps, and the like.

Naesala was a true savior with all her handy spells, potions, and magical devices. We certainly couldn't have gotten this far without her help.

"It's safe to talk now," Jeondar said.

"How did it go?" Arabis asked.

Kalyll explained quickly, told them we were to have dinner with Mythorne, and instructed them to get acquainted with the castle as only servants could. They were to figure out an escape route we could use if the need arose.

After all of that was settled, I went into my assigned room. It wouldn't do for a daughter to spend her entire time in her father's chamber. It would look suspicious, for sure.

On tenterhooks, I waited for dinner time to arrive—my chambermaid, Arabis, helping me get ready to appear as enticing and "touchable" as possible. The objective was to tempt Mythorne to come close and lay his hands on me. It would be far easier if he came to me, but if he didn't take the bait, the bait would go to him.

CHAPTER 30
DANIELLA

The dinner table was about twenty feet in length, and Kalyll and I had been instructed to sit at the opposite end to Mythorne, as far away from arm's reach as possible.

It was a stupidly impractical sitting arrangement, which made me worry he suspected something. But if he did, why not capture us as soon as we entered his domain?

I stabbed the meat on my plate, a stringy, brown chunk with some sort of gravy splashed around it, and wondered if I should worry about its source. Under the table, Kalyll nudged me with his foot, staring pointedly at the mystery culprit. Holding my breath, I stuffed the small piece in my mouth and swallowed straightaway, then pretended to chew. My gag reflex almost activated at the gamey taste, but I managed to keep it under control.

"My troops have arrived at the Winter Court," Mythorne said, sounding pleased. "The Winter King will receive them and join his armies with mine. Without hoping to gain anything."

"We cannot help it if Naeduin lacks creativity and political acumen," Kalyll said unapologetically.

I resisted the urge to glare at him and instead decided to

learn the way things worked among these Fae Royals. From this example, it seemed that straight-up words were the leading choice when dealing with barbed comments that would be useless to deny.

"Indeed." Mythorne chuckled, then took a sip of his wine.

He was again accompanied by Cardian, who sat quietly and meekly as if not allowed to issue a sound lest the king stabbed him with his steak knife.

"Lady Mylendra," the Unseelie King shifted his attention to me, "tell me about your interests and pursuits. I would love to learn what things we have in common."

Well, for starters, I love to torture helpless people. Would it get me brownie points if I told him that?

Instead, I went over the boring spiel I'd rehearsed with Kryn.

"One of my favorite pastimes is literature," I said. "I also enjoy horseback riding."

Mylendra had other interests, but we chose to keep it short in case someone decided to discuss things I knew nothing about, like for instance, battle strategies. Apparently, the earl had insisted on both Kryn and his sister learning all about the intricacies of war.

To my left, Kalyll sat seemingly at ease. He appeared as unbothered as if he were at his own table, and watching his calm demeanor helped me keep my own cool.

"I hear you're an accomplished archer," Mythorne said with a sidelong glance at Cardian, the fucking tattletale.

"Um, I certainly am."

"I love to hear it. I do love a female who can handle herself during the hunt. Perhaps you and I can have some fun out in my woods at some point."

Not a chance, you asshole. You'll be an empty husk as soon as I get my hands on you.

"And do you have any . . . special skills?" Mythorne gestured toward a servant to take away his plate.

"I don't," I replied, knowing that by special he meant magical.

He grunted. "That is unfortunate. I hear you are a shadow-drifter, Earl Qierlan, a fact you've kept well hidden up until now. I bet you wish you'd passed some of that on to your *offspring.*"

The way he said *offspring* made me wonder if he suspected the earl was Kalyll's father. Whatever the case, it was a moot point, especially when Queen Eithne had made sure to create a narrative that assured everyone King Beathan had sired Kalyll.

"The earl" sipped his wine, then answered, "I certainly wish my son had inherited *something* from me. He's good for nothing. He disappoints me at every turn."

"What a pity. There's nothing more satisfying and pride-inducing than . . . seeing yourself in your son."

There was a hint of pain in the Unseelie King's words. I paused and glanced in his direction, and for a moment, thought I caught proof of that pain in his gaze, but it all happened too fast to be sure.

When dinner was over, Mythorne stood and addressed me with gentleness. "Lady, I would love to take a walk with you in my gardens. I believe you will appreciate their . . . wild beauty."

The thought of going anywhere with him put my teeth on edge, but this was exactly what we wanted.

I set down my napkin on my unfinished food. "It would be a pleasure."

Kalyll stood to pull my chair back. He offered his hand and helped me stand. I strolled toward the front of the table, acting unhurried as I composed myself. Kalyll followed several paces behind me.

Mythorne shook his head. "There's no need for your presence, Earl Qierlan."

"I will not allow her to go without a chaperone," Kalyll said.

"Do you not trust me?" The question was loaded, the kind that didn't need to be asked because there was only one acceptable answer.

I glanced back over my shoulder and gave Kalyll a reassuring smile. I could defend myself all too well, and he knew it. This was our opportunity.

"I promise to remain well away from her," the Unseelie King said.

A curious thing to say, and once more, I found myself wondering if he knew exactly who we were.

"Very well." Kalyll inclined his head, looking pleasant, though I could tell from the stormy look in his eyes that he was fighting not to let Wölfe take control of the situation.

I kept walking, praying that he would prevail over his wilder side. It wouldn't do to cause a confrontation that could end badly when we had the means to quietly dismantle his dark court.

As we exited the dining hall, Mythorne walked briskly ahead of me, moving as lithely as only the Fae can. I went after him, memorizing the winding halls in case I needed to find my way back by myself. This side of the castle was as dark and foreboding as the rest. I didn't like this place at all. The shut-in feel, the lack of proper light. It made me feel as if I was trapped inside a mausoleum. I could almost smell the dank rot and the sweet decay of dead flowers, but I was sure it was all my imagination.

When I passed through a narrow door, and a cool breeze caressed my face, it was a relief. Though it was dampened by the lack of good lighting. It took my eyes a moment to adjust and take in the gardens that Mythorne assumed I would enjoy.

The moon shone meekly over the exotic landscape, illuminating a host of strange plants and bushes such I had never seen. The air was filled with a poignant mixture of smells, also unrecognizable.

In the center, a large tree sent its branches reaching up to the sky. White flowers in the shape of wine glasses seemed to shiver. A pool of water gurgled near the tree, its surface dark and oily. A variety of plants grew around it, their leaves leathery and glossy. A twisted plant with leaves like feathers caught my eye. What in the world?

Mythorne stood ahead of me on a wide cobbled path. With a hand gesture, he invited me to join him. I did so, closing the distance between us, a distance that he quickly widened, pushing to the very edge of the path.

"I promised your father I would keep my distance," he said, starting an easy stroll.

He either was very honorable, didn't trust anyone getting close to him or suspected something. Of course, my vote was on one of the last two options. This bastard didn't have one honorable bone in his body.

He cast a glance around the garden. "I'm sure the specimens here are unlike anything you're used to."

"You are correct." I followed his gaze to a bush with perfectly round leaves.

"Many wouldn't consider this garden beautiful, and I would call them shortsighted. There is no beauty in useless things, and there's nothing useless about any of these plants. Each one of them has a use. Some heal, some inebriate, others kill, like that bush we just saw."

"Fascinating." And it really was. I knew a lot about plants and their many attributes. My knowledge could be called extensive by many, but I'd never seen any of the specimens found here. They drove my curiosity to no end.

"It seems you have a true affinity to plants," Mythorne said, noticing my interest.

Kryn hadn't mentioned anything about his sister liking plants, so I needed to tread carefully.

I made a noncommittal gesture with my hand. "Anything can hold my attention when expressed with such zeal. You've managed to make me very curious." I added the last bit in an insinuating tone.

Our gazes locked and held. I smiled and took a step closer.

He made a disapproving sound in the back of his throat. "We better keep our distance, my lady. We wouldn't want your father growing angry."

"I never took you for a male preoccupied with propriety."

"I am when it pertains to the female I might marry."

Behind Mythorne, the slightest movement of a shadow caught my eye. It slithered over the ground, so quickly that I might've missed it if I'd blinked.

Kalyll?

Once he moved closer, I became certain it was him. I felt him in my bones as if they were made of iron, and he was a magnet.

I shook myself and forced my attention back to Mythorne. "I am glad to hear you are considering me."

"Are you, really? My court is not the best place for someone like you. I would think you would hate coming here."

I leaned down to look closer at a flowering plant in front of us. I pretended to examine it, and when I glanced up I caught Mythorne admiring my boobs . . . well, Mylendra's boobs. They were substantial, bigger than mine. I hadn't gotten used to them.

"If you do not think I'm tough enough," I said, "you must not know much about my father."

"Oh, I know enough. You may think yourself hardened, but you are as soft as the first rays of morning light. I'm afraid there may be no room for that here."

"You forget that light is insidious," I retorted, walking closer and pretending to examine the plants.

He casually walked backward, keeping the distance between us steady. I did my best to hide my frustration, but this was getting ridiculous. Maybe he was a germaphobe, and that was why he had so many plants that could heal . . . just in case he caught some deadly virus. Honestly, at this point, a biological agent seemed like a much better weapon than me.

How long would it take to gain his trust? Days? Weeks? We did not have enough time or potion for that. His troops were already at the Winter Court and would be joined by the Fall Court regiment. And what then? What orders would they receive from their commander?

Would they immediately move on to attack Imbermore, Jeondar's beautiful home? It was the closest opposing court. And even if the Spring Court rose to the occasion and joined Jeondar's father, would they be strong enough to hold three armies back?

"And what of me?" the Unseelie King asked, gesturing toward his face.

"What of you?"

I acted as if I didn't know what he meant. He was not a good-looking male by any stretch of the imagination, on the contrary. He was way too thin, and his hook nose made him look like a malnourished parrot. Though it wasn't only his discordant features that made him unattractive. There was more to it. The windows to his soul told me he was far uglier inside. Despite the manners and diplomacy he had shown so far, his gaze swirled with malice, the kind that knew no bounds and rejoiced at the suffering of others.

He blew air through his nose and ignored my question. "I must admit, I am intrigued by you, Lady Goren. You don't shy away the way most females do in my presence. You hold my gaze and talk with confidence. Even people who have known me for a long time are unable to do that much."

"Are you trying to scare me, King Mythorne?"

"Scare you?"

"Yes. You are saying that even those you allow to keep on living fear you."

He only shrugged in answer.

"Do you like people to fear you?"

"It has its advantages."

"I can only imagine. No one has ever feared me." I bobbed

my head from side to side as if considering. "Well, maybe one chambermaid or two."

He laughed at that.

I smiled, which was an effort.

"Yes." He nodded slowly. "I'm definitely intrigued by you."

CHAPTER 31
KALYLL

I did not like the way Mythorne was looking at her. It was nearly impossible to sit in the shadows, doing nothing, waiting for Daniella's opportunity to get close to him.

This was the plan, I knew, but what if his rumored secret powers were only that: a rumor? I wasn't afraid of him, and I wouldn't mind fighting him and finding out who was more powerful.

—Let me kill him.

No. We won't endanger the others.

—I can take him, if you're too afraid to do it.

We're in a bed of snakes. They will rear their heads and strike at the slightest sign of trouble.

I would never forgive myself if my rash behavior got my friends or my beloved hurt.

So I remained one with the shadows and watched as he ogled her. Logically, I knew it was Mylendra's body he was admiring, but I couldn't shake off the uneasy feeling that he could see further. The way he was acting, staying away from her reach. Perhaps it was just caution since one never knew the extent of what others could do. He certainly was adept at keeping such things secret. He understood the advantage it gave him. So naturally, his own strategy would make him wary of others. Or perhaps it had to do with what happened to his pet sorcerer, Runik. Mythorne knew there was someone out there who could kill him with a single touch.

But did he know about Naesala Roka? Did he know she was so crafty and powerful that she could make one person look exactly like another? Did he know she was at our disposal? I didn't think so, but it all depended on how much Cardian had fathomed from Varamede's run-in with me in Elyndell. Or maybe it didn't.

If I knew my brother well, I had to believe that he'd kept that little incident from the Unseelie King. Cardian didn't like to admit his failures, and confessing that he'd transferred to Nerethien in a fit of panic believing that I had escaped was no small blunder.

Though Daniella never had the opportunity to come close enough to touch Mythorne, I was relieved when they started walking back toward the door. I followed them, staying at a safe distance, and didn't breathe easily until he bid her good night, and they went their separate ways.

As Daniella walked toward the guest wing, her steps echoed against the dark-stone walls, with not a tapestry to dampen the sound. When she entered the final hall, she stopped, looked around, then turned in my direction.

"I can feel you there," she said, her voice sounding strange, a mixture between Mylendra's deeper tone and Daniella's sweeter one.

I let my shadows rise higher, climbing from the floor to the wall, then I peeled away, taking corporeal form.

She blinked at the sight of me, rushed to my side, took me by the elbow, and pushed me into the chamber.

"Your hair," she hissed. "It's blue."

"And your voice."

She touched her throat. "The elixir is wearing off."

"We're back just in time, then."

"That was close. I hope Mythorne didn't notice anything."

"I doubt it. I just did, and I know you much better than he ever will."

She nodded and walked away, wringing her hands. She sat down and glanced over at the cloth-covered listening device. "I can't put a finger on that male."

"Yes, he is definitely . . . slippery."

"Exactly! He's a snake." She shuddered. "And snakes don't trust anyone because they think everyone is like them."

"Which makes it ironic when Cardian stands next to him."

"That must have been hard to witness."

"It was hard not to lunge in his direction and kill him. It's what Wölfe wants to do."

She peered at me with her warm brown eyes, and my murderous instincts dissolved. We sat across from each other in silence for a long time, lost in our own thoughts. Over the course of ten minutes, I watched her figure change, the dress she wore becoming a bit looser around her body. A pressure that I hadn't realized was there eased from my chest as I took her in.

"You're back to normal," I said.

"You are too." She smiled, and I could see the same relief I felt in her features.

A knock came at the door. I jumped to my feet. The knock was followed by three more. Two fast, one slow. Daniella and I exchanged a glance and nodded.

I cracked the door open and found Jeondar in his guise, standing on the other side. I allowed him entry and secured the lock behind him.

He frowned at my appearance. "How . . . did it go?"

We explained what had happened, and when we were done, he appeared as uneasy as I felt.

"Perhaps tomorrow," he said.

"Perhaps."

"For our part, we were given rooms in the very bowels of the castle. The servants treat us with distrust and keep a close eye on our every move. The steward seems to be some sort of spymaster to whom they all report. Regardless, it wasn't hard to find a quick passage out of here. They seem indifferent to our comings and goings outside the castle walls. It is only when we step inside that they lurk about, dusting and straightening things in our wake."

"Let them waste their time," Daniella said. "Maybe they'll burn Mythorne's dinner."

"We'd better make some progress quickly," Jeondar said. "We only have two more days, worth of the transformation potion."

"I'll get it done," Daniella said with conviction.

Jeondar nodded. "I'll be off then."

As his steps echoed outside, I said, "Stay with me tonight. I don't want you sleeping by yourself. Go and pretend to get ready for bed and then sneak out."

She didn't argue, and within ten minutes she was back,

wearing a silk gown with a matching robe over it. Lace trimmed the hem, brushing the top of her bare feet. I secured the door, turned off the lights except for one lamp, and we got into bed.

We lay on our sides and faced each other. She sandwiched her hands under her cheek and watched me, love brimming in her eyes.

"I missed your tattoo while you were the earl." She traced the outline from my forehead down to my jaw, giving me a chill.

"You don't think it mars my face? That's what my mother said when I got it."

"It doesn't. No one could ever be more handsome than you."

"I must agree."

She punched my shoulder. "Conceited much?" We laughed, then she asked, "What does it mean?"

"The tattoo?"

She nodded.

"It's a dragon. I got it after the Battle of Fheraigh. I was drunk after our victory against their host. I rode a dragon that day, hence the moniker *Dragon Soul* which many have used to refer to me since that day. I was young and let it go to my head."

"Holy shit. You really are legendary."

"Again, I must agree."

She rolled her eyes and pursed her lips, looking adorable.

After we were quiet for a long moment, she tapped my nose. "Everything all right?"

The thoughts that had been swirling inside my head spilled out. "I wish for peace."

Despite my somber words, my hand traced the contour of her waist and hips.

She looked down. "Do you happen to associate sex with peace?"

I smirked.

Her hand slid under my waistband.

"What are you doing, woman?" I growled, hitching my hips up a little bit to make sure she felt my malehood to the fullest.

"Mmm, I'm just trying to . . . get a handle on this peace of yours." Her hand abandoned her delicious ministrations and rested on the bed between us as she sobered. "I've only known peace my entire life. I wish you could say the same."

"I am happy about that. Your realm has seen terrible wars, but I'm glad you've remained untouched by them. I suppose I've been alive too long, and it is inevitable. Sooner or later you're bound to experience it. Many creatures seem to crave conflict, and the Fae are no exception."

"I know I've been fortunate. Peace is certainly something that many in my realm take for granted. I will do everything in my power to get your realm the peace it deserves."

By Erilena! When did I become lucky enough to deserve her?

"Healer of kingdoms," I said.

"What?"

"You are a healer of kingdoms."

She touched my forehead. "Do you have a fever?"

"I am serious. You healed me. You healed Jeondar's father, and now he will heal Nerethien. Mythorne is a blight. You see the terrible symptoms of his rule in his people's eyes. They suffer. They fear. When he's gone, you will give them hope, the medicine they need to believe in a brighter future."

"You give me too much credit. I've only done what anyone else in my place would have done."

"Doubtful."

I leaned over and kissed her lips, and too quickly my gratefulness turned into desire. I climbed on top of her, spreading her legs apart, and settled myself there. When I leaned to kiss her, she welcomed me with the warmth of her tongue and the scent of her immediate arousal.

I would oblige.

CHAPTER 32
DANIELLA

I sighed as he settled between my legs. His lips crashed against mine, his tongue sweeping across the length of my bottom lip. He tasted of the dinner wine, except infinitely sweeter. He abandoned my mouth to trace a path down my neck. He wiggled the tip back and forth, exerting pressure in a very suggestive way as he kept going down, down, down. Heat flooded my core, as he started pushing up my gown, and though I craved to feel the pressure of his lips against that aching nub in my center, the craving for something else was much stronger.

"Nah-ah." I shook my head and forced him to lie down on his back. I had to push on his shoulders when he tried to sit up, resisting me.

"What is this about, melynthi? Is there something we need to discuss?"

"Discuss? No, nothing like that," I said as I kneeled between his legs.

His eyes widened. He was always so hungry that he'd not once allowed me to enjoy him in this manner, but tonight I would brook no argument.

"Let me pleasure you first."

He tried to sit up again.

"Nope." I waggled my finger at him, then proceeded to untie his sleeping trousers, which were tented beautifully, stretching the fabric.

He made a sound in the back of his throat. "I don't think I can—"

"Shh, would you be quiet? You promised to let me make my own claim whenever I wanted, remember?"

He grunted in disapproval.

I sat back on my heels, placed my hands on my hips, and looked down at him. "This will give me untold pleasure. Do you want to deny me?"

"Never, melynthi." He fisted the sheets and pushed his hips forward to give me better access.

I squirmed as a jolt of pleasure thundered down my belly. My hands trembled from excitement as I finished undoing the lace and freeing his impressive length.

He was superb, thick and with a large head. The underside was flushed and throbbing, begging to be licked. A bead of moisture shone at the very tip. I held him in my hand. He purred deeply in his chest, his features turning sharp. I lapped up the moisture.

"Dani," he purred my name.

I licked my lips, then took him in, making him hiss as his eyes closed. Opening wider, I took him in further. All six-foot-three of him shuddered.

"Let me take you," he growled.

I moved my head from side to side to tell him *no* at the same time that I lapped the length of him.

"That would be excellent," I said. "But this is delicious too, and I can't stop."

Working up and down, I sucked and licked his girth.

My jaw ached as I exerted myself, but it was impossible to be thorough. He was too big. Still, I did my best, taking him in all the way, out for a brief moment to lick at his full length, then repeating the process again, loving how he felt.

Making eye contact, I paused at his tip, taking him in my mouth, then wrapping a hand around the base. All at once, he was hard as steel and soft as velvet. My hand glided up and down while my mouth took in what it could.

He started moving back and forth, eyes tightly shut. The sounds he was making drove me crazy. He was putty in my hands. I moaned in response, a twinge of pleasure electrifying my core. My hand moved faster as I kept sucking.

As he tensed, my legs clenched together, and just when I thought I would climax from the way he throbbed, he bit his lower lip to contain what would have surely been a roar of pleasure.

I tasted him fully, savoring the way he shuddered under my care. My powerful prince, my king, my mate reduced to nothing. I pulled back a little with one final lick. He practically whimpered.

Witchlights, he's delicious.

"Melynthi, you are . . ." but he didn't finish. Instead, he switched spots with me, flipping me onto my back so fast that I got dizzy. "Time to repay the favor," he rumbled, then put his tongue to good use.

CHAPTER 33
DANIELLA

The next morning, I woke up in the chamber assigned to me. It seemed as if I'd slept, but I didn't feel rested at all. I only slid out of bed when our secret knock came at the door. I let Arabis in, who was carrying a tray with tea and what looked like cookies.

"Good morning, my lady," she said.

I mouthed *good morning* but only gave an audible grunt. Royals here, and perhaps everywhere, weren't known by their manners toward their servants.

"One of King Mythorne's servants said to inform you that he will be occupied most of the day. He said to make yourself comfortable, and that this afternoon you're invited to join his hunting party in the castle grounds. He said it is a previous engagement with several attendants, which he cannot cancel despite his special guests, but he wishes fervently that you'll attend."

Fervently? Really?

I made as if to gag myself. "I see. Well, that is kind of him to invite us. I never imagined he would be so considerate."

Arabis pressed her lips together to restrain a laugh.

I served myself tea and bit into a cookie. It wasn't half bad, much better than anything they'd served last night for dinner. I couldn't place the main flavor, but it was sort of minty.

"What shall we do with our free time?" I mused.

She shrugged.

"I guess I'll talk to Father. He may have some ideas. Honestly, I wouldn't mind staying in, reading a book. I'm tired from so much travel."

"Not a bad idea, my lady."

I mimed drinking one of Naesala's potions and pointed at a clock on the wall, trying to indicate that staying in would buy us additional time—not to mention that I would get to stay in my body. She nodded, seeming to understand.

Taking my teacup and another cookie, I gestured toward the door. "I think I'll propose that to Father."

Catching on, Arabis went to the door and peeked into the hall. Once she made sure the coast was clear, she waved me ahead, and we slunk to Kalyll's room. Jeondar was there. He'd brought a similar tray with the same cookies for Kalyll, but he hadn't touched them. He was pacing, appearing worried.

"We should inform the others of this hunting party," he said.

Jeondar nodded. "I agree. We might have an opportunity against Mythorne. If he gets separated, we could ambush him."

"Ambush him? What are you talking about?" I said. "We have a plan. We should stick to it."

Kalyll frowned. "The longer we stay under Mythorne's roof, the more likely we are to be discovered."

"So far he's buying the ruse. We have enough elixir for

another day. Maybe more if we don't take a new batch until it's time to meet him later today."

"I'm worried our plan won't work," Kalyll admitted. "He is too distrustful, so if we have an opportunity out there, we will take it. Inform the others to be ready."

"You don't trust that I can get it done." I set my teacup on the untouched tray.

"It isn't that."

"You don't sound so convincing." I stopped right in front of him and glowered.

He held my gaze.

I narrowed my eyes, unblinking.

"All right," he broke our staring contest. "I'm worried that if you actually manage to get close, he will hurt you. We don't know what magical powers he possesses."

"For all we know he has none." I threw my hands up in the air, frustrated. "We've already been through this."

"Yes, we have been through this, and we concluded that he's likely very powerful based on what his son could do. You do remember all the people he killed in Elyndell?"

"Fine! Risk the others, but I will continue trying to get close to him."

"Daniella, perhaps you should stay here and not risk going hunting."

"Are you kidding me?"

"Well, you have no idea how to shoot a bow and arrow."

"And you don't know how to kill someone with a single touch. I'm going."

"He'll expect you to *actually hunt*."

"I'll figure something out."

"Please."

"What?" I lifted my chin. "Did you forget your promise?"

"Fine. You keep trying, but the others are coming too."

Despite his acquiescence, I knew I would pay for contradicting him in front of the others. His eyes had grown dark and his features had acquired Wölfe's sharp edges. If he intended to scare me, he was mistaken. I loved it anytime his dark side came out to play. Trying to tame him was quickly becoming a fun challenge.

So, in the end, the plan was for Kalyll and me to stay in our chambers in order to save our potion supply, while Jeondar and Arabis went to inform the others of the new developments. I hoped we would accomplish our goal today, but just in case we didn't, saving our resources was critical. With their constant comings and goings, Jeondar and Arabis were using more of the potion than Kalyll and me, so we needed to be thrifty.

Twenty minutes before we were due to meet Mythorne, I drank the potion and once I endured the transformation, I changed into a comfortable tunic, leggings, and a pair of supple brown boots. I tied Mylendra's red curls back to keep them away from my face and applied a light layer of makeup.

Kalyll came to my door back in the earl's shape. He still appeared angry at me, but he had no right. He had promised to let me fight, and I wasn't going to let him change his mind. If I didn't stand up for myself, his overprotectiveness would likely lead him to treat me like a porcelain doll, and I didn't want a future where I was constantly stifled.

We made our way to the same garden Mythorne had shown me last night. In daylight, the many plants looked even stranger than under the moonlight, displaying features that I hadn't noticed before: shining thorns, leaves with veins that seemed to run with red blood, translucent bark, exposed roots that writhed toward the sun, and more.

Jeondar and Arabis were waiting for us there, ready to guide us to the meeting place the servants had informed them about.

"Did you contact the others?" Kalyll asked them in a low whisper.

They nodded.

"Run into any trouble?"

"Someone tried to follow us, but we shook them off easily."

"Mythorne's surely paranoid," I said.

"And with good reason." Kalyll squeezed my hand as if to indicate how deadly I could be. He seemed to have come to terms with the fact that I was doing this. "Don't you think?"

I smiled and had to agree that the Unseelie King had a right to be distrustful.

We tracked down one side of the castle. The path was steep and narrow and flanked by thorny bushes on either side. As we exited through an iron gate, the din of voices filled the air.

In a strip of clear ground, between the imposing wall and the edge of the woods, a large group of people milled about. I hadn't expected so many guests, including a good number of Mythorne's personal guards, all dressed in his livery, their suspicious eyes intent on the woods.

Already, this didn't bode well for Kalyll's new plan. I raised one eyebrow at him, feeling smug. It seemed the best chance of getting to the Unseelie King still rested with me.

"You exasperate me sometimes, woman," he hissed in my ear.

"Happy to oblige." I gave him a cheeky smile.

Jeondar and Arabis slipped away, and I knew they would soon find their way into the woods, where they would hope for an opportunity to attack.

"Ah, here you are," Mythorne said, pulling away from a group of stuffy-looking males who eyed us suspiciously as if they suspected we'd come to eat their dinner. Not for the first time, I wondered how many others had tried to throw their daughters at the Unseelie King, and yet, he had accepted no one—not officially anyhow. He'd had a son, and it was rumored that he had other offspring. I couldn't imagine living as long as he had and having no one to share my life with. Or perhaps, it was my shortsighted human perspective that made me look at things that way. Perhaps the thought of being attached to the same person for so long should be a scary thought instead. Would I get tired of Kalyll after a hundred years? Two hundred? More? Something told me I wouldn't.

"Allow me to introduce you to a few members of my council." Mythorne proceeded to spew a bunch of names that ran together and I would never remember.

I noted how he didn't keep his distance from them or anyone else for that matter, though he still was careful to stay far away from Kalyll and me.

While everyone was introduced, I acted meekly as they would expect a female to do, and allowed Kalyll to make niceties with them, something he did flawlessly, all while cataloging every single person he met, an undertaking that was evident in his calculating eyes.

I was watching him closely when his eyes flashed, growing

dark and feral, evidence that his shadowdrifter blood was stirring. I followed his gaze to find Cardian joining the group alongside none other than Varamede.

Surreptitiously, I joined Kalyll's side and wrapped my hand around his wrist, tugging slightly on his life force. My chest tightened as I took in his energy. He blinked and looked down at me.

I got on my tiptoes and whispered in his ear. "Come to your senses. You will ruin everything if you do something stupid now." I pulled away and laughed, as if I'd made a joke.

He inhaled sharply and forced a laugh to match mine, though his eyes seemed to have trouble focusing as he dealt with the sudden loss of energy.

"Are you going to behave?" I asked, pretending to arrange his already pristine collar.

He managed one nod.

With my hand still around his wrist, I allowed the energy I'd taken to flow back into him. Color returned to his cheeks, and we smiled at each other, acting as if we were just having a cute father-and-daughter moment. When I peeled away from him, however, I noticed Mythorne's inquisitive dark eyes examining us carefully.

I waved at him coquettishly, all the while trying to hold back a scream and tamping down the urge to run away. Mythorne smiled thinly and returned to his conversation with a tall female dressed in leather armor. *Sheesh*, what did she think we were hunting? Dragons? No one else was dressed like that.

Kalyll's gaze kept wandering to Varamede. He could curb his desire for revenge when it came to his brother, but the thunderlord wasn't that lucky. When I'd been lost in my dark sleep, Kalyll had promised to avenge me, and it seemed he still expected someone to pay for the pain they'd caused me.

"The horses are ready as is everything else," an attendant announced, gesturing toward a group of horses aligned along the edge of the forest. "The weapons are over there. There are swords, bows and arrows, and spears. Each weapon is spelled to keep count of how many mud-spriggans you kill. The winner will receive a special prize from King Mythorne."

A wave of questions went over the crowd as they all wondered what the prize could be. For my part, I was trying to remember if I'd ever heard of mud-spriggans. Whatever they were, judging by Kalyll's reaction at their mention, it wasn't the type of creature he would use for sport. I wanted to ask him about them, but people had clustered together, and I was afraid of being overheard.

Everyone hurried to retrieve a weapon from the set of wooden racks that held them. Kalyll chose a sword, and as he weighed it in his hand with a glint in his eyes, my mouth went dry. I really hoped it hadn't occurred to him to do something heroic. I quickly chose a spear. It made the most sense considering that I didn't know how to hold a sword or a bow and arrow properly.

"A spear?" Mythorne asked. "I thought you would choose a bow and arrow."

"I would like a challenge today." I shifted my attention to him and smiled. "What is your weapon of choice?"

He stepped in front of the rack, examined the swords, then pulled one out. He sliced it in the air, making it sing and demonstrating his skill as he twirled it and cut at the air.

"A king shall always choose a sword," he declared, giving Kalyll a sidelong glance.

"Rightly so." I tried to look at him with admiration, but I feared I was coming up short.

"Will you ride with me, Lady Mylendra?" Mythorne moved toward the remaining horses. We were the stragglers, and the rest were already scattering on horseback, weaving their way through the thick woods in search of mud-spriggans.

"I will be delighted." My heart beat faster. Perhaps it wasn't such a bad idea that the others were here. The thought of Jeondar, Cylea, Kryn, Silver, and Arabis hiding somewhere in the forest gave me a modicum of confidence that set my mind at ease. Besides, Kalyll was here, he would be riding with us too.

"Earl Qierlan." Cardian rode from the side on a dappled steed. "It would be my honor if you join me. There are a few war-related issues I would like to discuss with you."

Kalyll froze, looking up at his brother, then at me. "Perhaps we can talk later. I want to accompany my daughter."

Mythorne stepped forward. "Earl, didn't we go over this last night? I promise your daughter is safe with me."

It was clear in Kalyll's expression that he didn't want to let me go alone with the Unseelie King but refusing would be an outright insult at this point. Besides, discussing the war should be one of the earl's priorities.

"I'll be all right, Father," I said. "I assure you, King Mythorne was a complete gentleman last night."

Kalyll grunted as if he didn't believe that for a second. Tension crackled in the air, especially when Varamede trotted closer.

"Very well, King Cardian," Kalyll said, "my daughter has a spear after all, and I am very interested in hearing about the role the Seelie Court will play in the war."

I walked to one of the three remaining horses, a brown gelding that appeared diminutive next to the black stallion that stood next to it. A page boy held the stallion's reins, which was clearly meant for Mythorne.

As I reached my horse, I tried to catch Kalyll's eyes, but he never looked my way. A seed of fear embedded itself deep in my gut. What if he tried to attack Varamede? If he did, could he take him? God, this wasn't how things were supposed to go.

My horse was beautiful with a blond mane and tail. I wondered briefly if Mylendra would be able to mount while holding the spear, then decided it didn't matter because there was no way *I* could do it.

"Hold this for me." I thrust the spear toward the page boy. He took it, eyes cast to the ground. Once I mounted, I took the spear back, resisting the urge to try different grips to find the most comfortable one. Instead, I tried to look as if I knew what the hell I was doing.

Mythorne got on his horse in one swift motion, looking just as capable as Kalyll in the saddle, which was saying a lot. He pulled the reins left, the opposite direction Kalyll was going. I took my time, glancing through the trees to my right, where Kalyll's figure retreated. I had wanted to prove myself. Well, here was my chance.

I spurred my horse forward, following the path Mythorne's stallion was carving. Something moved in my hair, and I nearly swatted at it, thinking it was a bug until I heard a familiar voice.

"You won't be alone, Dani," Larina whispered.

"What are you doing here?!" I hissed.

"You didn't think I was going to stay at the inn while everyone else came to help, did you?"

"That was the plan."

Mythorne glanced over his shoulder, frowning.

I leaned forward and patted the horse's neck. "You're so soft and pretty," I said in a whisper.

His upper lip twitched, and he faced forward again, his expression signaling that he thought I was foolish for talking to a horse.

"Stay hidden no matter what, Larina. Okay?" I didn't want her to get hurt.

She didn't reply.

"Please don't do anything stupid."

"I won't."

She was so tiny and fragile and could get hurt so easily. Then again, she was a pro at going unnoticed.

CHAPTER 34
KALYLL

The reins creaked in my hands as I twisted them, and pain shot up my jaw from the force of my bite. It was all I could do not to leap from the horse and wrap my hands around Varamede's throat.

—*Kill him*, Wölfe said in my mind.

Patience, I replied.

In this, we were in agreement. The thunderlord had to die, but the time wasn't right. Mythorne was the priority, and once he was dead, Varamede would get my full attention.

—*Cardian too*, that familiar dark force whispered inside my head.

He will live, for our mother's sake.

—*Bah.*

Wölfe didn't mind being a monster, but I wasn't ready to abandon all sense of morality, even if my brother deserved to share Varamede's fate.

"What news of the troops?" I forced myself to ask. "Are they with King Naeduin?"

Cardian ignored my question. "A nice day for hunting mud-spriggans, wouldn't you say?"

I grunted and made no comment. Making sport of the

creatures was despicable and exactly what I would expect from someone like Mythorne. The creatures were suspected to be self-aware. They exhibited interesting behavior and were known for their rudimentary use of tools. When left alone, they were harmless and even helpful, keeping vermin in check. But when they were mistreated or their land encroached on, they turned territorial and mischievous, becoming pests.

"Indeed," I responded, sure that Earl Qierlan wouldn't mind making sport of the minor folk.

"It's been some time since I enjoyed your company?" Cardian said.

I narrowed my eyes, pretending to search for prey in the underbrush. I had no idea when Cardian had seen the earl last. Was this a test? Did this mean he suspected we might not be who we said we were? If I answered incorrectly, he would have his proof. So I didn't say anything. Instead, I simply shrugged.

"You lied to me," Cardian said with sudden anger. "And I'm not happy about it."

What is this about? Was it part of the test? Or had the earl actually done something to anger Cardian?

I turned on my saddle and faced him full-on. "I thought we were here to hunt, not to discuss platitudes."

"Platitudes? That is what you call your betrayal."

I ignored him once more and urged my steed forward, twirling my sword in a way that displayed the considerable skill I knew the earl to possess. My intent was for the action to appear threatening in hopes that Cardian would shut his mouth. Though it was very likely a waste of time. He had his thunderlord by his side, and he always felt untouchable when Varamede was around.

"You promised me Mylendra," Cardian spat. "And now you're here, slithering about Mythorne's feet, thrusting her at him instead."

So this was it then, the reason why Cardian had appeared so upset when we first arrived. This was no test then.

"From one snake to another," I said, "slithering is what we do. Not to mention betrayal."

Cardian's upper lip trembled. I knew the tic very well. It manifested when he was angry, fit to burst.

Warily, I glanced sideways at Varamede, who appeared alert to any command from my brother. "I don't owe you anything, *boy*. Once I realized who was really in control, I knew what I had to do."

"And what of the gold I gave you," Cardian barked.

Gold? There had been a bribe involved? Cardian had paid for a wife? Worse yet, the earl, my father, had literally sold his daughter. And I'd thought they couldn't get any lower.

My fingers cracked as my hand closed into a tight fist. I looked at it as it trembled. The action had been involuntary— or more to the point, caused by Wölfe.

—Rip his head off.

I took a deep breath, regaining a shred of calm, barely enough to keep me from letting my dark side erupt.

"You will pay it back," Cardian said. "Every last bit of it. Three thousand gold coins."

Three thousand?! This had to be a joke.

Cardian's gaze roved over my face, expectantly.

"Sure," I said. "Come by Thellanora one day, and you can have it back."

He scoffed, then smiled crookedly, leaning down to pet the thick column of his mount's neck. "It seems you don't mind paying me back with interest, *Earl Qierlan*," Cardian said.

Fuck.

The clever asshole had alluded to a much larger sum than he'd actually given the earl, knowing that he should balk at being asked for more.

His eyes flicked in Varamede's direction, and he gave a curt nod. The thunderlord whipped a hand in my direction and released a bolt of electricity, aimed directly at my chest.

CHAPTER 35
DANIELLA

A creature the size of a Great Dane slashed across the path in front of us, running from the cover of one bush to another. It seemed to be made from broken branches and mud and had a huge rack on top of its head like a buck. Lichen hung from its body in strips, and it moved half upright and half on four legs.

"Our first mud-spriggan," Mythorne said, urging his horse forward. The animal's hooves tamped down a group of flowering plants, kicking back black soil.

I followed, racking my brain, trying to figure out how I was going to manage to get my hands on the bastard.

Ahead, the bushes ran out, giving way to a clearing and a tall outcrop of rocks. The creature looked right and left, and finding itself trapped, whirled, and bared its teeth at us with a growl.

I came to a halt behind Mythorne, who dismounted, sword in hand.

What the hell? It didn't seem wise to face such a creature face to face. With luck, it would tear the Unseelie King to pieces and save me a heap of trouble.

Mythorne twirled his sword. I couldn't see his face as his

back was to me, but his smooth movements telegraphed his overconfidence.

The mud-spriggan sidestepped, drool dripping from its jaws. Its eyes were full of calculation and hatred, and something in its depths made me look closer. I gasped as the strangest thought entered my mind.

Those are not the eyes of an animal.

There was intelligence behind those large yellow orbs, and maybe . . . resignation, like it knew it didn't stand a chance against its opponent.

Mythorne advanced, his movements lithe, his blade glinting in the weak rays of sunshine that managed to seep through the heavy canopy.

Out of the corner of my eye, I noticed a slight movement in the bushes to our left. My horse stomped the ground, snorting. I scanned the heavy brush, searching for the source of the sound, and noticed a second pair of yellow eyes. They met mine. Another mud-spriggan. It bared its teeth, ready to lunge at me. I shook my head and mouthed the word *no*.

The creature paused. It understood I meant it no harm.

I inclined my head in Mythorne's direction, inviting it to help its friend, and for an instant, I thought I saw gratitude in its expression. Quickly, it turned its attention to the Unseelie King, who had corralled the creature against the rock wall.

The second creature lunged from the bushes, maw angled perfectly toward Mythorne's neck. As it attacked, two things happened at once. Mythorne twirled toward the newcomer, his sword held at an angle, and my horse reared back, kicking its front legs toward the sky.

My one-handed grip on the reins slipped, and I was thrown

backward off my horse, dropping the spear as I futilely attempted to hold on. With a scream, I sailed through the air and watched as Mythorne's blade sliced the lunging mud-spriggan in half. In the same motion, he finished twirling and stabbed the other one as it cowered against the rocks. All before I thudded to the ground.

My spine and skull cracked as I crashed against rocky soil. A warm feeling slid down the back of my head. Blood. I cried out once more, baring my teeth in pain. My first instinct was to allow healing magic to course through my body, but I remembered in time that Mylendra didn't have such powers. My second instinct was to search for Larina. Was she all right? Had I flattened her when I hit the ground? Oh, God! I was near panic when I noticed her hiding in a bush.

Mythorne walked in my direction. I watched him through narrowed eyes. Looking down at me, he stabbed his sword into the ground and scanned me without a shred of sympathy in his eyes.

"Are you all right, Lady Goren?" he asked in a half-amused tone.

I almost said *yes* and attempted to stand on my own. I didn't want to give the asshole the satisfaction of seeing me suffer in any way, but then I realized this was the perfect opportunity to lure him closer.

"No, I'm not all right." Working up some tears, I slid my hand into my hair and touched the wound. I pulled it back and looked at it, blinking to force out the tears. "I'm bleeding. By Erilena, I'm bleeding." I sounded a little hysterical, which was exactly my goal.

Mythorne huffed, appearing aggravated. He glanced back at

the fallen mud-spriggans, seeming mad that I'd ruined his game.

With a sigh of resignation, he looked down at me again. "Can you walk?"

"I . . . I don't know." I tried to push up on my elbows, then fell back again, though it wasn't all a show. My head was spinning. Maybe I had a minor concussion. I'd knocked my head pretty good.

Grudgingly, he offered me a hand. He was wearing gloves, but I couldn't complain. This was progress. I reached out, and he seized my wrist and yanked me up with one strong tug that threatened to dislocate my shoulder. As soon as I was on my feet, he let me go. I swayed precariously and threw my arms out in an effort to keep my balance, except I started to fall again.

I thought Mythorne would let me collapse, but in the last instant, he wrapped an arm around my waist and held me in place. I closed my eyes and pressed my forehead to his chest until the dizziness passed. Slowly, I glanced up to meet his gaze.

He was looking at me strangely, a deep frown cutting across his forehead. His gaze fell to my lips and quickly moved back up. It seemed he found Mylendra pleasing, after all.

"It seems . . . you're in need of a healer." His voice was halting for the first time.

"I am." I sounded pathetic, to say the least, but it seemed my helplessness was bringing out his male protective instincts.

My hands inched up his arms. If I could wrap them around his neck . . . I licked my lips and blinked slowly.

"I feel like such a fool," I said. "That creature came out of nowhere. I would've struck it with my spear if the horse hadn't . . . Oh, to think it might've hurt you. I'm so sorry."

"I was never in any danger. I promise you." Now his voice was husky.

I have you now, I thought, my hands moving up with more confidence.

He inclined his head to one side, mouth parting, and leaned closer.

Oh God, he's going to kiss me.

Bile rose up my throat, and it was all I could do to keep an inviting expression on my face. My hands raced toward his neck. If I could touch him there before his lips reached mine, the sacrifice of kissing this monster would not be necessary.

My fingers were only an inch from his neck when a deafening thunderclap resonated through the forest.

CHAPTER 36
KALYLL

Melting into shadows, I slithered over the ground, dodging Varamede's attack. The bolt hit the ground, sent a spray of dirt into the air, and set a nearby tree on fire.

"Where did he go?" Cardian demanded. "There!"

Varamede released another bolt of lightning. This time, getting away was far easier as I was already nothing but shadows. I didn't know if such an attack could harm me in this state, but I wasn't going to risk finding out.

"Get him!" Cardian ordered.

Another bolt exploded a few inches behind me. A dry shrub ignited with a *whoosh*.

Heading in Varamede's direction, I zigzagged along the ground.

"You're too slow," Cardian barked, his horse backing away and rearing its head.

I sensed anger from the thunderlord, but not toward me . . . toward Cardian. It couldn't be easy receiving orders from someone so useless. But he had chosen this path, and in so doing, he'd meddled with the wrong person. The moment he attacked my mate, he signed his death sentence.

My shadowy form slid over the ground at a prodigious

speed. Varamede tried to back away as he shot multiple bursts of lightning at the ground, filling the air with dust and the smell of ozone.

When I was a couple of feet from him, he finally realized his powers were nothing against me in this form. Whirling on his heel, he ran, but it was a useless attempt. I was much faster, and when I reached him—my shadows coalescing around his feet—I dismissed the darkness and invited the beast.

I rose from the ground, the shadows forming an insubstantial body that quickly solidified. Releasing a powerful roar, I reached out with a clawed hand and took hold of Varamede's shoulder. Yanking him back, I slammed him against the ground and pounced on him. His eyes went wide as I opened my maw and let out a second roar.

My hand tightened around his neck, claws digging into his flesh. In response, he electrified his entire body, doing his best to repel me. As the current hit me, my limbs spasmed, but it wasn't to his advantage. Instead, my hold grew tighter, and warm blood spilled from his neck as my claws punctured an artery. He opened his mouth, making a gurgling sound, feet thrashing behind me.

My teeth were clenched of their own accord, and I bore down on him even as his electric power coursed through me, singeing my hair, and filling the air with its burnt scent. As the thunderlord's life dimmed from his eyes, I was vaguely aware of hooves pounding the ground in retreat.

By degrees, Varamede's power diminished as did my body spasms. We remained locked for a few more beats until he went utterly still and his power released me. My tensed muscles and joints unhinged. I rolled off him and hit the ground.

I stared at the quickly darkening sky through a gap between the thick leaves overhead. The beast's senses were sharper than my own, and the sound of Cardian's retreating horse still pounded in my ears.

—*Get up!* A deep voice, Wölfe's voice, echoed in my head. *Go after him.*

I rolled over and got on hands and knees. I had morphed into a shape close to my own, but to reach him I would be better served by a proper wolf.

Lunging into the air, I took off after my brother. As I sailed forward, I morphed once more. Large paws hit the ground running, my sensitive ears pointed at the retreating sounds. As trees rushed by, I passed a couple of hunters from Mythorne's party. Thinking it good sport to kill the biggest beast, they gave chase.

Arrows zinged by me and embedded themselves in the ground. I weaved through the trees to make their job harder, all the while focused on my target. I could see Cardian now. He was forty yards ahead, glancing back over his shoulder as he mercilessly beat his horse with his crop, demanding more speed.

—*There is no beast fast enough that can save you from me, little brother.*

My claws tore the ground, sending chunks flying back. A spear thwacked mere inches from me and stabbed a patch of grass. I veered left around a thick tree with low branches. One of the riders behind me didn't think much of my path choice, never considering that I was a creature capable of making intelligent decisions. Too late, he realized his mistake. A quick glance over my shoulder showed me the male attempting to duck and failing. A branch knocked him clean off his horse, and as he fell, his head smashed against a rock with a satisfying crunch.

I was closer to Cardian now, and I could see the desperation on his face every time he glanced back. He knew who was after him, and the reckoning that was coming his way.

No, we will not kill him.

—He deserves to die.

Death will be too swift a punishment.

—You will not trick me into offering him any sort of mercy but that which my teeth and claws can offer.

I could almost feel the metallic taste of blood in my mouth as Wölfe yearned to clasp his jaws around Cardian's neck. But there was no use in arguing. Words would not sway my darker side.

The *twang* of an arrow sounded behind me. I dodged to the right, avoiding it. It bounced against a tree and fell into a bush.

When the tail of Cardian's horse tickled my maw, I leaped, ramming my weight against the animal's hindquarters and knocking it off kilter. The horse cried out as it tumbled to the ground, sending its rider soaring through the air. As soon as my brother slammed against the roots of a tree I was on him.

The remaining pursuer brought his steed to a stop and nocked an arrow. My head jerked in his direction, and I met his gaze as I slowly morphed into a half-Fae creature. He gasped at the sight of me and hesitated for only a moment, then aimed again.

"You will stay out of this if you know what's good for you," I said in a voice that sounded like rocks tumbling inside a collapsing cave.

Cardian whimpered beneath me, and the male thought better of it. Putting the arrow back in its quiver, he urged his horse back the way he'd come and quickly disappeared, leaving me to deal with the biggest weasel I'd ever known. I had no doubt the rider would soon be back with others, but I didn't need long to deal with this coward.

"You won't get away with this." Cardian's voice trembled as he spoke.

"It doesn't sound as if you believe yourself," I rumbled in his face.

My clawed hand wrapped around his neck, slowly tightening.

He kicked with all his strength, but my own brute force made his attempt appear childlike. When he realized the futility of his efforts, he changed tactics.

"You would kill your own brother?" His voice was pleading now, and his eyes full of the sickening tears he used to deliver when he was a child and found himself in need of sympathy.

"And why not? You would have killed me. The only difference is that I will do it with my own hands, and you instead sent Mythorne's son to do it, and then Varamede."

My grip around his neck tightened until my sharp claws drew blood. Something wet and warm spread between his legs and the stench of urine filled the air. Oddly enough, it was my disgust for his pathetic existence that gave me the strength to overcome my dark side.

I released him. He went limp with relief.

"You are not worth the air you breathe," I spat. "Death would be such an easy way out for you, which is all your life has ever been. Instead, you will spend the rest of your days in a prison cell, making good use of your hands."

At that, he frowned, but I didn't elaborate. He would find out his fate soon enough. He would not be idle. He would have to work for his meals and the luxury of a clean cell.

But I'd wasted enough time with him. I had to find Daniella, except I couldn't leave Cardian like this. I had to make sure he didn't get away.

Grabbing the lapels of his jacket, claws tearing into the fabric, I hoisted him up, then towed him up the tree. I climbed using only one hand, pushing with my clawed feet, tearing off chunks of bark as I went. When I reached the top, and the branches started bending toward the ground with our weight, I let him go.

"You'd better hold on, *little brother*. Move too much and the branch might break." I started climbing down.

He hugged the branch, wrapping his arms and legs around it. "You can't leave me here."

"I can do whatever I want with you," I growled back. "You're only alive because Mother wouldn't wish me to feel remorse for murdering my own blood. Though I'm not so sure I would feel any, so don't tempt me or I might change my mind."

Practically sliding down the length of the tree, barely using my claws to slow down my descent, I made it back to the ground. As I turned, I heard hooves headed in my direction. The rider back with reinforcements, I was sure.

Well, I wasn't going to stay here for them, and I wasn't worried about them helping Cardian. He was too far up. Besides, I doubted Mythorne's court would have any sympathy for him, though they might be entertained by the sight.

I leaped over a row of bushes and started in the direction that the Unseelie King had taken Daniella.

"It was right here," I heard the rider who had chased me tell the others. "We should fan out and find it. We can't allow foul shadowdrifters in our land."

"Oh, thank Erilena!" Cardian exclaimed from up the tree. "Someone help me get down, please."

I smirked and kept going, making sure to remain hidden from view, treading silently over the underbrush.

But in the next instant, the need for stealth became a luxury. A cry rent the air.

It was Daniella!

I shifted into a wolf and ran at full pelt.

CHAPTER 37
DANIELLA

As soon as the thunderclap reverberated through the forest, Mythorne's gloved hand wrapped around my neck.

He lifted me off the ground as if I were nothing but a child, and held me aloft and at a distance. Panic burst through my veins, and for a shocked moment, I could do nothing more than kick and try to scream again, which was impossible with his fingers digging into my windpipe.

Only a rasp came out as I struggled to take in air.

Then I remembered, I wasn't helpless. I had power . . . the ability to make him wither like a cut flower left in the sun. Bringing my hands to his wrist, I started pushing his sleeve up, peeling away layers to expose his flesh.

His eyebrows drew together as he tried to make sense of my actions, and as I'd nearly managed to uncover his arm, he dropped me and backed away.

As my feet hit the ground, I bent my knees and went in a crouch.

"What are you?" he demanded.

"I am your reckoning," I said and leaped in his direction.

At the same time, Larina flew up from the bush where she'd been hiding and came flying at a prodigious speed.

Moving with the kind of agility I'd only seen in Kalyll, the Unseelie King sidestepped me, easily avoiding me. But he wasn't counting on a tiny pixie appearing out of nowhere. More yet, she was carrying a spear—the one she'd taken from Shadow the day she tried to take Kryn's eye out for doubting her loyalty. And it seemed Larina had taken a page from the sprite's book, attempting the same attack.

Time slowed. The whir of Larina's wings filled my ears. The tip of her needle-like spear glinted. Mythorne's foot settled on the ground as he finished the quick maneuver that had helped him steer clear of me.

Too late, he spotted the second attacker, and before he had time to react, Larina's weapon embedded itself in his eye with a *squish*.

Mythorne growled in pain and blindly batted a hand at the air, hitting Larina and sending her sailing across the clearing. With a delicate *thump*, she crashed against a wide tree trunk and dropped to the ground.

"No!" I ran to her side and dropped to my knees, immediately calling healing energy to the tips of my fingers. "Larina."

Fingers hovering over her small body, I assessed her injuries and vitals. The former were extensive, but the latter . . . I got nothing.

"No, no, no. Please no."

I allowed a little bit of healing energy through my finger, just enough for someone her size. "You'll be all right. You'll be all right," I repeated, even when I knew it wasn't true, even when my skills were telling me there was nothing to be done, nothing that could repair the vast injuries her fragile body had sustained.

Tears clouded my eyes. "Why did you do that?"

Mythorne growled behind me, and I could hear his foot-steps approaching. Eyes blurred by tears, I turned to face him.

He took a few steps to the right and picked up my discarded spear, already calculating his shot. I felt so numb, I didn't react. Larina was dead, and she'd died to save me. She was my dearest friend in Elf-hame. We had grown to care for each other, and I'd imagined her by my side. I'd even daydreamed about taking her to my realm, so my family could meet her and see I was sur-rounded by wonderful people. But now she was gone.

The Unseelie King pulled the weapon back. Blood smeared the left side of his face and empty eye socket. His lips curled into a cruel grimace, and his remaining eye gleamed with malice.

He would impale me, and I would rest next to Larina—no better company.

My unexpected deliverance came in the shape of an arrow whizzing through the air, aimed directly at Mythorne's chest. Cylea!

But it couldn't have been that easy. At least not as easy as Mythorne flicking his arm and knocking the arrow down with the spear. He twirled the weapon expertly, parrying two more arrows and avoiding injury.

There was a sound to the right. My eyes cut in that direc-tion. Kryn stomped into the clearing, a sword in his hand and a wicked grin twisting his mouth.

And he was not the only one. Silver, Cylea, Jeondar, and Arabis—the last two looking like themselves again—came from behind the trees to form a circle around the Unseelie King.

At the sight of them, hope returned, and with it came fury and a deeper desire for revenge. He had hurt the people I cared about the most in this realm, and he would pay.

I stood, my entire body quivering with rage.

Mythorne's face betrayed surprise only for an instant at seeing everyone there. "It seems I wasn't as careful as I thought. You will have to tell me later how you managed to infest my lands, thus I can make sure nothing of the sort ever happens again."

Silver reclined against a tree, looking nonchalant. "Sure. We'll tell you—not that it'll do you any good. But as dying wishes go, I've heard of worse ones."

I imagined Mythorne was talking about torturing every little detail out of us before he killed us, but I liked Silver's interpretation better. It was six against one, after all. We could take him. And yet, the Unseelie King appeared unbothered. Why? What advantage did he have over us?

"Lay down your weapon." Arabis's Susurro command cut through the clearing. I felt it like a slithering caress against my skin, and if I'd had any weapons, I was sure I would have dropped them, even if the command wasn't directed at me.

"I'm afraid I can't oblige." Mythorne appeared completely oblivious to Arabis's powerful skill.

How?!

Silver pushed away from the tree, cocking his head to one side and regarding the Unseelie King with curiosity. Moving as swiftly as the wind, Silver shot a hand forward and released a stream of frigid ice. The current enveloped Mythorne, hiding him from view for a second, then shards of ice clinked to the ground, one after the other, leaving him standing there, untouched.

"What the hell?" I muttered.

"Anyone else care to try?" Mythorne glanced toward Jeondar. "How about you, Prince Lywynn? That is who you are. Correct?"

Jeondar didn't need another invitation. Hands moving in a blur, he created a large ball of fire and launched it at Mythorne. Like Silver's magic, it enveloped him, then slid to the ground, melting the ice that lay at his feet and making a puddle of water.

Mythorne laughed. "Anyone else have any magic?" He glanced sideways in my direction. "You do, don't you? What is it then? How did you kill Runik? Is it in your hands?"

"Come here and let me show you," I spat.

Using his teeth, he removed one of his gloves and extended a hand toward me. "You're welcome to try."

I took a step forward.

"Dani, no," Arabis warned.

Halting, I glared at Mythorne. He was trying to lure me closer, probably to catch me and use me as a bargaining chip. He wasn't worried about my power because he was … immune to magic? Was that it?

But if that was the case, why had he been so careful to stay away from me? Was he susceptible to some types of magic and not others? If he was, I doubted he would take a chance to find out which type I possessed. He didn't intend to let me touch him. That was clear. Either way, I was going to try.

For the pain he'd inflicted on Kalyll.

For Larina.

My hands inched closer.

"My blade can cut through your flesh as well as anyone else's," Kryn said, then lunged forward, sword high up in the air.

Mythorne twirled with grace, retrieving his sword from the ground as he made an impossible somersault. He landed, planting his feet on the ground and meeting Kryn's blade with his. The sound of metal against metal rang through the trees.

The others jumped in, surrounding and attacking the Unseelie King with everything they had, while I could do nothing more than stand off to the side, hoping one of them would strike a blow. But as the seconds ticked by and Mythorne blocked each attack and delivered several of his own—not at all overwhelmed as he should be—I quickly lost hope.

Jeondar ducked. Mythorne's blade whizzed a mere inch from the top of his head. Releasing a burst of fire, Jeondar hit his attacker's sword. The extreme heat should have melted the weapon, but it seemed the magical immunity extended to it as well.

Unexpectedly, Mythorne kicked back, slamming his foot against Silver's stomach. With the air knocked out of him, Silver staggered and crashed against the base of a tree. I ran to his side, ready to pour healing magic into him, but he shook his head.

"No. Save your energy. Shoot him with your light," he hissed with what little breath was left in him.

What light? My battery wasn't charged.

Taking huge breaths, Silver clambered to his feet, ready to go back in. Mythorne was moving just as fast, showing no sign of fatigue. In fact, he appeared even stronger, and a strange red aura had started building around him, forming an outline around his body.

"What is this?!" somebody shouted from the side, and in seconds, we were surrounded by mounted Unseelie Court guards.

Without hesitation, they jumped into the fray to aid their king. And just like that, we were the ones outnumbered. Not that Mythorne seemed to care. He was an army all unto himself.

As my friends found themselves attacked from different angles, Silver pushed me out of the way, raised his sword, and blocked an attack from a barrel-chested male. I lurched sideways, then whirled and turned to help. Our opponent held a huge ax over his head, ready to split Silver in two.

"No!" I ran and jumped onto the male's back, taking hold of a thick braid and pulling on it. His head whipped back, and I took my chance.

Fingernails digging in, I slapped my hand on the back of his neck and drew on his life force. The giant male immediately went down on his knees, then face-planted with me on top. Silver's blue eyes were wide as they met mine. He had never seen me use this power. In fact, few had.

My ribcage tightened as the energy I'd drawn settled.

"Well done," Silver said as he charged into the battle, sword raised above his head and a fierce battle cry on his lips.

Glancing around at the chaos, I wondered where Kalyll

was. That thunderclap, it had been Varamede. He must have attacked Kalyll, and I was sure it had served as a signal to Mythorne, an agreed-upon indicator that we were impostors.

I wanted to tear through the forest to find him, but I had to trust that he could take care of himself. Besides, I was needed here, and I shouldn't lose sight of our goal.

The Unseelie King.

I quickly tracked him in the melee. He was fighting Kryn, whose tremendous skill with the sword made him look like a child playing chess against the Grand Master. My chest felt tight, but I was still ready to siphon every last bit of his energy until Mythorne was nothing but an empty shell. And if that didn't work . . . then I would unleash my light and let him have it in a single blow. If I could deliver a blast straight to his head or heart, his immunity might not matter. I could only hope because I had to try something. I couldn't just watch while the others fought.

Ducking past Silver's opponent, I rushed in Mythorne's direction, my fingers flexing as if hungry for more. A guard stepped in front of me, teeth bare, sword ready to slice my throat. I ducked and tackled him, gripping his forearm in the process. His eyes rolled back, and he fell backward. I let him go before he took me down with him.

I'd barely regained my bearings when I had to twirl to avoid Cylea's opponent as he collapsed, a dagger through his eye. Luck wasn't on my side because I found myself in front of yet another guard. He stabbed his sword toward my middle, and he would have skewered me if not for Cylea's quick reflexes, which helped her block the blow. The guard forgot about me and pivoted toward the opponent who was wielding an actual weapon. And that was his mistake because I leaped forward and took hold of his arm. He face-planted on the ground before Cylea made her next move.

My ribs ached as his life force filled me, and for a moment, it was hard to draw breath. But quickly, the energy seemed to find places to fill other than my chest, and I was finally able to inhale.

"Gotta go," I said to Cylea and continued on my path toward Mythorne.

As I rushed past, Kryn noticed me out of the corner of his eye. Guessing what I was trying to do, he shuffled to one side, forcing Mythorne to turn his back on me.

My steps were light and silent, and when I found myself only a few feet from the Unseelie King, I jumped up, anchoring my hands around his neck, flesh to flesh. Teeth clenched, I worked my healing powers in reverse, determined to suck him dry.

Nothing happened.

Nothing except me flying above Mythorne's head and landing in front of him, flat on my back. A jolt of pain traveled up my spine and drove nails into my head. I winced, seeing flashes of white light, which intertwined with Kryn's agile feet as he positioned himself between me and the Unseelie freak.

A ball of fire streaked past right above me, smashing into a horned female as tall and wide as Kryn. She used a magic-imbued sword to block the attack. It split in two, but part of it struck her arm, singeing her flesh and sending the stomach-roiling scent of charred meat into the air.

I sat up groggily, my back cracking like popping corn. I struggled to get my bearings. More fire, ice, and arrows whizzed by. The din of metal against metal filled my ears. The scene before me swam.

A scream came from Cylea. I glanced in her direction and saw her limping backward, a huge gash across the side of her leg. Behind her, Arabis ordered a male to impale himself, and as he did, another one jumped on top of her, pressing a hand to her mouth before she could issue more orders. The male, who was twice her size, pulled out a dagger to stab her.

I jumped to my feet, hoping to aid her, but she bit his hand. Her lips barely moved with a command, and he drove the dagger into his own neck, splashing her face with a jet of blood. She sputtered, her bared teeth and blue eyes two beacons in her crimson-stained face.

A female that looked like the mix between an orc and a zombie came running at me, a huge mallet twirling from a leather strap wrapped around her hand, ready to do my head in. I saw my life flash by in an instant. I closed my eyes. The hiss of Silver's magic resounded in my ears. When the blow didn't come, I opened my eyes to find the female's ugly mug frozen right in front of mine.

"We're even," Silver said as he released another stream of ice at another foe, though this attack was met by a shield with enough magic to withstand the blow.

The world around me kept tumbling. Nausea hit my stomach. The blow to my head had been too much, and I was having all the symptoms of a pretty wicked concussion. But I couldn't let that stop me. There was one more thing I needed to try.

Everything went quiet. The fighting had ceased, the last of the guards dead.

A growl from Kryn drew my attention back to him. I found him on his knees, his arms trembling as he held his sword above his head. With glee in his eyes, the Unseelie King bore down on my friend, ready to kill him.

No, you won't. I was on his blind side, so he didn't see when I thrust my hands forward and unleashed all the energy I'd drawn in, catching him unprepared.

A blinding light filled the clearing. I shut my eyes and turned my head, but kept my laser beam focused on Mythorne.

Everyone around me went silent, and I felt like a mote floating in a sunbeam.

At first, there was no opposition from the Unseelie King. In fact, he felt like some sort of vessel for the magic I was pouring into him. But then something changed. Mythorne shoved back, the same way Varamede had. Even though I was blinded, I somehow understood exactly what was happening.

Mythorne was like me. He was not immune to magic. He had consumed every attack that had struck him, the way I consumed people's life force. And when I'd jumped on him and tried to draw his life force, it hadn't worked because his ability allowed him to hold on to energy until he was willing to let it go.

And now, he was.

He was full to the brim, and he'd decided it was time to return the favor.

Today, he had drunk a lot of power, and I had too, but was it enough?

I had no way of knowing. All I could do was meet his power with mine, letting it spill out to the last drop if that was what it took to kill him.

You can't do that, the voice of reason shouted in my head. *The last time you barely survived. This time you might not.*

But I couldn't back down now. I had to keep going.

Mythorne pushed, and I felt the connected streams of our energy reaching a balance, his force reaching the apex, then getting closer to me, inch by inch.

I leaned forward, teeth gritted, every last bit of power I'd stolen spewing out of me along with my hatred. For an instant, my magic shoved his back, but then he also redoubled his efforts, and he came closer still.

No. Not today.

Digging deep, deep, deep, I gathered more of myself and let the surge out.

CHAPTER 38
KALYLL

P anic and determination combined in an explosion of energy inside my chest as a burst of bright light swept through the trees. I felt it like a gust of wind, the brightness piercing my eyes sharp enough to hurt.

Blinded, I kept running forward, with only the memory of the trees to guide me forward. On that memory alone, I veered left. My side scraped against rough bark, tearing at my fur, but I didn't slow down. I barreled through, dodging sightlessly.

Soon that map inside my mind came to an end. I opened my eyes a sliver. A large dark shape loomed in front of me. In the last instant, I leaped to one side, avoiding a thick tree by mere inches. Squinting, I did little more than perceive shapes, but it was enough.

Dani, I'm coming!

As long as that light shone, I knew she lived. I had seen a similar display from her when she fought Varamede. Now, I had no idea who she was fighting or why such a violent release of power was necessary, but I would not lose her again—not to the deep slumber that had taken her before, not to anything at all.

My paws thudded against the ground as I galloped at a dizzying speed. Finally, I reached a clearing. My limited eyesight and my other senses alerted me to the presence of others. I smelled blood and fear. I heard moans and grunts, as well as a familiar voice.

"We need to do something," Jeondar was saying.

In the middle, the brilliance of a small sun dominated the scene. It was like the fight with Varamede all over again, except this time, the tableau displayed light fighting against light.

I skidded to a stop, unsure of what to do. I had no idea who she was fighting. It was impossible to tell, but whoever it was, their energy was starting to overpower hers.

NO!

She had already given so much for me, and for a realm that wasn't her own. I would not allow anyone to hurt her.

The stream of light stretched before me, its source masked by the brilliance. I tried to catch Dani's scent to determine her exact location, but there was no hint of it. What in all the realms?!

"I can get through." Kryn's voice came from the other side of the luminance.

I didn't know if he was in trouble, but I wouldn't be distracted by him or anyone. Instead, I focused on the light, opening my eyes a little wider than a mere sliver. Tears filled them. I shook my head and cleared my sight.

Then I knew: the exact shade of my mate's magic. She was to my left, and her opponent to my right.

Roaring, I pushed on my hind legs and took a mighty leap.

I crashed against an invisible barrier and fell to the ground.

What was this? There was some sort of force field around her, a barrier not of her making. I could tell by the foul feel of it.

It was Mythorne!

He was her opponent, and he had locked everyone out to ensure he could destroy her, to prevent us from coming to her aid.

I scrambled to my feet, already knowing what I must do to get to her.

Wasting no time, I let myself dissolve into shadows.

CHAPTER 39
DANIELLA

My eyes were wide open now. Light poured out of them as well as from every pore in my body. It was pure energy, a radioactive mass of power.

The brilliance around me was beautiful and absolute. I spread my arms out and wiggled my fingers. I no longer needed to direct my attack at my enemy. I could simply will it so. A feeling of ecstasy filled me. I knew it would be brief, knew that Mythorne had stored more magic than me, and I would run out first.

But it was all right.

When I was gone, he would be weak, and my friends would be here to take him. Elf-hame would be free of his tyranny, and the land would remain untouched by war. Kalyll and the others would make sure of that.

There was no better way to meet my end.

My legs faltered, and I took a step forward. I was near the edge, teetering. I only had a tiny bit more to give.

The beautiful brilliance turned murky. Shadows rose from the ground, climbing toward the sky, quickly forming a dome around me. Around Mythorne.

At first, I didn't understand what was happening, but

then that sliver of darkness that lived inside me nodded its head in acknowledgment as it sensed its match.

Kalyll was here.

I could almost taste his presence, sharp and lethal.

For a beat, I reveled in the knowledge that he was here, then that feeling of joy and relief melted into dread.

No! What are you doing?

—I'm here for you, melynthi.

Somehow we were communicating inside our minds. That part of him that lived in me heard him now.

The shadows drifted away from me, sliding down the cupola that surrounded us like a bowl trapping vermin underneath it. What was it? Some sort of force shield, I realized, and Wölfe had entered it, had drifted in like smoke under a door.

Stop! You don't know what you're doing. He drinks magic. He will consume you.

—I love you, Dani. For all your pain, I'm sorry, and for all you have given me, thank you.

Stop right this moment! I ordered.

But he wasn't listening anymore. Instead, through our link, he sent a feeling of peace and love, the idea that everything would be okay, that I would be safe and well.

No, no, no.

I scrambled to think of something. Anything. But I couldn't stop him. He was shadow and I was light, and here and now, we seemed to slip through each other's fingers.

The brilliance attacking my own was abruptly engulfed by the darkness, like Kalyll trapping Mythorne in the palm of his hand. Under the now dark and moonless sky, it took my eyes some time to adjust.

Unbalanced, I fell forward, my knees smashing into the ground.

"No!" I tried to crawl forward, a hand reaching out toward the dark, shapeless miasma that floated in the air, pulsing as the light tried to pierce through the shadows, poking, jabbing, fighting.

My friends and others stood around me, palms or knuckles pressed to their eye sockets as they tried to clear their vision, tried to get a glimpse of this incomprehensible situation: the Seelie and Unseelie King incorporeal, locked in a battle of wills while all we could do was watch.

My heart ached with desperation.

The shape throbbed, a giant heart, ten feet off the ground.

Legs wobbling, I stood and stumbled under the large mass. If I released what little was left in me, could I tear them apart? I wanted Kalyll away from Mythorne's evil, even if he was the one willingly trapping the Unseelie King. To hell with preventing war. We needed to get the fuck out of here.

I raised my hands, determined to try what little I could.

Someone swept in from the side, wrapping their arms around my waist and scooping me off the ground. The next thing I knew, I was being carried away and delivered behind the safety of a tree.

"Let me go!" I pounded on Jeondar's chest, smearing my fingers with blood. He was wounded, but I didn't care.

"Kalyll wouldn't want you doing that, Dani."

"He's not the only one who gets to decide." I shoved him hard.

He staggered back, pressing a hand to his chest.

Walking drunkenly, I rounded the tree, heading back.

The shape had shrunk considerably. A moment ago, it had been as big as a car, now it was half that size. Abruptly, it shrank further, right before my eyes, turning no bigger than a transfer token.

Before I could take another step, all that was left was a pinprick, something so impossibly small that it could hardly contain a dust mote.

"Kalyll!"

The pinprick expanded, becoming so giant that it seemed to envelop everything around us. I felt Kalyll in the brush of that power, his energy, his soul.

I reached out with everything that made me who I was and tried to snatch him from the air, lure him to me, but he slipped away like water draining through tightly cupped hands.

"Please, no, no."

A loud boom reverberated through the air as the energy that surrounded us, unable to continue expanding, ruptured. There was a flash of light that quickly dissipated, then we were left under the dark evening sky, while the shreds of shadows scattered in every direction, the only remnants from the explosion.

I cried out, desperately batting at the air, hopelessly trying to capture the little bits that floated around me.

"No. Come to me. Where are you?"

I caught a bit of shadow no bigger than ash fall and zealously hugged it to my chest, but when I looked, there was nothing there.

"Oh, God! Please." I whirled and whirled, looking up at the sky as the dark snowfall peppered my face. "Pleaaase. Not Kalyll too." Tears slid down my cheeks.

Arabis limped to my side, her eyes wavering.

"Where did he go?" I demanded.

She only shook her head, reached out a hand as if to comfort me, but I batted it away. I didn't need comfort. I needed Kalyll.

I stood in the middle of the clearing and screamed his name at the top of my lungs. He was out there. He had to be.

The dark sky and trees and people around me spun. My legs trembled. I had so little left in me I collapsed to my knees, crying. I stared at my hands, at a tiny dark flake resting between my knuckles.

The nonsensical idea that this flake was a part of Kalyll assaulted me. That powerful male couldn't be reduced to little more than dust. He was bigger than life. He was my everything.

"Dani," Cylea's voice called from the side. "We . . . need to leave."

"No!" Was she out of her mind? We couldn't leave.

"He's gone, Dani." Kryn was at my side, grabbing my arm.

"No, he's not." I pounded a fist against his chest as he dragged me to my feet.

A silver line of tears shone in his eyes. "We have to go. It's what he would want you to do."

"What the hell do you know?" I pushed him away. "How can you give up on him? We have . . . we have to . . . gather him."

He frowned and shook his head. "What are you talking about?"

"He's all around. Can't you see? Help me." I kneeled and started scooping dust into my hands.

They didn't help me. They just stood there like idiots, and

I wanted to scream loud enough to do their heads in for being so useless, but I didn't have time for that.

I was dimly aware of the sounds of approaching horses.

"Take this token." Kryn reached a hand toward Cylea. "Go with the others. I'll take care of her."

Cylea stepped to Arabis's side, and in a moment, they dematerialized.

"Fine! Leave! Cowards!" I yelled as I stuffed dust into my pockets.

Cylea was back in an instant. She took Silver next.

Kryn tightened his hand around a second transfer token, the one I'd taken from Cardian, and tried to grab my arm. I leaped out of reach and scampered away on hands and knees.

Cylea was back for Jeondar. The Summer Court prince didn't want to leave, but Kryn assured him he would get me.

"Go!" he ordered as he came at me again.

"How can you just abandon your brother? He's right here." I swept a hand over the clearing.

"You're in distress, Dani. He's gone."

"He's *not* gone."

"Then where is he, huh? Where?!"

"He's . . . he's . . ." My eyes roved the clearing. "He's . . . the shadows."

"What shadows?"

My thoughts seemed as slow as cold honey. The shadows . . . they . . . they were weak. Night had fallen, and there was no moon.

"I know what I have to do!" I exclaimed.

"Yes, you have to come with me." Kryn reached for me for

a third time, but I scurried to the side, and giving him no chance to try again, I pointed my hands toward the ground and let the last of my healing magic glow, my power helping the trees and rocks cast stronger, darker versions of themselves because without light . . . shadows can't exist.

Without me, there was no Kalyll. No Wölfe.

CHAPTER 40
KALYLL

Drifting. My consciousness growing thin. I didn't know how or when, but I'd lost track of Mythorne.

He was . . . scattered.

No, not exactly. Gone, he was gone. And my mate, she was safe.

We had done it, and now I could get back to her. We had done it.

Eager to hold Daniella in my arms, I attempted to gather myself and consolidate my shadowy form.

Nothing happened.

I reached out again.

For the first time, I realized I was the one who was scattered.

In the explosion—there had been an explosion, I now recalled—I'd been ripped into thousands of dandelion-fuzz particles. I felt each fragment disseminated all over the clearing. I writhed and twisted, trying to bring each scrap toward a common center, but they barely shifted. It was useless. I was too weak. The shadows that made up my body were fragile, insubstantial. They slipped through cracks in the ground and drifted away with the slightest stir.

I was trapped in my own darkness, unable to escape. Time slipped away and so did I. Death was closing in around me, and there was no way to fight it. No way at all.

Resignation filled me as I understood my time had come. The Envoy had promised that Daniella would be my queen, and she had been. In my heart, she was my wife. My everything.

I love you. Be well.

She would live, enjoy a full existence, free of the peril I had brought her way.

I could let go, relinquish myself to the void, knowing she would go forth, shining her light.

Surrendering, I dismissed the shadows to their homes at the base of night-darkened trees and gloomy holes between rocks.

It wasn't a bad death.

A weak light, warm and gentle, shone nearby. It flickered, nearly sputtering out. Like the finest silk, it draped over the ground, the trees, the rocks. It was the only gleam of hope under the dark sky and absent moon.

Where was it coming from?

As soon as the question formed, I knew the answer.

Daniella.

It was her glow, the luminescence of her very soul. She was weak and battered, but she burned for me, her being calling mine.

Please, you have to come back. You can't leave me.

—I . . . can't.

Yes, you can.

—I'm too w-weak.

INGRID SEYMOUR

*Dammit. I don't care. You're my mate and without you,
what kind of life will I lead? You have to get your ass back here.*
—But I'm . . . so far gone.
See my light? See me? All you have to do is follow me.
And so I did.

CHAPTER 41
DANIELLA

My strength was dwindling, and the light I'd sent out across the clearing was growing dimmer and dimmer by the second. It would not last. I knew that much. This last-ditch effort to save Kalyll had a fast expiration date.

Kalyll, I called him.

Only silence.

Please, you have to come back. You can't leave me.

—I . . . can't, he answered, sounding like the echo of a vanishing thought.

Yes, you can.

—I'm too w-weak.

Dammit. I don't care. You're my mate and without you, what kind of life will I lead? You have to get your ass back here.

—But I'm . . . so far gone.

See my light? See me? All you have to do is follow me.

I sensed the moment he gathered the last dregs of his strength and started following me. My light, even weak as it was, made the trees, the rocks, my body cast stronger versions of themselves onto the ground, and wherever those deeper shadows touched, Kalyll's scattered fragments grew stronger, denser.

Bit by bit, they drifted closer to each other, forming bigger pieces, bigger shadows. Then those pieces joined others and grew in turn.

Soon, the ground seemed alive, shifting and changing like the surface of a gloomy lake. I sensed Kryn standing next to me, still as a statue, his body casting its own shadow.

My light grew softer, and the world around us dimmer.

I panicked for an instant, then realized that the newly assembled pieces were quickly coming closer to my dying light and dimming shadow.

A thought occurred to me.

"Kryn, get down here. Next to me!"

Without asking questions, he kneeled by my side.

"Put your hand next to mine." I shook my left hand up and down to indicate where to set his up.

Quickly, he aligned his arm with mine from the tip of our pinkies through the length of our forearms.

With that done, I slowly let my light dim further, guiding the shadows inward, then I channeled all the remnants of my energy through my right hand, positioning it right about our lined-up arms.

Together, we cast a smaller, yet more concentrated shadow, a shadow under which all the scattered pieces convened, joining like drops of water that soon became a small puddle.

"This way. I see a light," someone called through the trees.

"More guards are here," Kryn hissed.

Kalyll, hurry!

To my relief, the puddle doubled, tripled, quadrupled in an instant. Then, all at once, the shadows elongated, stretching up into the air. Kryn and I reared back, watching eagerly.

The shape solidified, then Kalyll stood there. He placed a hand on his chest as if to feel he was real.

Joy and relief filled me, then what little strength had been holding me upright leaked out of me, and my entire body unhinged.

Before I hit the ground, Kalyll scooped me up and cradled me in his arms.

"Melynthi, you saved me." He buried his face in my hair, and I weakly wrapped an arm around his neck.

"I hate to interrupt this tender moment," Kryn said, "but we have to get out of here. Here." He pushed his open hand in front of Kalyll's face. It held the transfer token. "Take her to safety."

"There they are," someone screamed, then the light of torches and the beat of hooves filled the clearing.

"Go!" Kryn pressed the token into one of Kalyll's hands. "Now!"

"Wait, no. Larina. Put me down." I pushed against Kalyll's chest.

Kalyll didn't argue and set my feet on the ground. I stumbled in Larina's direction and fell to my knees. Gently, I scooped her in my hands and cradled her close to my chest. Glancing at Kalyll, I nodded. A thousand questions brimmed in his eyes, but he only wrapped an arm around me and looked over at Kryn.

"I'll be right back for you," he said.

We dematerialized in an instant. That familiar feeling of nausea assaulted me, and as our surroundings washed away in bleeding colors, I nearly lost consciousness. We reappeared at the prearranged spot, a patch of forest outside of Imbermore.

"Where is Kryn?!" Arabis demanded.

"I'm going back for him." Kalyll quickly deposited me on the ground and was gone.

"No." I reached out, batting at the air.

"I've got to go back. Give me the token." Arabis reached out for Cylea's hand.

"Kalyll has gone back for him." Cylea pulled her hand away. "You don't have to go."

We waited, holding our breaths. Seconds ticked by, then a whole minute. Wobbling, I tried to get on my feet. Jeondar came to my side and helped me up the rest of the way as we stared at the empty air, waiting for Kalyll to reappear with his brother.

"Where are they?" Arabis demanded. "It's taking too long. Give me that token." She reached for Cylea once more.

"No use in risking your life too." Cylea pushed Arabis, whose face turned bright red with anger.

Jeondar stepped forward. "I think we all need to go back."

"Looks that way." Silver took his spot next to Jeondar, looking ready for a fight. Blood covered one side of his head, turning his platinum hair crimson and smudging the front of his pointed ear and sharp jaw.

In fact, everyone seemed to have some sort of injury. How could they fight again?

"Don't make me use my power on you," Arabis growled.

Cylea shook her head. "They'll be back any second. They know what they're doing." She didn't sound so certain.

Arabis put her hand out, an intense glare in her blue eyes.

Cylea hesitated only for an instant, then tipped her hand

over Arabis's. The transfer token dropped, and the instant it hit her palm, two shapes materialized behind her.

I whimpered in relief. Arabis turned very slowly and took in Kryn and Kalyll standing there, the former slumping, one hand pressed to his stomach, and the other holding on to Kalyll, who slowly eased him to the ground.

A trail of blood stained Kryn's tunic and leggings. Arabis's face crumpled and she fell to her knees next to him. She took his free hand in hers, then looked at me. *Can you heal him?* her desperate eyes asked.

I inched closer on shaky legs, Jeondar helping me forward.

"Take energy from me." Kalyll stepped forward.

"Are you strong enough?" I asked.

"I am. You just put me back together, remember?" He offered me both hands.

I pulled my cupped hand away from my chest and held Larina forward. Cylea gasped and blinking rapidly took the pixie from me and held her reverently and tenderly.

"Just hold on," Arabis told Kryn.

"A-re you worried . . . about me?" Kryn coughed.

"Shut up!" Arabis snapped.

He groaned and winced, shrinking into himself.

"Please hurry. He's so pale," Arabis urged.

Quickly, I took Kalyll's hand, found his life force, and drew on it, careful not to take too much. In an instant, strength flooded me. My knees straightened from their bent position, the wound in the back of my head healed. My lungs drew in a deep breath, and the fog that seemed to have fallen over my eyes cleared.

"A-rabis," Kryn mumbled, his voice a fading light that despite its dimness demanded to be heard.

"Save your breath," she ordered him.

"I'm tired . . . of doing that. Al-ways holding back. I love you. Forever. Even if you . . . never . . . forgive me. I won't stop. I—"

"You will stop now." She shushed him with a kiss, her lips upon his as she clenched her eyes shut and a tear slid down her cheek.

With my strength restored, I kneeled by his side, pulled his bloody hand away from his wound, and got to work, repairing his injuries. With my skill, I sensed his punctured liver and heavy internal bleeding.

I knitted his vital organs and torn veins first. When that was done, I focused on the wide wound, which had pierced him almost all the way through, surely the vicious stab from a broadsword. As the gash sealed, he gasped in a breath, then let it go in relief.

Arabis pulled away and peered into my face. I nodded to reassure her he would be all right. Color returned to Kryn's face, and when she noticed it, she started to pull away. Kryn grabbed her wrist.

"Oh no, you don't. Not again," he said. "You deserve to be happy. And I promise you that nothing will ever get in the way again. Not in a million years."

Arabis seemed uncertain.

I pulled away from them and went to Kalyll. He was reclining against a tree, taking deep deliberate breaths.

"Did I take too much?" I asked.

He shook his head and gestured toward Kryn and Arabis. "I'll say it was all worth it."

I glanced back to find Arabis's arms wrapped tightly around Kryn's neck, holding on as if she would never, ever, let him go again.

Turning to my mate, I did the same.

CHAPTER 42
DANIELLA

I stood at the edge of the small pond in Imbermore, the Summer Court capital, wearing a blue gown that tried and failed to match the lovely shade of Larina's skin. A small pedestal with her body rested in front of me, surrounded by a circle of flowers.

Kalyll and the rest of the Sub Rosa were there, their heads bowed. My heart was heavy with a mixture of sadness and gratitude. I took a deep breath and began to speak, my voice shaking with emotion.

"Larina, we're here to honor your bravery and sacrifice. You were a true friend, and I will miss you dearly." I stifled a sob.

Kalyll rested his hand on my shoulder, lending me his support.

My voice steadier now, I continued. "Your courage and selflessness saved so many lives. Elf-hame owes you a debt of gratitude. Forever and ever."

I spoke of her kindness toward Valeriana and her unabashed affection. I told her how much her friendship meant to me, and how I would think of her every day. I spoke of how getting to know her opened my eyes to the unjust way the minor folk were sometimes treated, and I vowed to make things better for them in her memory. Only Kalyll's comforting presence gave me the courage to finish speaking.

The brooch he gave me was the only thing of value I possessed here, so I placed it on the pedestal next to her.

I met Kalyll's gaze. *Is it okay?*

He nodded without hesitation.

As I stood back, a light breeze rustled through the flowers, and the sun shone brightly on Larina's translucent wings, giving them a soft glow.

A small boat appeared on the placid waters of the pond, slowly making its way toward us. Realizing it was for Larina, my heart ached. The boat was adorned with more flowers and glimmering crystals. As it approached, her body dissolved into a shower of glitter and floated onto the boat.

I couldn't help but feel a sense of awe as I watched the small vessel make its way around the pond, slowly disappearing from view. I knew Larina was on her way to The Blessed Fields, the final resting place of all Fae.

My friends placed their hands on my shoulders, a show of support and shared grief. Despite the pain of her loss, a sense of peace floated in the air. Larina was at rest.

As we turned away, Kalyll wrapped me in his arms. "I'm here for you, always. I love you." His words felt like a balm to my sorrowful heart, and I leaned into the embrace, finding comfort in his arms.

As we all made our way back to the castle, I felt a sense of purpose. I knew that Larina's sacrifice hadn't been in vain. Many would live on because of her, and I would fight for the minor folk and so would Kalyll. Together, he and I could do anything.

In the distance, a beautiful display of colors filled the sky. It was a reminder that even during difficult times, there was still beauty to be found.

KALYLL
A WEEK LATER

"Ridding the court of all the traitors may be an impossible task," I complained to Kryn.

He kept walking, his eyes lost in a faraway point ahead.

"I'm talking to you."

"Oh, what were you saying?"

"That ridding the court of all the traitors may be an impossible task."

"I believe that's an understatement."

Everyone was stabbing each other in the back and doing somersaults to avoid being identified as a Cardian supporter. Honestly, there were days I wished to get rid of all of them, and it wasn't because they had chosen to follow my brother or because of their ambition, but because they'd been willing to destroy our peace in a war orchestrated by Kellam Mythorne.

That was unforgivable.

I suspected some of them were still holding out hope that

Cardian would come back. By the time I returned to the tree where I'd stashed him, he was gone, and no one knew where he'd gone. Perhaps it was better this way.

Kryn had gone back to looking like a childling in a playing field. He had been this way ever since Arabis forgave him, and I suspected he would remain this way for a very long time. Not that I could blame him. I was also rushing away from the irritating council meeting we'd just attended. It had been unpleasant, to say the least, torture compared to the two females who awaited us in the Eastside garden.

There would be enough meetings to attend and weasels to flush out for weeks to come, so the goal at the moment was to enjoy my time away from kingly duties to the fullest.

As we exited into the garden, I caught sight of Arabis and Daniella, working diligently on the rose bushes. Daniella hated being idle, so she had gotten a hold of some garden tools and worked every morning on the task, which she found relaxing and satisfying.

Kryn ran ahead, scooped Arabis off the ground, and twirled her around. Daniella smiled, watching them, then walked in my direction.

"They put us to shame," she said, planting a quick kiss on my lips.

"They do." I took her hands in mine and kissed each one in turn. "Miss me?"

"Not really."

I placed a hand on my heart, acting injured. She smiled that beautiful smile that left me breathless.

"How did it go with the council?" she asked.

I shook my head. "Torture."

"I'm sorry."

"It will take some time, but I'll take care of it."

"I have no doubt."

"Naesala is here," Arabis said, pulling Kryn along by the hand. "Better not to keep her waiting." They started walking down the path, leading the way.

"Are you ready, melynthi?" I asked.

"Yes?"

"You don't sound so sure."

"I can't help but worry about your people not accepting me."

"We've been through this."

"I know. It's just the last few days have been so easy. I've had a good time with you, and no one seems to care about who I am. The moment I go back to looking human, everything will change."

Today, Naesala was to undo the spell that changed Daniella's human features to make her appear Fae. When I introduced her to the court as my future wife, she would be wearing her own beautiful semblance. I wouldn't have it any other way, and neither would she. Moreover, Daniella wanted to visit her family, but going back in any shape other than her own was not an option.

Besides giving back her human features, the sorceress would also begin to teach Daniella how to extend her human life.

Still, I could tell she wasn't ready. Not yet.

She was right. The last few days had been peaceful, and despite my duties, we'd been able to spend a lot of time together. And each night had been—

WÖLFE

I wrapped an arm around her waist and roughly pulled her to me. "If you're not ready, Dani, I will not make you."

"Hey, there."

"Hey back."

"What are you doing here?" Her smile twisted to one side as if she were trying to repress it.

"I've come to take you away."

She blinked. "Is that so?"

"That is so."

"And where will you take me?"

I pulled the transfer token from my trousers' pocket and twirled it in my fingers. "There is a place near Mount Ruin that I can't forget about."

Her cheeks flushed, her chagrin making me even hungrier for her.

"I promised you I would take you back."

"I thought Kalyll had promised that."

"You thought wrong and should know better, woman."

I tightened my hand around the token, and in an instant, we stood on moss-covered ground.

Daniella pulled away and pressed a hand to her stomach. "I've never liked that feeling."

"Don't worry. I'll give you something that you'll like." I pulled her against me once more, making sure she felt my erection.

"Oh, dear, someone is quite ahead of the game. Did you forget about foreplay?"

"I didn't forget anything. If it's a game you want, I'll play it until I make you beg again."

She looked affronted at the reminder of the time I'd made her beg me to fuck her.

Tapping my chin with her finger, she said, "I think it will be your turn to beg, my king."

I laughed. "And how do you plan to accomplish that?"

She slipped from my grip and moving faster than I'd ever seen her do, she rushed behind a tree.

"How?" I asked, bewildered.

"Another side effect of your shadowdrifter magic. I discovered it in Nerethien. But that doesn't matter. What matters is that you'll have to beg me to let you touch me."

"You cunning woman, keeping such a secret from me. I think I need to teach you a lesson." I darted toward her, using the vastness of my speed, and to my utter surprise, she'd disappeared.

"Hey, over here," she called from behind the safety of another tree.

I tried again. Once more, she was faster than me.

For five minutes, I attempted to catch her, but every time, she eluded me. I stopped in the middle of the clearing. "I'm getting angry," I rumbled.

"That is a *you* problem. All his majesty has to do is beg."

Beg? Beg?! Was she—

KALYLL

I dropped to my knees. "I beg you, melynthi."
"No. Not you," she said. "Wölfe."

WÖLFE

"Oh, what the devil." I slowly unbuttoned my shirt and let it drop to the ground.

The wicked woman peered at me from behind the tree trunk, her eyes hungry, but her expression just as resolute. The set of her jaw told me she wasn't going to give me what I wanted until I begged.

Bitting down my pride, I placed my hands together in the gesture that supplicants used in her realm.

"Please, Dani. I beg you."

Wearing a satisfied smile, she sashayed into the clearing, freeing her hair and letting her dress fall around her ankles.

Her luscious shape made me instantly harder. Walking on my knees, I came to a stop in front of her. She glanced down, her long hair cascading over her breasts.

"Take me then," she said.

She didn't have to ask me twice. That night, we fucked and made love, made love and fucked without a care in the world.

The Envoy had been right the first time I visited her. *You will travel to Mount Ruin without the aid of a transfer token, and during the journey, you will find what you never thought you would ever possess.*

True happiness.

THE SPRITE
SHADOW

T he sprite moved like a shadow, paying homage to her name. She was a Sunnarian, born to a warrior clan, bred to kill, and though she hadn't been in a battle in over a hundred years, her instincts were as sharp as they had ever been. It was in her blood, the hunger to kill when justice needed to be served.

And in this instance, justice was overdue.

When the sprite was a young warrior, recently marked by the elders after her first ten kills, she had been boastful and rash. She'd thought herself invincible, unstoppable.

She had been wrong. So wrong.

Disobeying orders from her commanding officer, Shadow had attempted to rescue a group of kidnapped Sunnarians, peaceful members of her clan, who were taken by slavers to be sold into bondage or indenture.

She imagined herself returning to her village with the abducted clan members and being hailed as a hero. Instead, she ended up a prisoner herself, locked up with all the others, and shipped far away from home. The slavers had a powerful sorcerer, who used his powers for evil and profit.

It was never a fair fight: Shadow's spear and courage against magic.

A month later, she was sold to the highest bidder to serve as a lowly spy, a fly on the rafters, as her overlord called her. Bound by magic that prevented her from escaping, she was forced to serve that awful male for over twenty years.

She despaired, thought she would forever be his subject, until one day, the Seelie King and Queen came to the overlord's mansion on official business.

Per usual, her overlord sent Shadow to spy on his guests. He wanted to find out what it would take for the Seelie King to offer him the vacant council member post he'd lusted over for so long.

As Shadow hid in the monarchs' assigned chamber, the Seelie Queen immediately sensed her presence.

"Come down, sprite," the queen commanded, staring straight toward Shadow's hiding spot near the ceiling.

Unsure how the female had spotted her—this had never happened to Shadow before—she flew down and landed gracefully on the queen's boudoir.

"What are you doing here?" Queen Eithne demanded.

There was no magic to prevent Shadow from speaking the truth, so she did. "My overlord sent me to spy on you and the king."

The queen's cold gaze bore into Shadow, carefully assessing her. After a moment, she nodded. "I see. And what information does he hope to gain?"

"He wants to know how to win your husband's favor and be allowed to become a council member of the Seelie Court."

The queen thought for a moment, then said, "Tell your

lord that it takes more than spying to win the favor of the Seelie King. Tell him that it takes loyalty, honor, and above all, trust."

Shadow clenched her jaw. If she relayed these words to her overlord, he would have her tortured by his sorcerer.

"What is the matter?" the queen asked.

"Nothing. I shall give him your message."

Shadow flew up from the boudoir and headed for the door, bracing herself for the pain to come.

"On second thought," the queen said. "I will come with you."

That day, the Seelie Queen confronted Shadow's overlord, swore to him that he would never be a council member, and paid a large sum of gold to purchase Shadow. Or at least that was what the sprite thought was happening. In fact, what Queen Eithne had done was to buy Shadow's freedom. Expecting nothing in exchange, the queen told the sprite she was free to go back to her people.

But Shadow was ashamed to go home. Moreover, she felt she owed the queen a debt, for the queen had upheld justice, the way Shadow had been born to do. So instead, the sprite offered her services to the queen, as a spy or whatever else the queen desired.

And for a hundred years, Shadow had stayed by Eithne's side, and during that time, the sprite was never asked to do anything at all, except offer her companionship, and thus a true friendship developed between them.

Now, that friendship had been severed. Forever.

Justice had to be served. That was why Shadow was here.

She had found him. It hadn't been hard. He thought

nothing of the minor folk, thought them incapable of anything noteworthy, like the spy network they possessed. And he would never learn otherwise because his life was forfeit.

Flying as silently as the wind, Shadow descended from her spot in the rafters. The once-prince lay sleeping on a bed that he surely considered beneath him. He had taken refuge in an inn located in a small town outside of Nerethien. He had sold his gaudy jewels and was on his way to retrieve the treasure he had hidden in case his plans took a bad turn, which they had.

He snored slightly, blond hair matted to a sweaty forehead.

Alighting on the pillow softer than a feather, Shadow pressed her spear to Cardian's neck. His blue eyes sprang open.

"Don't move," Shadow warned.

She could have killed him without him realizing death was upon him, but she wanted Cardian to know who had ended him. More importantly, she wanted him to know why.

"My name is Shadow Eira, and I am here to impart justice for the death of my friend Eithne Adanorin."

"Shadow, what are you . . . doing?" he asked in nervous spurts. "This is me, your prince."

"You are no prince of mine. You are a murderer." She leaned into the spear, pressing it to a throbbing vein in Cardian's neck.

"Stop. I have treasure. Lots of gold. I'll give it to you. All of it."

"Gold means nothing to me, and now it will mean nothing to you too."

He tried to move, but he was slow, no match for a Sunnarian warrior's reflexes. The needle-like spear lanced through the vital artery. With one swift motion, the sprite dragged the weapon down, down, down, ripping a wide hole through which a river of blood gushed out, staining the yellow sheets even as Cardian tried hopelessly to staunch the bleeding.

With that done, Shadow slipped out of the room through a crack in the window and flew into the night sky. There was someone else who would get a visit from her tonight. A certain overlord who, as promised, would never get to be a council member in the Seelie Court.

After that, Shadow would surrender herself to the mercy of Kalyll Adanorin. Whatever he decided her fate should be, she would face it with dignity.

HE NEEDS MY HELP,
BUT HE'LL BE MY DOWNFALL.

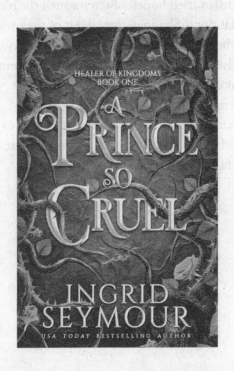

OUT NOW.

HEADLINE
ETERNAL

THE PRINCE WOULD CHOOSE
TO SAVE HIS REALM.
BUT THE BEAST WOULD FOLLOW
HIS HEART . . . TO ME.

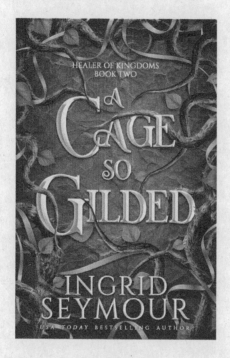

OUT NOW.

HEADLINE
ETERNAL

HEADLINE ETERNAL

FIND YOUR HEART'S DESIRE...

VISIT OUR WEBSITE: www.headlineeternal.com
FIND US ON FACEBOOK: facebook.com/eternalromance
CONNECT WITH US ON X: @eternal_books
FOLLOW US ON INSTAGRAM: @headlineeternal
EMAIL US: eternalromance@headline.co.uk